Praise for *Kissing Sin*

"*Kissing Sin* will captivate readers from page one with its kick-ass heroine's struggle to do what's right without losing herself. . . . Keri Arthur's unique characters and the imaginative world she's created will make this series one that readers won't want to miss."
—*A Romance Review*

Praise for *Tempting Evil*

"Riley Jenson is kick-ass . . . genuinely tough and strong, but still vulnerable enough to make her interesting. . . . Arthur is not derivative of early [Laurell K.] Hamilton—far from it—but the intensity of her writing and the complexity of her heroine and her stories are reminiscent."
—*All About Romance*

"This paranormal romance series gets better and better with each new book. . . . An exciting adventure that delivers all you need for a fabulous read—sexy shapeshifters, hot vampires, wild uncontrollable sex and the slightest hint of a love that's meant to be forever."
—*Fresh Fiction*

"An amazingly awesome book that completely blew me away. Ms. Arthur's world building skills are absolutely second to none. . . . I simply must have more please, as soon as humanly possible. Five cups."
—*Coffee Time Romance*

"Pure sexy action adventure . . . If you like your erotic scenes hot, fast, and frequent, your heroine sassy, sexy, and tough, and your stories packed with hard-hitting action in a vividly realized fantasy world, then *Tempting Evil* and its companion novels could be just what you're looking for."　　　　　　　—*SF Revu*

"Keri Arthur's Riley Jenson series just keeps getting better and better and is sure to call to fans of other authors with kick-ass heroines such as Christine Feehan and Laurell K. Hamilton. I have become a steadfast fan of this marvelous series and I am greatly looking forward to finding out what is next in store for this fascinating and strong character."　　　—*A Romance Review*

Praise for *Dangerous Games*

Finalist for the 2008 Fantasm Award for Best Urban Fantasy Romance

"*Dangerous Games* is by far one of the best books I have ever read. . . . The storyline is so exciting I did not realize I was literally sitting on the edge of my chair seat. . . . With this series, Ms. Arthur has a real winner on her hands. Five cups."　　　—*Coffee Time Romance*

"The depths of emotion, the tense plot, and the conflict of powerful driving forces inside the heroine made for [an] absorbing read."　　　　　—*SF Revu*

"This series is phenomenal! *Dangerous Games* is an incredibly original and devastatingly sexy story. It keeps you spellbound and mesmerized on every page. Absolutely perfect!!"　　　　　　—*Fresh Fiction*

Praise for *Embraced by Darkness*

"Arthur is positively one of the best urban fantasy authors in print today. The characters have been well-drawn from the start and the mysteries just keep getting better. A creative, sexy and adventure-filled world that readers will just love escaping to."
—*Darque Reviews*

"A great continuation of the Riley Jenson Guardian series . . . Each book has been thrilling, suspenseful, and outside the box. . . . Arthur continues to get better and better and I can't wait to see what she has in store for us next." —*Night Owl Romance*

"Arthur's storytelling is getting better and better with each book. *Embraced by Darkness* has suspense, interesting concepts, terrific main and secondary characters, well developed story arcs, and the world-building is highly entertaining." —Reuters.com

"Once again, Keri Arthur has created a perfect, exciting and thrilling read with intensity that kept me vigilantly turning each page, hoping it would never end."
—*Fresh Fiction*

"Arthur's fifth Guardian novel is just as fabulous as the first. . . . Fast paced and attention grabbing, *Embraced by Darkness* is a must read and a necessary possession. Five cups." —*Coffee Time Romance*

Also by Keri Arthur

KERI ARTHUR

Mercy
Burns

DELL
NEW YORK

A Dell Mass Market Original

Copyright © 2011 by Keri Arthur
Excerpt from *Darkness Unbound* by Keri Arthur
copyright © 2011 by Keri Arthur

Published in the United States by Dell, an imprint of
The Random House Publishing Group, a division of
Random House, Inc., New York.

DELL is a registered trademark of Random House, Inc., and the
colophon is a trademark of Random House, Inc.

This book contains an excerpt from the forthcoming book
Darkness Unbound by Keri Arthur. The excerpt has been set
for this edition only and may not reflect the final content
of the forthcoming edition.

ISBN 978-0-440-24570-4

Cover design: Lynn Andreozzi
Cover illustration: Juliana Kolesova

Printed in the United States of America

www.bantamdell.com

2 4 6 8 9 7 5 3 1

Acknowledgments

I'd like to thank:

Everyone at Dell who helped polish this book—most especially my editor, Anne; assistant editor, David; all the line and copy editors who make sense of my Aussie English; and cover artist Juliana Kolesova.

I'd also like to send a special thank-you to my agent, Miriam, for her support and guidance; the Deadline Dames for being totally ace women and fab writers; my crit buddies and best mates—Robyn, Mel, Chris, Carolyn, and Freya; and finally Kasey, for just being an awesome kid.

You all rock, ladies.

Mercy Burns

Chapter One

"We'll have you out in a minute, ma'am. Just keep still awhile longer."

The voice rolled across the gray mist enshrouding my mind—a soothing sound that brought no comfort, only confusion. Why would he say I shouldn't move?

And why was he saying it just to me? Why wasn't he saying anything to Rainey, who'd been driving the car?

Ignoring the advice, I shifted, trying to get more comfortable, trying to *feel*. Pain shot through my side, spreading out in heated waves across my body and reverberating through my brain. The sensation was oddly comforting even as it tore a scream from my throat.

If I could feel, then I wasn't dead.

Should I be?

Yes, something inside me whispered. *Yes*.

I swallowed heavily, trying to ease the dryness in my throat. What the hell had happened to us? And why did it suddenly feel like I was missing hours of my life?

The thing that was digging into my side felt jagged and fat, like a serrated knife with a thicker, heavier edge, yet there were no knives in the car. People like me and Rainey didn't need knives or guns or any other sort of human weapon, because we were born with our own. And it was just as dangerous, just as accurate, as any gun or knife.

So why did it feel like I had a knife in my side?

I tried to open my eyes, suddenly desperate to see where I was, to find Rainey, to understand what was going on. But I couldn't force them open and I had no idea why.

Alarm snaked through the haze, fueling my growing sense that something was *very* wrong.

I sucked in a deep breath, trying to keep calm, trying to keep still as the stranger had advised. The air was cool, yet sunshine ran through it, hinting that dawn had passed and that the day was already here. But that *couldn't* be right. Rainey and I had been driving through sunset, not sunrise, enjoying the last rays before the night stole the heat from us.

Moisture rolled down the side of my cheek. Not a tear; it was too warm to be a tear.

Blood.

There was blood on my face, blood running through my hair. My stomach clenched and the fear surged to new heights, making it difficult to breathe. What the hell had happened? And where the hell was Rainey?

Had we been in some sort of accident?

No, came the answer from the foggy depths of my mind. *This was no accident.*

Memories surged at the thought, though the resulting images were little more than fractured flashes mixed with snatches of sound, as if there were bits my memory couldn't—or wouldn't—recall. There was the deep, oddly familiar voice on the phone who'd given us our first decent clue in weeks. And Rainey's excitement over the possible lead—our chance to discover not only what had happened to her sister, but also to everyone else who had once lived in the town of Stillwater. Our mad, off-key singing as we'd sped through the mountains, heading back to San Francisco and our meeting with the man who just might hold some answers.

Then the truck lights that had appeared out of nowhere and raced toward us. The realization that the driver wasn't keeping to his own side of the road, that he was heading directly for us. Rainey's desperate, useless attempts to avoid him. The screeching, crumpling sound of metal as the truck smashed into us, sending us spinning. The screaming of tires as Rainey stomped on the brakes, trying to stop us from being shunted through the guardrail. The roar of the truck's engine being gunned, and a second, more crushing sideways blow that buckled the doors and forced us through the very railing we'd been so desperate to avoid. The fear and the panic and the realization that we couldn't get out, couldn't get free, as the car dropped over the ledge and smashed into the rocks below, rolling over, and over, and over . . .

The sound of sobbing shattered the reeling images— deep, sobbing gasps that spoke of pain and fear. Mine. I sought desperately to gain some control, to quiet the sobs and suck down some air. Hysteria wouldn't help. Hysteria *never* helped.

Something pricked my arm. A needle. I wanted to

tell them that whatever they were giving me probably wouldn't work because human medicine almost never did on us, but the words stuck somewhere in my throat. Not because I couldn't speak, but because I'd learned the hard way never to say anything that might hint to the humans that they were not alone in this world.

And yet, despite my certainty that the drug wouldn't work, my awareness seemed to strengthen. I became conscious of the hiss of air and of the screech and groan of metal being forced apart. Close by, someone breathed heavily; I could smell his sweat and fear. Farther away was the murmur of conversation, the rattle of chains, and the forlorn sighing of the wind. It had an echo, making it sound as if we were on the edge of a precipice.

What was absent was Rainey's sweet, summery scent. I should have been able to smell her. In the little hatchback there wasn't much distance between the passenger seat and the driver's, yet I had no sense of her.

Fear surged anew and I raised a hand, ignoring the sharp, angry stabbing in my side as I swiped at my eyes. Something flaked away and a crack of warm light penetrated. I swiped again, then a hand grabbed mine, the fingers cool and strong. I struggled against the grip but couldn't break free, and that scared me even more. He was human, and I wasn't. Not entirely. There was no way on this earth he should have been able to restrain me so easily.

"Don't," he said, gravelly voice calm and soothing, showing no trace of the fear I could smell on him.

"There's a cut above your eye and you'll only make the bleeding worse."

It couldn't get worse, I wanted to say. And I meant the situation, not the wound. Yet that little voice inside me whispered that the pain wasn't over yet, that there was a whole lot more to come.

I clenched my fingers against the stranger's, suddenly needing the security of his touch. At least it was something real in a world that had seemingly gone mad.

The screeching of metal stopped, and the thick silence was almost as frightening. Yet welcome. If only the pounding in my head would stop . . .

"Almost there, ma'am. Just keep calm a little longer."

"Where . . ." My voice came out little more than a harsh whisper and my throat burned in protest. I swallowed heavily and tried again. "Where is Rainey?"

He hesitated. "Your friend?"

"Yes."

His hesitation lasted longer. "Let's just concentrate on getting you out and safe."

There was something in his voice that had alarm bells ringing. An edge that spoke of sorrow and death and all those things I didn't want to contemplate or believe.

"Where is she?" I said, almost desperately. "I need to know she's okay."

"She's being taken care of by someone else," he said, and I sensed the lie in his words.

No, I thought. *No!*

Rainey had to be alive. *Had* to be. She wasn't just my friend, she was my strength, my courage, and my confidante. She'd hauled me out of more scrapes than I could remember. She *couldn't* be gone.

Fear and disbelief surged. I tore my hand from his and scrubbed urgently at my eyes. Warmth began to flow anew, but I was finally able to see.

And what I saw was the crumpled steering wheel, the smashed remains of the windshield, the smears of blood on the jagged, twisted front end of the car.

No, no, NO!

She couldn't be dead. She *couldn't*. I'd survived, and she was stronger—tougher—than me. How could she die? How could that be possible?

And then I saw something else.

Bright sunlight.

Dawn had well and truly passed.

That's why my rescuer had been so vague about Rainey. They couldn't find her. And no matter how much they looked, they never would. The flesh of a dead dragon incinerated at the first touch of sunrise.

I began to scream then, and there was nothing anyone could do to make me stop. Because they didn't understand what a dragon dying unaccompanied at dawn meant.

But I did. And it tore me apart.

Though in the end, I *did* stop—but only because the pain of being wrenched free of the twisted, broken wreck finally swept me into unconsciousness.

Chapter Two

I left the hospital as soon as I was physically able.

The staff had tried to make me stay. They'd tried to convince me that one day after an operation to remove a six-inch piece of steel from my side, I should be flat on my back and recovering, not strolling around like there was nothing wrong with me.

But they didn't understand what I was. I couldn't have stayed there even if I'd wanted to, and not just because they would have noticed how fast I healed and started asking questions.

No, the real reason was Rainey.

Her soul still had a chance to move on.

Sunset wasn't only the time where day met night, it was the time when the dead could mingle more freely with those who lived. Some of those ghosts would be dragons who died without someone to pray for them, destined to roam this earth forever—insubstantial beings who could never move on, never feel, and never experience life again. But those who had died *before* their time had one small lifeline. If I caught and killed those responsible for Rainey's demise within seven days of her death, I could then pray for her soul on the fall of the final day and she would be able to move on.

I had five of those seven days left, and there was no way on this earth I was going to waste them lying in a hospital bed. No matter how much it still hurt to walk around.

Which was why I was sitting here, in this dark and dingy bar, waiting for the man we'd arranged to meet before that truck had barreled into us.

I reached for my Coke and did a quick scan of the place. It wasn't anywhere I would have chosen, though I could see the appeal to a sea dragon. Situated in the Marina district of San Francisco, the bar was dark and smoky, and the air thick with the scent of beer, sweaty men, and secrets. Tables hid in dim corners, those sitting at them barely visible in the nebulous light.

There was no one human in those shadows.

A long wooden bar dominated one side of the venue, and the gleaming brass foot rail and old-style stools reminded me of something out of the Old West—although the décor of the rest of the place was more ship-related than Western-themed, with old rope ladders, furled sails, and a ship's wheel taking pride of place on the various walls.

I'd attracted plenty of attention when I'd walked in, and I wasn't entirely sure whether it was due to the fact that I was the only female in the place, or the rather prominent scar on my forehead. Most of the men had quickly lost interest once I'd sent a few scowls their way, but the bartender—a big, swarthy man of indeterminate age—seemed to be keeping an eye on me. While some part of me figured he simply didn't want trouble, something about it bothered me nonetheless.

Then the door to my right opened, briefly silhouetting the figure of a man. He was thickset but tall, and his hair was a wild mix of black, blue, and green, as if some artist had spilled a palette of sea-colored paints over his head.

When my gaze met his, he nodded once, then stepped into the room.

I took another sip of Coke and waited. He weaved his way through the mess of tables and chairs, his movements deft and sure, exhibiting a fluid grace so rare in most people.

Of course, he *wasn't* most people. He was one of the other ones. One of the monsters.

"Angus Dougall, at your service," he said, his deep, somewhat gruff voice holding only the barest hint of a Scottish burr. "Sorry I was so late, but there were protestors up on Mission Street and the traffic was hell. You want another drink?"

"Not at the moment, thanks. And why meet here if it was so far out of your way?"

"Because I know these parts well enough."

Implying that he felt safer here than anywhere else, I guessed. He took off a blue woolen peacoat that had seen better years and tossed it over the back of the chair opposite, then walked to the bar. He was, I thought with amusement, very much the image of a sea captain of old, complete with jaunty cap and a pipe shoved in his back pocket. His multicolored hair was wild and scraggly, his skin burned nut-brown by the sun, and his beard was as unkempt as his hair. All that was missing was the parrot on his shoulder. And the wrinkles—because despite looking like an old-style sea captain, he couldn't have been any older than his mid-forties.

Only I doubt he'd ever been near a boat in his life. Sea dragons had no need for that mode of transport. Not according to Leith—a friend who was currently running a background check on Dougall. And he should know, because he was a sea dragon himself.

Angus came back with a beer in his hand and sat down. His gaze swept my face, lingering on the half-healed wound that snuck out from my hair to create a jagged line across half my forehead. Once it was fully healed, it would be barely visible, but right now it was fucking ugly.

Which was a small price to pay, considering the other option. Tears touched my eyes and I blinked them away rapidly. Now was *not* the time to grieve. I had far too much to do before I could give in to the pain and hurt and loss.

Angus took a sip of his beer then said, "I wasn't actually expecting you to make it today. I thought you'd been in an accident?"

Fear prickled my spine. I took a drink to ease the sudden dryness in my throat and wondered if he'd been behind the wheel of that truck. Wondered just how safe I was in this bar, even with the dozen or so strangers around us.

"I was."

"You look okay."

"I am." My fingers tightened around the glass. "Who told you about the accident?"

Certainly *I* hadn't mentioned it when I'd finally received my possessions from the mangled car and had given him another call. In fact, I hadn't told anyone—although that hadn't stopped Leith from calling the hospital frantically to see if I was all right. But then, he had other methods of finding these things out.

Angus shrugged. "I saw it mentioned in the *Chronicle*."

If the *Chronicle* had run an article on the accident, why hadn't they contacted me? I was, after all, one of their reporters. But I could sense no lie in his words or in his expression, and reading a newspaper had been the last thing on my mind when I'd awoken in the hospital. For all I knew, he *was* telling the truth. Yet there was a strange tension emanating from him, and that made me uneasy. I eased my grip a little on the glass and took a sip.

"I was also told you're draman," he continued.

Meaning someone *had* been checking up on me. And given the accident that wasn't, that couldn't be a good thing—especially considering I wasn't exactly popular at home. I knew for a fact that many in my clique hoarded a grudge as avidly as they collected all things shiny—which was the reason behind my original move to San Francisco.

It was entirely possible that one of those long-hoarded grudges was the reason behind Rainey's death. After all, someone had given that deep-voiced man my cell phone number, and Mom still lived within the clique's compound. She was extraordinarily trusting when it came to the dragons that she lived with and loved.

And just because I was presuming it was linked to our quest to discover the reason behind the death of Rainey's sister didn't mean that it actually was.

And if I was wrong, then Rainey would pay.

But I wasn't wrong. I felt that with every inch of my being.

"What does it matter to you what I am?" I asked, wondering if he, like many full dragons, held a grudge against those of us who weren't.

It was a sad fact that most full-bloods considered us a blight on the dragon name. In times past, it had been common practice among the dragon cliques to regularly cull the draman ranks. These days, such practices were outlawed by the dragon council, but I very much doubted it was done to protect us. The fact was, humans were encroaching on dragon land more and more, and mass cleansings—as they were called— were bound to attract notice sooner or later. It said something about the council's desperation to avoid human notice that they were allowing our numbers to increase.

But if Angus was one of *those* dragons, then I wasn't entirely sure what my next step would be. I desperately needed the information he apparently had, but he was a sea dragon and a man besides. He had me bested in both strength *and* skill.

He took a sip of beer, his face giving little away. White froth briefly decorated his wiry beard before he wiped it away. "You're a member of the Jamieson clique, aren't you?"

Again that sliver of fear ran down my spine. Maybe

I'd stepped out of the frying pan and into the fire— and this wasn't the sort of heat I could control. Not if things went wrong. "How do you know that?"

"Because I'm not stupid enough to meet anyone without checking up on them first."

"And if you're inferring that I am, then you're mistaken." Although he wasn't. Not entirely.

A smile briefly touched his mouth before disappearing. "Jamieson's one of the oldest ones, isn't it?"

I raised an eyebrow. "They're all old, simply because there are no new cliques. There haven't been, for hundreds of years."

The rogue towns certainly didn't count. Not yet, anyway—although I had no doubt that the council would move on them sooner or later. They seemed to think the only way to stop the humans from discovering us was to rule us all with the iron fist of fear and retribution.

Which is why Rainey and I had thought that the council might be behind the cleansings of both Stillwater and Desert Springs. But the clues weren't really adding any support to that.

Angus took another sip of beer then leaned forward, blue eyes wary as he said, "Prove you are who you say."

"What? Why?"

"Because I need to be sure it's not a trap."

"Why would you agree to meet me if you think it's a trap?" And why would he even *think* I was trying to trap him?

Hell, even Rainey wouldn't have tried something like that, and she'd had the full spectrum of dragon powers. But she'd also had a lot more respect for full-bloods, despite what we'd gone through growing up.

Angus's smile had a bitter edge. "You ask that, two days after a serious accident that landed you in the hospital and left your best friend dead?" He shook his head. "You'd be better off walking away right now, little draman."

He was probably right. I knew that, even if I had no intention of ever doing it. "I can't."

"Even knowing you could be risking your life? These people aren't the type to let anyone off easily. We both bear the scars to prove that."

"What they've done has only strengthened my determination to track them down." Tears welled and I blinked them away quickly, internally repeating the mantra that had become a theme for me this last day and a bit. *Don't think, don't feel.* Not until it was all over, one way or another. "And if you've got scars, where the hell are they?"

Angus shoved an arm across the table and pushed up the sleeve of his shirt. His leathery skin was criss-crossed with a myriad of thickly healed wounds. "My whole body bears the evidence of their attack. They're not going to get a second shot."

My gaze jumped from the scars to his eyes, and I saw the glint of determination and fury there. And suddenly, I knew *why* he'd chosen this bar. Not because it was a refuge for would-be sea dogs, but because it was close to the sea. Which was his to call, like fire was for dragons. He'd drown everyone if he thought I was in any way here to trap him.

I blew out a breath, then said, "What do you want me to do?"

"If you are who you say you are, show me your stain and prove it."

The stain was a leathery, luminescent strip of skin that swirled around the spines of all dragons, whether they were of the air or sea, or were a half-breed like myself. The colors varied depending on clique and parentage, but usually involved a myriad of iridescent colors. I'd never been able to shift shape and attain dragon form so, unlike most stains, mine was just a boring brown.

But there were only a few people who could know that—past lovers, my mom, and my brother.

Neither my mom nor my brother would give out personal information like that, so that left past lovers. And while I could name a couple of those who'd delight in not only telling all but in getting back at me in any way possible, they'd left the clique well before Rainey and I had.

"I'm not stripping in public just to prove who I am." Especially *not* in a bar filled with shadowy men who maybe weren't less-than-savory types, but who were still unknowns all the same.

And you never trusted an unknown. It was a motto that had saved my skin many a time growing up, and I wasn't about to abandon it now, no matter how badly I wanted information.

Angus studied me for a moment, then said, voice still flat, "Then dance fire across your fingertips. I'm told you have extraordinary control."

I frowned. I didn't like using dragon skills in public—in fact, not using them *anywhere* humans were likely to see them had been hammered into my brain since birth. There might be no humans currently in this bar, but there was nothing stopping them from walking in at the wrong moment. "Why is this so important to you?"

"It's important because I've been caught unawares before and have paid the price for it." Bleakness flared in his eyes, and his somewhat fierce expression was touched fleetingly with sadness, a sadness that tore at my heart and made the reporter in me want to ask what was wrong. But I very much doubted he'd answer that question when he didn't even trust me with the information I was going to pay him for.

Then the sadness was gone and he took another sip of beer before adding, in a voice that was edgy and sharp, "And I've discovered the hard way that lies and entrapments fall from the prettiest tongue as easily as the ugliest."

"Well, I hope I fall into the former group rather than the latter," I said, a little alarmed by the sudden fierceness in his tone. Something was very off, but I wasn't sure what. Then my gaze flicked to his arm. Maybe his fierceness *was* understandable. With scars like those, survival must have been touch and go, even for a dragon who could heal far better than any human.

"Do it," he said, "or I walk out of here now and you'll never get your answers."

I looked around the room, seeing no one looking our way or showing any undue interest. That might change given what I was about to do, but there wasn't much I could change about that. Not if I wanted my answers.

If this guy *could* provide answers and wasn't just yanking my chain.

I mean, the voice on the phone that had given us

this lead had been oddly familiar, and that alone had raised questions. But Rainey had convinced me that we needed to take the chance if we were ever to get some answers. And now Rainey was dead and I was here talking to a stranger who might not only be connected to her death, but who might well be here to trap me—the one who had escaped from their little "accident."

And while Leith and his people *were* doing the background check on Angus, I simply didn't have the time to sit back and wait for the answers. Hence the reason I was here, taking this god-awful chance.

I had no other choice if I wanted to save Rainey.

I pushed the Coke back then held up a hand, keeping it close to my chest so that there was less likelihood of anyone else noticing.

Then I reached deep down into that place in my soul where the dragon resided. She came roaring forward in answer, heating my skin and making it tingle. But she was all flame and no substance, as usual. I focused on the energy burning through my body, controlling and restricting it until it was little more than flickers dancing joyfully across my fingertips.

Few dragons could do that with their fire. Most had full flame or nothing.

I met Angus's gaze. "Satisfied?"

He nodded, but oddly he didn't seem to relax. In fact, the tension that was knotting his shoulders and arms seemed worse than ever.

"So tell me," I added, "what you know about the cleansings."

He laced his fingers together, then leaned forward. "I know where the bodies are."

His voice was little more than a husky whisper and, for a moment, I wasn't sure I'd heard him right. "How can there be bodies? After death, a dragon's flesh is incinerated by the touch of the day's first rays."

His smile was grim. "The sun has to touch the flesh to incinerate it. If the body is underground by then, no amount of sunshine will burn it."

As a dragon—or half-dragon—I was horrified at the thought of flesh being left underground to rot. It wasn't only a sign of disrespect, but utter and total disregard. "Why would anyone do that? Hell, if nothing else, it's leaving evidence behind for others to find."

"Aye, but when a dragon dies and is gifted the sun's caress one last time, is not the passing of his or her soul felt by those close to them?"

I nodded. It was the only reason that Rainey had realized something had happened to her sister, and one of the major reasons behind my desperation to find Rainey's killer. She'd only had the one sibling and, unlike me, wasn't close to her mother. In fact, she hadn't seen her since she was five. This wasn't rare in our clique, as children tended to be raised in crèches rather than family settings, but my mom had made the effort to be involved in both my and Trae's upbringing, so we knew not only her but her relatives—although I doubted they actually realized we were half dragon. But most other mothers—whether human or dragon— didn't bother with their children. For Rainey, this meant that there was no one who cared enough to find out what had happened or to try and save her soul.

Only me.

"Then why," Angus continued, "would the people

behind these slaughters risk the sun setting the souls of their victims free and thereby notifying their kin that something had happened?"

"I guess they wouldn't." But it meant something had gone wrong when it came to Rainey's sister, because Rainey had definitely felt her passing.

"Exactly. So the remains are there to find. It's just that no one has been left alive to tell the tale."

It also meant that the men behind these slaughters were experts at covering their tracks. We'd certainly seen nothing that had looked like graves—or even freshly dug earth—at either Stillwater or Desert Springs.

But was that so surprising? If the people behind this were clever enough to make the population of two small towns disappear without anyone getting suspicious, then they were clever enough to disguise the graves.

I took a drink. The remaining ice clinked merrily against the sides of the glass—a sound at odds with the somber feel of the bar. "So you really did survive one of the cleansings?"

"Aye, I did."

"Then why have you never come forward to tell your story before now?"

He snorted softly and leaned back in his chair. "Who was I going to come forward to? The council? They wouldn't have given a damn. Outcasts are outcasts because the cliques don't want them. And I could hardly go to the human authorities, now, could I?" He took a long drink of beer then added, "Besides, I was only fifteen when it happened."

"Fifteen? But that means it had to have happened

years ago." And if that were the case, then there wasn't likely to be much in the way of evidence left.

"Thirty-one years ago, to be precise."

"But—" I stopped. We might have been operating on the assumption that the two destroyed towns we'd seen were the only ones involved, but there was no logical reason why this couldn't have happened before. After all, dragons had a long history of not wanting too many draman around. "So why agree to this meeting now?"

"Because I heard whispers that the killings had started again, and it needs to be stopped." His expression was an odd mix of guilt and anger, but the glint in his blue eyes was something else entirely.

Cold determination.

It sent another chill down my spine—though again, I wasn't entirely sure why.

"Meaning you're trying to stop them yourself?"

He gave me a smile that was part sadness, part grief, and a whole lot of anger. And again, I got that odd feeling of something deeper going on here. Something I just wasn't catching.

"No. I'm afraid sea dragons generally aren't the brave-soldier type. We leave that up to our fiery cousins."

But Leith was a sea dragon, and he could fight with the best of them. "Then you're not actually offering to help hunt down these people?"

"No." He shrugged—a casual motion that seemed at odds with the tension still riding him—and added, "But if telling you what I know helps bring these bastards down, then that's a small price to pay for the nightmares remembering brings. Just be careful, that's all I ask. I don't want another death on my conscience."

I leaned back in my chair and wondered if he meant Rainey or someone else entirely. While I believed he was telling the truth as far as it went, I also believed there was a whole lot more that he *wasn't* saying.

And that intrigued me—even as all the senses honed by years of watching my back and recognizing trouble before it hit were warning that this man was just *that*. Trouble.

It was a damn shame they couldn't actually tell me whether he was a major instigator or merely a foot soldier.

"The problem is, you're not telling your story for free, are you?"

His sudden smile was grim. "Nothing is free nowadays, lass. And the money will come in handy for the booze it'll take to drown the memories again."

"How much do you want?"

He pulled at his beard for a moment, as if considering the question, although we both knew he'd had a figure in mind from the moment he'd walked in the door.

"A thousand will do."

A grand wasn't a whole lot in the scheme of things—not if it led me to the answers I needed.

"I'll give you two thousand," I said slowly, and watched his eyes light. "Five hundred for telling me your story now, and the rest if you lead me to where the bodies are."

"I don't know—"

"You asked me to prove myself," I cut in. "And I'm offering you a lot of money. It's only fair that you prove the truth behind *your* words."

"My scars are my proof."

"Your scars could have been caused by anything. You're the one who said you know where the bodies lie. I want you to show me."

He picked up his beer and drained the glass in one gulp. He wiped the froth from his beard with the back of his hand, then said, "I just have to show you? I don't have to do any more than that?"

"No more. I just want proof." What I'd do with it once I had it, I wasn't entirely sure.

Nor was I sure how finding bodies from a cleansing that had happened over thirty years ago would help my quest or find Rainey's sister, but I had to try. Hell, merely having some evidence might just get the council to take me more seriously. Reporting the empty, gutted towns had caused little more than uninterested disdain.

Angus studied me, blue eyes still holding that cold determination. "Why do you want proof? It's not like you can go to the cops, and if you think the council will care, you're not exactly living in reality. And you're not going to threaten these people, especially considering you're just one lone draman."

"I never said I was alone." Although to all intents and purposes, I *was*. Leith was ready, willing, and able to help, but I'd already lost one good friend to this quest. I had no intention of losing another. "I just want to stop what is going on. Finding the bodies is one more step along that road."

"But why? That's what I don't get. Especially after what they tried to do to you." He studied me for a moment then added, "Was someone you loved killed in one of the cleansings?"

"No." I hesitated, then added, "But Rainey lost a sister in one."

"That wasn't mentioned when we arranged the original meet."

"No," I said, and wondered why the hell he even thought it should have been. It wasn't something you mentioned on a phone to a complete stranger.

I gulped down the rest of the Coke and wished it were something stronger. I'd never been one for alcohol, but a little something to help push the memories back into their box would have been handy right now.

Angus—who was watching me like a hawk—said, "You want another drink? Perhaps something with a little bite?"

I grimaced. "Not at this hour. But another Coke would be good. Thanks."

He snapped his fingers at the bartender, who gave a nod. Obviously, Angus was pretty well known here. I couldn't imagine the gruff-looking bartender playing waiter for any old stranger.

Angus looked at me and said, "Okay, it's a deal."

I took my wallet from my pocket and dragged out the cash, but I didn't hand it over yet. "Tell me how a sea dragon came to be in a town of outcast draman."

He smiled. Again, it was a bitter thing. "It was bad timing, nothing more. My parents and I were swimming to Australia to spend the winter, but a bad storm caught us. I was small for my age, so Mom decided to make for shore." He hesitated, and the ghosts of the past seemed to crowd the room for just a moment. I shivered and rubbed my arms. "The little seaside town seemed ideal."

"Seaside?" That surprised me. Both Stillwater and

Desert Springs were situated in the semiarid wastes of Nevada. There were rogue towns outside Nevada, of course, but as far as I was aware, none of those had been hit as yet.

Of course, I couldn't *actually* be one hundred percent certain, because no one really knew just how many rogue draman towns there were. As Angus had said—and I'd discovered—the council didn't give two hoots about them. Their main concern was keeping the thirteen main cliques in line.

The bartender arrived with our drinks and a strange, forced smile. Obviously, he wasn't *that* happy about being treated like a waiter. Angus paid the man, then waited until he'd gone before saying, "Aye, and a pretty spot it is, too."

"You've been back there, then?"

Again, sadness briefly clouded his eyes. "I lost my parents in that town. I go back there every year, on the anniversary of their deaths."

"So is the town still vacant? Or has civilization encroached?"

"Only ghosts reside there, even now." He shrugged. "I'm told the kin of the people who owned the land are keeping it as some sort of memorial."

"So is the land draman-owned?"

"Dragon-owned. At least it is now."

"Who by?"

He smiled, but there was nothing warm about it. "Jamieson."

My clique. Great.

And while that didn't mean they were in on this whole cleansing business, I wouldn't put it past them. The bastard we called king certainly wouldn't be above a little outlawed cleansing if it suited his purposes—and if he thought he could get away with it.

"But you've never seen anyone else there?"

"No." He shrugged again. "I just lay my flowers and leave, lass. That's enough for me."

It would probably be enough for anyone. I dragged the Coke toward me and took a sip. The chill of it sent a shiver down my spine. "Has this town got a name?"

He hesitated. "Whale Point."

I took another drink of Coke, then said, "Never heard of the place."

"Well, yeah, because the town and the road into it are all but destroyed."

It was a reasonable-sounding statement, and yet there was an edge to his voice. My gaze flickered to his arms. If not for those scars—which fit every scrap of information I knew about the destruction of the dra-man towns—I might have been tempted to believe that this was some odd con. "Meaning the town isn't on the Cabrillo Highway?"

"No. The highway bypasses Whale Point and most of the surrounding area is state park. The track running into the town has been left to ruin, and it's easy to miss if you don't know what to look for."

His voice held a tiredness that made me want to believe him. And yet, part of me didn't. I wasn't sure if it was my long history of distrusting the motives of just about everyone, or whether it was simply disbelief that answers might finally be at hand after months of Rainey and I finding nothing but ruins and dead ends.

And now I had only five days to find my answers and solve this crime.

Panic swirled, briefly making it hard to breathe. I pushed it away fiercely. I could do this.

I *had* to do this.

He took a long swig of beer, then added, "Whale Point's down by Limekiln Beach State Park, a good two and a half hours' drive from here. When do you want to go?"

I glanced at my watch. It was nearing four now, and I didn't fancy walking around an abandoned town at dusk, let alone at night. I might not be bereft of fire come darkness—an oddity no one could explain given most dragons and draman were—but I still wasn't about to be caught at night in a place I didn't know and with a man I didn't trust.

"Given the time, perhaps it would be better to start tomorrow."

He nodded. "You got a truck or a car?"

"Car. Why?"

"Because as I said, the track was in pretty bad shape last year, and it has probably degenerated since. You'll need a four-wheel drive."

"Then I'll meet you at the beginning of the road into Whale Point, and you can drive from there."

There was no way I was getting caught out in the middle of nowhere without transport, either. Not when I couldn't fly. He wasn't to know that, of course, and that's just the way I intended to keep it. The more he thought I was one of those draman who'd inherited full skills, the less chance there'd be of him pulling something funny when we were out there alone.

Or was that just my suspicious nature rearing its ugly head again?

"It'd be easier if I simply drove all the way there, but

we'll play it your way. You're the gal with the money, after all."

It was pointedly said, so I pushed the money across the table. He scooped it up quickly, then reached into his coat pocket and drew out a pen and a business card. He scrawled several lines on the back, then slid it across the table. "Driving directions."

I picked up the card and had a look. As directions went, they were pretty detailed, but I guess if this place had been easy to find, more people would have known about it. I flicked the card over. The Captain's Bay Cruises, it said, in big bold letters. I'll be damned. He *was* a sea captain.

I shoved it in my pocket and took another drink. The ice was melting fast—an indication of just how hot this bar was becoming. I blew out a breath, lifting the damp hair from my forehead, then said, "How did you manage to survive the destruction when no else did?"

"Blind luck." Once again, the memory of the past seemed to crowd close. "I'd been out of the water too long and my skin was itchy, so I headed down to the beach."

I nodded. According to Leith, sea dragons needed water as much as air dragons needed the sun to fuel their flames. Only for the sea-born, it was a daily necessity, whereas air dragons could survive days on end without being out in the sun.

"And that's where you were attacked?"

He nodded. "I heard screaming and had started to run back, but was confronted by several men with long blades."

"Blades?"

"Blades," he confirmed grimly. "Big brave men that they were, they felt the need to attack a lone teenager in a pack." He shook his head. "It was lucky that I was still close to the water. I went under and stayed there."

"So you didn't actually see the destruction?"

He hesitated. "Some. I poked my head up occasionally, but it was all flame and death. There was nothing I could have done to stop it. There were just too many of them."

"But the town was right next to the sea—you could have flooded the place and washed them away."

"The sea rarely answers the call of one so young." He grimaced. "Which didn't stop me from trying, believe me."

"So why didn't your parents—"

"My parents," he interrupted, voice terse, "must have been among the first to die. Otherwise, they would have."

And he felt guilty about their deaths. Or rather, he felt guilty about surviving when everyone else had not. It was all there to be seen in the shadowed depths of his eyes.

"Did you see any of them at all?"

"Not really." He drained his glass. "They wore masks, all of them. Ski masks."

"Why would they hide their faces if they intended to destroy the whole town? That makes no sense at all."

He shrugged. "Maybe they simply wanted to ensure that if someone *did* escape, they wouldn't be able to identify them."

Who in the hell would they identify them to? As Angus had already pointed out, neither the human cops nor the dragon council were likely prospects, no matter how many people had died. And the cliques weren't any different. The ones who had died were the unwanted.

Then again, maybe this *was* the council's way of taking care of the draman problem. Anything was possible.

I drank some more Coke, then asked, "Have you ever tried to find any of the men involved?"

He hesitated, and emotion flashed in his eyes. Anger, regret, and something else I couldn't really name, but which stirred a response in me nevertheless. I licked my lips and ignored muscles twitching with the need to be gone. Now. I could defend myself. I'd proven that time and again. And one lone sea dragon didn't pose half the threat that my clique had over the years.

"Hard to get revenge on folk when you never saw their faces," he said.

And *that* was his first complete lie. I could taste it, could practically feel the air curling away from the poisonous words. Trae, my half brother, might have the dragon knack of stealing, but I'd inherited something far more useful—the ability to sense falsehoods.

Of course, it wasn't infallible, as the scars on my back and side would attest, but it had saved my life more often than not, and I wasn't about to doubt it now.

"You said they wore ski masks. If you were close enough to see that, then you were close enough to notice other things."

He studied me for a moment, his eyes suddenly as flat as his expression. "Like what?"

"Were they human or dragon kind, for a start?"

He snorted softly. "Humans would have been nei-ther fast enough nor strong enough to overpower a whole town of draman."

That was true, but the question still had to be asked. Not all draman inherited dragon powers. Some fell on the human side when it came to capabilities. "What about plate numbers? Or voices?"

"I never heard or saw any cars. And I would have, if they'd driven."

If they'd flown, they must have landed away from the town, so as not to alert the townsfolk of their ap-proach. The rush of wind past a dragon's wing wasn't exactly quiet.

He finished the dregs of his beer then shoved back the chair and stood. "What time do you want to ren-dezvous tomorrow?"

I hesitated, wondering if I would need backup. I might be able to defend myself, but something about this dragon made me wary, and it wasn't just the lies and half-truths I was sensing. "How about eleven?"

I could ring Leith when I got back home to see if he would accompany me. And if not, maybe he could lend me one of his investigators. I'd feel better if my back was covered. Hell, if I knew where my brother was, I'd ring him, but he was off somewhere again.

"Eleven would be good. And don't forget to bring the rest of the money." Angus gave me a nod, then turned and walked out of the bar.

I drained my Coke, then stood. The room spun for a moment, and I grabbed at the tabletop to steady my-self. Sweat broke out across my brow and I swiped at it irritably. Lord, I didn't think it was *that* hot in here.

Or maybe it wasn't the heat. The doctors had

warned me something like this was likely to happen after the blood loss I'd suffered in the accident, which meant I needed to go home and rest, just like they'd ordered.

I grabbed my jacket from the back of the chair, then gave the bartender a nod and walked out. I could feel his gaze in the middle of my back, like an itch I couldn't quite scratch, and again unease washed through me.

It was a relief to hit the street again, although the brightness of the dying day had me blinking after the dark of the bar. I raised my face to the sunshine, feeling the power of the oncoming dusk beginning to rise and letting it slither through me to stir the fires in my soul. Yet neither that energy nor the accompanying breeze did much to clear my spinning head.

I flicked a droplet of sweat from my nose, then turned and headed up the street. Once I got home, I could grab a shower. That would cool me down.

But my legs felt shaky and the footpath seemed to be swaying and my stomach was roaring up my throat. I swallowed back bile and grabbed at the nearby wall, trying to steady myself. Lord, maybe I *should* have stayed in the hospital after all. Or maybe the drugs they'd given me were finally beginning to take effect.

Drugs . . .

No, I thought, suddenly remembering the forced half smile the bartender had given me when he'd brought over the drinks. *It couldn't be.*

Why in the hell would the bartender want to drug me? And why would he even bother? It made no sense.

Unless . . .

Unless he was a part of this whole deal. Unless he was one of those who had helped kill Rainey.

I shoved a shaking hand into the pocket of my jacket, dragged out my cell phone, and flipped it open. The little number pad blurred and danced before my eyes. I swore and swiped at a button, trying to get the phone book up. The screen went white and tiny little icons jigged about happily.

Again bile burned the back of my throat. I swallowed heavily and hit a button. Another screen flashed up, but I couldn't read it. The characters were just a blur.

Then my fingers lost their strength and the phone hit the ground. Before I could grab it, a passerby kicked it away. It skidded off the pavement and into the path of a car. The wheels squashed it flat.

Fuck.

I needed help and I needed it fast. I tried to grab at someone as they passed, but it felt like my limbs were trapped in treacle, and I was unable to complete the motion. The movement unbalanced me and I went down hard while the person strode on, oblivious. Pain radiated from both my knee and my barely healed side—red-hot pokers that did little to clear the fog.

"Are you all right, lass?" someone said

Angus.

"What?" It came out croaky, and I licked dry lips. "What have you done?"

"What I had to do," he said, and I swear there was a note of sorrow in his voice. "Give me your hand."

"Go fuck yourself."

He sighed and grabbed my arm, hauling me to my feet. I reached down, deep into the part of me that was dragon, and called to the fire. But for the first time in my life, she didn't answer. She was as drugged and confused as the rest of me, and even the flames in my soul seemed dimmer.

Fear swept through me. God, what had he done?

I tried to hit him, but my fist swished through thin air and unbalanced me even more. And then unconsciousness claimed me once again.

Chapter Three

Voices invaded the darkness.

Voices that were gruff one moment, and oddly urbane the next. One was far stronger than the other, but together they formed a chorus that made no actual sense. What they were saying remained tantalizingly beyond my reach, swimming in a thick soup of incomprehensibility.

But as my thoughts traveled slowly toward consciousness, the rhythm of speech and the words became things I could grasp and understand.

The stronger of the voices belonged to Angus. The other one—although almost tinny in its tones—was vaguely familiar. A ghost from the past I couldn't quite put my finger on.

And whoever he was, he had no smell. The only person who seemed to be here—wherever the hell here was—besides me was Angus, which meant he was probably talking on the phone.

"For the third and final time, yes, I'm sure it's her."

There was a distinct edge riding through Angus's gruff tones and it had confusion swirling. It spoke of anger and hate, but that made no sense if Angus was working for the men behind all this.

He continued. "And no, I didn't see her stain, because she refused to show it. But it's her. Aside from the scar from the accident your man botched, she matched the picture you sent me perfectly."

Oh God, the other man had arranged the truck accident. Which meant that I was close to finding out who he was. If I survived whatever they currently had planned for me, that is.

But if they were going to kill me, why drug me first? They'd certainly shown no compunction about trying to kill me before, so why hesitate now? Or was that what waited for me once these men finished talking?

Fear rose, then drifted away. And suddenly, being drugged seemed like a good thing.

"She won't be restrained by darkness. The bitch never could be." The familiar voice held a hint of sophistication that came with money and a cultured upbringing, which was odd because I really didn't know anyone who matched either of those criteria.

Yet there was something about the voice that chilled me.

It was a voice that held no sense of life, no sense of compassion. Just a cold determination to do what had to be done. Once upon a time I'd known a man like that. It was he who'd given me my scars, and he'd made my teenage years hell.

Of course, there *were* some who said I'd deserved

it. I'd struck back and disfigured him—something few half-breeds ever had the skill or the gumption to do.

But this *couldn't* be him. Aside from the fact that Seth had apparently died in an accident, there'd never been anything cultured about his manner or his tone.

Although it still sounded like him.

"The drug will keep her out for twenty-four hours. At least." Was I imagining it, or was the edge I sensed in Angus's voice filled with bitterness? He sure didn't sound like a willing henchman, but maybe the fact that my mind seemed to be drifting a layer or two below true wakefulness was affecting my perceptions. Especially given the sense of wrongness I'd been getting about Angus in the bar.

"Trust me, the bitch can never be relied on to do the expected. Throw her in the box with the muerte. If he can't get out, no one can." He hesitated, and a hint of cold amusement came into his voice. "And it'll have the side benefit of bringing back some very delicious memories for her."

Confusion rolled through me. The man I was remembering hadn't known me in *that* way. Oh, he'd wanted to, hence his scars and, subsequently, mine. So why would he imply otherwise?

Angus merely grunted. It wasn't a happy sound.

"Evan will warn us if anybody comes looking for her, won't he?" the urbane man added.

Evan? Not a name I knew, but one I could file away for later.

If there *was* a later.

"That's what we pay him for." Again, that bitterness. It just didn't jell with a man who was only doing his job.

"Good," the urbane man continued. "Tell Albert and Jay I'll be there tomorrow night."

"Will do."

"And tell them to keep an eye on that fucking muerte. Just because he's flamed out doesn't mean he's not dangerous."

"If he's such a problem, then why don't you just kill the bastard?"

"Because we need to know who set him on to us. The order didn't come from the council as a whole, but someone on the council *must* suspect. Muerte rarely move without orders."

Angus grunted. A second later there was a soft beep, then a clunk, as if something light had hit a seat. The phone, probably.

God, I'd have to find some way to escape before his planned rendezvous tomorrow night. Whoever he might have been in my past, this was the man who'd ordered the hit on Rainey, and I had no doubt he planned to do the same to me. I might need to kill him to free Rainey's soul, but even in my confused state, I had little hope that he'd face me alone. One full dragon I could cope with. Two was out of my league.

And I needed to survive the encounter to perform the ceremony that would free Rainey.

The throaty roar of an engine invaded the brief silence and the metal flooring underneath me began to vibrate. I was in a van, obviously, but the knowledge did me little good. I remained as I was, caught between consciousness and oblivion, struggling against the odd lethargy that held my body so still. I wished I could do something, anything, to fight these men, but my body remained frozen and unresponsive. Sound was my only ally, and even that was distant, the rumble of the van consuming all other noises. Angus might be at the wheel, but he was as quiet as death.

I'm not sure how long we drove but, in my disconnected state, it seemed to be for only a few minutes. The rumble and vibration of the van stopped and sweet silence filled the void. Then a door slammed, another opened, and hands were grabbing me, hauling me roughly along the metal flooring until I was flung like a sack over the shoulder of someone who smelled like sea and smoke.

The urge to fight, to kick and scream and run, swept through me again. But as hard as I tried to make my muscles respond, they wouldn't. Just like the dragon deep within.

What the hell had they given me?

It was a thought I pondered as more doors slammed open and closed, followed by the heavy sound of footsteps on wooden flooring.

"Albert, Jay, get your lazy asses down here immediately." Angus's voice was sharp and loud, echoing through the molasses of my thoughts.

There was a metallic click and Angus stopped abruptly. A soft, close voice said, "I've been watching you for the last two minutes. I could have shot you anytime I desired, sea dragon."

He said *sea dragon* like it was an insult. Obviously *not* a man who had any idea just how dangerous sea dragons could be.

Angus's snort was derisive, but I could feel the tension in him. "And that would have made the boss real happy, now wouldn't it?"

"I ain't afraid of the boss," the silky voice replied.

"Then you're a bigger fool than I thought. He'd kill his own fucking brother if he thought it would benefit him." He shifted my weight a little. "We've got another one for you to look after. The boss will be back tomorrow night to interview her."

A hand grabbed my hair and I heard an intake of breath, as if he were sniffing it. Then he yanked my head up. Suddenly I was glad my muscles weren't responding, because my instinctive reaction would have been to spit in his face—and I had a bad feeling that would *not* have been a good idea.

"Even with that scar, she's a pretty one."

"And she'll remain that way," Angus said sharply. "The boss wants her uncut and untouched until he gets here."

"The delay will only make her eventual interrogation that much sweeter," the other man said, and there was something in the way he said it that had chills skating down my spine. He let my head drop. "What has she done?"

"She's a reporter asking too many questions."

"Doing a story on the towns or the disappearances?"

"Both."

The other man grunted. "You'd think no one would be interested in ghosts these days. We locking her in darkness?"

"She's dragon, so it's best to." Footsteps echoed as we began to move again. "How's the muerte?"

"After more than a week of darkness, the fire has all but gone out of him."

Angus snorted again. "Thought those boys were tougher than that."

We seemed to be moving downward now, and the

bright sense of light faded into darkness and shadows. The realization gave me hope. If I was beginning to recognize light and shadow from behind closed eyelids, then maybe whatever drug they'd given me was starting to wear off.

Angus stopped and somewhere ahead a door creaked open. The shadows became true blackness and the air became stale, smelling faintly of mold. I was slung onto something hard and cold, my head hitting with enough force that stars danced behind my closed eyelids. Footsteps retreated, a door slammed, and thick, cold silence swirled all around me.

At least I wasn't alone.

The muerte was here. Even if those men hadn't said as much, I still would have known. The odd, tingling sort of awareness running through the part of me that wasn't human suggested as much. But it was an awareness that had been hit-and-miss most of my life—sometimes accurate, sometimes not—and it was a lottery that had caused me a lot of grief over the years.

Of course, I had no idea what a muerte actually was—aside from the fact that *muerte* meant "death" in Spanish.

That they were locking him away in darkness meant he was at least a dragon, because dragons—and most draman—needed the warmth of the sun to fuel their shape-shifting and fires. Locking them away from sunlight for any length of time robbed them of two dangerous weapons—which was a good thing in this case, because it meant he posed no immediate threat.

Not that the darkness presented any real problem to me, but that was a secret I kept closely guarded. I'd been shoved in more than one dark box over the years, and the terror I'd shown on release had been due to the length of my stay rather than the darkness itself. I'd never been sure if they'd release me or forget me.

If the voice on the phone *had* been someone from my past, maybe that's what they'd been referring to, rather than anything sexual.

Old fears stirred, but I shoved them away. I wouldn't be forgotten this time, even though *this* time it was probably the better option.

I swallowed, and centered my thoughts back on the man in the room with me. Angus had said he'd been over a week without sunlight. It was a long time for anyone, so why had Angus expected more from the muerte?

It was a question I pondered in the darkness, though no answers were ever likely to come to mind. My clique hadn't exactly exerted themselves to educate us half-breeds. Not when it came to dragon lore, anyway.

I have no idea how long I lay there before I realized I could move my fingers. It could have been hours, and it could have been minutes. There was no point of reference in this utter darkness, and my mind was still oddly disconnected. I tapped my fingers against the cool steel of my bed, strangely reassured by the movement. Gradually, the rest of my body began responding, and suddenly the dragon came roaring to the surface, until my whole body burned with the heat of her. The glow chased the chill from the blackness.

My gaze was drawn immediately to the man on the other side of the room. Like me, he lay on a bed that was little more than a slab of polished steel. Unlike me, he'd evidently put up quite a fight before capture. What remained of his clothes were bloody and torn, and the strong body visible beneath the many rents and tears was cut and bruised. There were several more recent wounds, some of them still bleeding, some of them barely beginning to bruise.

His face was as battered as his body, and his hair—which was as black as the darkness had been before my flames had returned—was matted with sweat and blood. His eyes were closed, his breathing even, and he showed no awareness of my being in the cell with him. I wondered if the cause was drugs or the beating he'd received.

My gaze lingered a little on the strong, straight length of his nose and the lushness of the lips underneath, before moving on to canvass the room. At which point, my stomach dropped.

I *had* been locked in a place like this once before. I'd barely been ten at the time, but even at that age I had gained a high degree of control over my flames. It was the only thing that had saved me when Seth and his friends had locked me into one of the clique's main freezers and left me there. Rainey had rescued me before I'd actually become a popsicle, but it had been a close thing.

And I'd been afraid of anything resembling a freezer ever since.

I closed my eyes and took several deep breaths, trying to calm the rush of fear, trying to stop the instinctive need to shiver and flame. This small, dark metal box *wasn't* cold. It wasn't a freezer, and I was in no danger of becoming a popsicle.

It was just a small, metal-lined basement—one obviously designed to contain dragons.

And best of all, I wasn't alone in *this* darkness.

I forced my eyes back open and tried to concentrate on realities, not fear. Five steps, if that, divided the four walls. Beyond the two steel beds and the solid metal door to my left, there was nothing else in the room. No windows, no vents—although they had to be here somewhere, because the air, although stale, stirred sluggishly. But there was also nothing that would provide any obvious form of escape. There wasn't even a smoke detector in the ceiling that I could flame and perhaps get help that way.

I swung my legs over the bed and slowly sat up. For a moment, the room spun around me and bile rose. I swallowed heavily and breathed deep and slow, until the spinning faded and the urge to throw up went away.

I waited several more seconds, just to be sure, then did a check of everything I had on me. My cell phone had been smashed by a car, and the only other things I'd been carrying were my keys and my wallet. My keys—like my jacket—were gone, but my wallet was still in my pocket. Okay, in a different pocket, which probably meant someone had been rifling through it. I took it out and discovered that while my cash, ATM card, and credit cards were still there, my drivers license and press card had gone. So they now knew not only who I was, but where I worked and lived.

They could find me again.

Not that they'd had any trouble finding me before. But the thought sent a chill down my spine and fear rose again, thick and fast. I thrust it away, back into that dark corner of my mind that held the grief. I needed to get out of this place before I started worrying about who these men were and how they knew so much about me.

Slowly, carefully, I pushed to my feet. My side twinged—a reminder that it hadn't yet healed—but my stomach remained still and the room didn't spin. I licked dry lips and wished I had some water to ease the metallic dryness in my throat. But that wasn't likely to happen unless I got out of this prison, and I couldn't do *that* without help. I shuffled forward carefully. It was only five steps, but it felt like a mile and left me tired and shaky. What the hell had they given me?

I dropped to my knees beside the stranger's bed, sucking in several breaths to stop the trembling and to feed some strength back into my limbs. It didn't seem to help much. It probably wouldn't until the drug leached out of my system.

I reached out and carefully touched the stranger's face. His skin was cold, almost clammy. It meant he'd spent far too long locked in this darkness. His body was beginning to slow down, getting ready for hibernation. It wasn't something most dragons attempted these days—simply because the number of humans who walked this earth meant it was no longer safe to do so—but I doubted this was deliberate. It was probably an instinctive reaction to the endless darkness, and it was something I'd have to stop if we were to get out of here.

I might be able to fight, but there were three men, at least, beyond this cell, and I wasn't stupid enough to think I could tackle them alone. I needed help, and this man was the only likely prospect around.

Of course, there was no guarantee that he *would* help me get out of here, but I couldn't imagine him wanting to remain in this darkness or take any more beatings.

I let my fingers drift from his chin, sliding them along the sinews of his neck then down underneath the torn and bloodied edges of his shirt. His breathing was soft and even, his chest muscular but not overly so. I let my hand rest in the middle of his chest, enjoying the feel of soft hair under my fingertips and the strong, steady beat of his heart. His slip toward hibernation must be a recent thing, because that rhythm would be much slower otherwise.

After another deep breath, I concentrated on the heat within my body, building up the fire until it was a maelstrom inside me. Then I channeled it forward, into my fingertips and down into his flesh. Chasing the chill from his skin, warming the inner dragon. I had no idea how long this would take, but hopefully it wouldn't . . .

The thought died as a hand grabbed mine and ripped it away from his body.

My heart just about stopped and a scream roared up my throat, but it came out as little more than a squeak as I clamped down on it hard. I didn't need my jailers to know I was awake. Didn't need them to know that the stranger was awake.

"What are you?" His voice was deep and smoky, thick with disuse and rich with a menace that sent a shiver down my spine.

"A prisoner, like you." I tried to pull my wrist from his grip, but it was stuck fast.

"Then why do you glow?"

"Because I was using my heat to warm you." I pulled at my wrist again. "Damn it, let me go."

He did so with a suddenness that had me sprawling backward. I picked myself up and scrambled to my side of the box, letting my fire die until it was little more than a muted glow that barely heated my skin, let alone the darkness.

But it was enough to see his eyes. They were as black as the shadows and as cold as hell.

I shivered. Not a man to be taken lightly.

"Dragons can't use their fire at night."

"Then it's just as well it's not night, isn't it?" Which wasn't exactly a lie, because the slivers of energy still riding the air suggested the last vestiges of daylight hadn't fully given way to darkness.

I pushed up onto the metal bench, but felt no better for being at eye level with the man. He could freeze an ocean with that stare of his.

I raised a hand and half covered the angry-looking scar on my forehead, then realized I was being stupid and let it drop. What I looked like or what he actually thought of me didn't matter. All that did was his willingness to help me.

"You were slipping into hibernation," I added, somewhat snippily. "Maybe I should have let you."

Since I *did* want his help, they probably weren't the wisest of words, but I just couldn't help it.

He raised a dark eyebrow. It lent him an arrogance that seemed appropriate given his strong nose and steely gaze. "So why didn't you?"

"Because there are three guards upstairs and that's one too many for me to handle." Hell, *two* was probably too many for me to handle, especially if they were all armed. I might have flames, but they couldn't beat back a bullet.

He smiled. Like his eyes, it was a cold, hard thing,

and yet it sent my pulse tripping. It was very easy to imagine those lips touched by the warmth of a real smile. Very easy to imagine the beauty of it.

"In case you haven't noticed, we're in a rather secure cell. It has no windows, it's lined with some sort of metal sheeting that is impervious to flames, and it has a rather thick metal door."

"I can see that. I'm not blind."

"Then how do you plan to escape?"

His tone was that of a parent humoring a well-meaning but errant child, and that irritated me even more than his stare. "I haven't been here very long. Give me a chance to think."

Again a smile teased the corners of his mouth, but this time, it hinted at amusement. My breath caught briefly in my throat. Lord help me if he actually flung a full smile my way. I had a feeling it would be devastating.

"Don't you think if there was a way out, I would have found it by now?"

"Well, considering you were unconscious and slipping into hibernation when they dropped me in here, I'd have to say no. I mean, it's hard to be proactive about escaping when you're out of it, isn't it?"

He studied me for a moment, then swung around on the bench and sat up. His long fingers gripped the base tightly for several seconds, hinting at either pain or dizziness—neither of which showed in his stony expression.

"Who are you?" he asked, after a moment.

"What are you?" I countered. I might want this man's help escaping, but I wasn't about to trust him with anything more vital than that. "The men upstairs were calling you a muerte. What the hell is that?"

"Literally, *muerte* means 'death.'"

And death had *never* looked so good. I mentally slapped the thought away, and said, "I realize that. I meant, why would they call *you* that?"

Amusement flirted with the night-dark depths of his eyes, a spark that did little to warm the chill of his countenance. "Because it's my occupation."

O-kay. I'd landed in a cell with a trained killer. Great. I shifted back on the seat a little, and the amusement in his eyes grew stronger.

Several limp black strands of hair fell across his forehead. He brushed them away with strong hands that were as bruised and as beaten as the rest of him, then said, "How does a dragon not know what a muerte is?"

I smiled, and saw something flicker in his eyes. Surprise, perhaps. It was a reaction as odd as the man himself. "I never said I was a dragon."

"You flame like a dragon."

"So I do." I pushed up from the bench too fast and pain flared, providing yet another reminder that I hadn't fully healed. I grimaced, grabbing at my side as I walked to the door. The stranger's gaze followed me— a weighted heat that caressed my skin and sent a tremor running through me. I did my best to ignore it—and him—and bent to study the door.

"It's solid," he said, the amusement that had been so evident in his eyes now reaching his voice.

"It certainly looks that way."

But I'd learned long ago that everything—and everyone—had a weak point, no matter how minor. This door might look rock solid, but that didn't mean it wouldn't give way if it was given the right sort of push.

I just had to uncover what sort of push that was.

There was no handle on this side, but that wasn't much of a surprise. Dragons were notorious thieves, and more than capable of cracking most of the locks and security devices currently on the market. Thieving was in a dragon's blood, and it was a skill learned—and honed—since birth. Hell, even draman could pick a lock faster than most humans could blink.

Not that my clique had actually taught us draman that trick, either, but some skills were easily picked up when they were being practiced all around you.

I peered into the small gap between the door and the frame. The metal bolt on the other side was at least an inch wide and who knew how thick.

"There's a rather large dead bolt out there," I said. "They're making sure you don't escape."

"You're in the same cell, remember." He studied me for a moment, then added, "Why is that? What did you do?"

"Asked a few too many questions, I think." I stepped back and studied the door as a whole. No hinges on this side. "What's your excuse?"

"Much the same thing, really."

I glanced at him. He looked healthier than he had five minutes ago, so obviously the warmth I'd lent him was chasing the coolness from his skin. But it wouldn't last long—not if he remained in this darkness.

"What questions were you asking that you shouldn't?"

"Lady, when you start answering my questions, I'll start answering yours."

"My name is Mercy Reynolds." Then I hesitated, wondering how much I should tell him. But really, what was the point of hiding anything? It wasn't like I actually knew anything vital. "And I was asking about two cleansed towns and missing draman."

"So was I."

"Then obviously someone doesn't want those questions asked." That was a point I was *all* too aware of already. I looked at the door and ignored the tendrils of pain and anger that rose with the thought. "What's the melting point of steel?"

"I have no idea."

I found myself grinning. "So Mr. Death doesn't know everything?"

"It's Damon—Damon Rey—not Death. And why would you want to know the melting point of steel? You think you can melt the door with your flames?"

His tone gently mocked and I met his gaze with a frown. "You think I can't?"

"Dragon fire is fierce, granted, but it's not concentrated enough to generate the sort of heat needed to melt *that* door. It's flameproof, like the walls."

Meaning he'd tried when he'd first arrived, obviously. "But I don't want to melt the door. I just want to heat the bolt enough so that it's pliable. Then we should be able to push it open."

"It still needs a concentrated heat."

That, I *could* do. Fire had been my only defense for a good part of my life, and I'd learned pretty quickly to make the most of it. Not even the dragons in my clique had my control—which didn't mean I was right and this man was wrong.

"So you did try to flame the door when you were first thrown in here?"

"Once, and they've pretty much kept me drugged since then. By the time they woke me to question me, I was sunshine-starved and had flamed out."

"So how long have you actually been in here?"

"What day is it?"

"Friday."

"And the date?"

"April fourth."

He swore softly under his breath. I raised my eyebrows. "Is that bad?"

His gaze came to mine again, dark eyes intense. Angry. And though that anger wasn't aimed at me, it was a frightening thing to behold.

"It means that I've been here for thirteen days."

Thirteen days? Without sunlight? Angus might not have been impressed, but I sure was. Most dragons could survive four or five days without sunlight, but to go thirteen—and still be lucid—took amazing strength.

"Are you going to be strong enough to handle those men if I can get us out of here?"

There was nothing pleasant or warm about his smile or the sudden glint in his cold, dark eyes. "You get us out of this room and I'll make sure we get free."

I believed him. It was impossible not to. Even so, I couldn't help wondering if Mr. Death himself might be more of a problem once we'd gotten out of here than the men upstairs.

But what other option did I have? There was only one thing that was certain—I didn't want to be here when that well-cultured man came back. One look at the mess Damon was in suggested their methods of getting information weren't ones I'd enjoy.

As if there'd ever been any doubt of that.

So I said, "Can you sense anyone nearby?"

"You really are going to try to melt the bolt, aren't you?"

Annoyance ran through me. "You got a better idea?"

"No. And if you can flame at night, why do you need me to sense the other dragons? Shouldn't you be able to tell that yourself?"

"I should, but I can't. Is there anyone near?"

He paused for a moment then shook his head. "They're both upstairs."

"Both? There should be three." Unless Angus had already left. But why would he do that? Was he really just a messenger boy or was something else going on?

"There aren't. Trust me."

Not as far as I can throw you. I turned away and studied the bolt again. It looked *really* solid—and despite my earlier boast, I'd never tried to do anything like this before. Not with steel, anyway.

I raised a hand and lightly pressed one finger against the gap between the door and the frame. With the bolt directly opposite my finger, I reached down and called to the waiting fire. It came in an explosive burst of energy that had heat radiating from my skin and the air churning. I frowned and concentrated the flames, channeling and intensifying them, forcing them away from my skin and down into my hand, into that one finger. Heat shot out from my fingertip, the glow of it so intense I had to close my eyes lest the image burn itself into my retinas.

I could still feel the heat of it, though. Could still see the glow of it, even through closed eyelids.

"I've never seen anyone control their flames with such precision."

Damon's words were little more than a whisper past my left ear. He was standing so close that the heat of his body washed across my bare shoulders and arms. So close that the raw, masculine scent of him— a scent that was an odd combination of musk, controlled violence, sweat, and blood—filled every breath, until it felt like his very essence was invading mine.

But perhaps what was even scarier was the fact that there'd been absolutely no sound to indicate he'd moved.

True to his name, he was as silent as a ghost.

I briefly opened an eye to check how I was doing and saw that the bolt was beginning to glow. It *was* working. But sweat was trickling down my forehead and my arm was beginning to shake. Worse, the maelstrom inside was rapidly losing its intensity. Generally, a dragon could flame for as long as she or he was awake and aware, simply because we were fueled by the heat of the sun. But it was now night, and my flames were drawing their energy directly from my body—a body that had lost a lot of blood in the accident and was still very battered and bruised.

I opened my eyes. The tight beam of fire was definitely less intense than it had been, but the bolt was glowing brighter.

I just had to keep going for a little bit longer, and we might be able to get out of here.

I bit my lip and concentrated on the flame, forcing as much energy as I could into it. The tremor in my arm spread to the rest of me, until my whole body seemed to be shaking with effort.

Hands touched my waist—just enough to hold me steady, and to catch me should my knees buckle. Damon's grip on my injured right side—though gentle—had the pain flaring again, but his touch was also heated and strong, and the dragon inside wanted to snatch and use it. It was a temptation I resisted. He needed to cope with the men upstairs, and who knew how much strength he actually had left? He might have lasted longer in darkness than I'd ever thought possible, but I doubted even Death could go on forever without the sun's warmth to fuel him.

The metal finally began to glow white hot. At first it was little more than a small pinprick right at the center of the flames, but it gradually spread, flowing outward across the hot metal.

Just a little bit more, I thought—and in that moment, the flames sputtered and died, and my legs went out from underneath me.

Damon caught me one-handed, pressing me against his side while he pushed his weight against the door. The muscles in his arm corded, and the exertion had his body shaking as much as mine.

For a minute I thought it might all be for naught, but slowly, surely, the door began to inch away from the frame. I broke free of his grip and grabbed at the wall to steady myself. Damon flung his full weight against the door and, with little ceremony, the bolt gave way.

The door sprang open. We were free of the cell.

Now we just had to get out of this place and away from the men.

Chapter Four

Damon barely stopped the door from crashing back against the wall. He looked at the melted bolt, at the strings of still glowing metal trailing from it, then at me. In the darkness, his eyes burned with an unearthly heat.

"That's an amazing thing you did there," he said, voice so soft it barely carried.

"Yeah." I blew out a breath and forced my shaking knees to lock. We weren't free yet, and as much as I wanted to sit down and recuperate, that wasn't an option right now. "Where are those men?"

He glanced up the stairs. "One to the left, one outside."

"I'm not going to be of much use on the fighting front at the moment."

His lips twitched, hinting at a smile, and for the second time that night, my breath hitched in reaction. I had an odd feeling this man didn't smile a whole lot, and that was probably a good thing if my reaction to the merest hint of one was anything to go by.

And that reaction was troubling. The last thing I needed was an attraction to a dangerous man—not when such an attraction had gone wrong so often in the past.

"You've upheld your end of the bargain. Time for me to uphold mine." He flexed his arms and his smile faded, his lips becoming as cold and harsh as his expression. "Wait here."

He didn't give me time to answer. He simply turned and melted into the darkness—a shadow that made no sound as he flowed upward and disappeared.

I grabbed the door and swung it closed again, just in case one of the men walked past the stairs. I trusted Damon to do his job, but even Death couldn't be in two places at once. It'd be just my luck that I'd get discovered on the verge of escape.

I pressed back against the wall, hoping the shadows were deep enough to cover my presence. And then I realized that was totally stupid. I mean, the guards were *dragons*. They'd sense me down here in the shadows regardless. I was better off hoping that I regained fire strength quickly so that I'd at least have something to protect myself with.

A clock ticked loudly into the silence and, as the minutes stretched, I wondered what was going on upstairs. I wondered if Damon was taking care of the men or simply getting the hell out. Maybe I was doing him an injustice by thinking that, but there'd been so many other dragons over the years who—in one way or another—had let me down.

I'm not sure how long I stood there before the

awareness that something was wrong began to steal through my soul. I pressed back harder against the brick wall, the chill of it seeping into my spine, making me feel colder than I'd ever thought possible.

I stared at the stairs, hating the fact that I didn't know what was happening up there. I took one step upward then stopped. I'd been told to wait here and it made sense to do so—especially given my fires were still little more than embers.

But if things *had* gone wrong—if Damon had been too weak to take care of both men—then staying here meant I'd be caught, too. And given I'd basically rendered the lock useless, who knew what they'd do to keep us still and quiet until tomorrow night?

I bit my lip, then slowly climbed the stairs, my heart racing so hard it felt like it was going to tear out of my chest as I strained to hear the slightest sound.

But nothing and no one else seemed to be moving.

Besides the clock, the house was deathly quiet. I reached the top step and paused. My dragon senses still weren't providing much in the way of information, which was damn frustrating because I really could have done with a little extra help.

But then, that was practically the story of my life. Things never went the way I wanted or expected them to.

Like Rainey. I pushed away the flare of pain and tried to concentrate on the here and now.

I peered carefully around the corner. Darkness lay to my right, but to the left, muted light filtered through huge ceiling-to-floor windows, highlighting the dust on the wooden floors and giving the cobwebs hanging from the cornices a silvery edge. Obviously, Albert and Jay weren't all that into housekeeping.

I looked at the darker end of the corridor. No windows, no filtered light. Nothing to indicate anyone or anything might be nearby.

It was the perfect place to hide.

Whether someone was, I couldn't say. My radar for that sort of information was still off-line. Which meant, unfortunately, there was only one way I was going to find out.

I slipped off my shoes, holding them in one hand while I felt along the wall with the other. Normally, dragons—and draman—could see pretty well in the darkness, but with my energy levels so low, it seemed "human" sight was all I was going to get.

My fingers hit a door frame and I hesitated. The clock's ticking suddenly seemed louder, and it was coming from beyond this doorway. I peered around cautiously. Floral patterned drapes framed the deep-set windows opposite, beyond which glowed the sullen, muted fire of an outside light. Little else was visible through the glass. The fog was too thick.

I scanned the small room, noting the plush chairs and mahogany furniture, the bookcases lined with books. This was someone's home rather than just a place being used as a prison.

I moved past the doorway and continued on. The ticking began to recede and the silence seemed to grow thicker. Another doorway—this time the entrance to a dining room that held a table longer than my entire kitchen. After checking it was empty, I moved on.

The hallway hooked left and led into the kitchen.

On the floor lay a lanky, dark man, the remains of a cup in his left hand and a pool of dark liquid gradually spreading out across the tiled floor. Ten feet beyond him lay Damon.

I swore under my breath and ran over, squatting down beside him and quickly touching his neck for a pulse. It was there, but felt too quick, as if his heart was straining. His skin was cool and edging toward clammy again, meaning the heat I'd loaned him hadn't been enough to keep him going. This wasn't surprising considering he'd been locked up for thirteen days, and that he had stopped me before I'd really had a chance to fuel him properly.

I lightly pinched his cheek, trying to get a response. He made a sound low down in his throat—a soft growl that echoed across the silence—but otherwise didn't move. But we couldn't stay here. Even if Damon had managed to take care of the second guard before he'd collapsed, there was no saying that Angus or someone else wasn't near.

I leaned down close. "Damon, we need to get out of here."

He didn't respond. I pinched his cheek again, harder this time, and he jerked away from my touch. His eyes flew open but his dark gaze was unfocused and his pupils large.

Behind us, something buzzed, and my heart jumped into my throat. I swung around, and saw the transmitter on the bench.

"Jay, where the hell are you? You were supposed to relieve me five minutes ago."

Though the voice was filled with annoyance, I recognized it nonetheless. It was the man with the silky voice—the one who'd looked forward to questioning me.

God, we *had* to get out of here. Now, before that man came up to check what was going on.

I pressed a hand against Damon's chest and reached for the fires deep inside me. They were still little more than smoldering embers, but I grabbed for them anyway, forcing the heat down through my fingers and into Damon's body. It left me cold and slightly dizzy, but he jerked under my touch and the unfocused look left his eyes.

"Jay, if you're asleep," that silky voice said again, "I'm going to kick your fucking butt."

The anger in the guard's voice was sharper. If he came up here to see what was going on, we'd be in trouble.

"We need to go," I said, pulling my hand from Damon's still cool flesh. He needed sunlight desperately. The little amount of heat he was getting from me just wasn't enough to keep his body going for very long.

I rose. My head spun again, but I resisted the urge to grab at the nearby countertop and offered him a hand instead. He ignored it and pushed to his feet, his jaw thrusting out and determination evident in the fierce glint in his eyes.

"Wait," he said, and staggered across to the man on the floor.

He dropped down beside him, his knees splashing into the edges of the coffee spill, and pressed a hand against the unconscious guard's chest. Flickers of flame jumped from the guard's skin to Damon's fingertips, and I realized that he was stealing the man's heat.

This was *not* a practice that had council approval—in any way, shape, or form—but I couldn't lend him more of my own heat, and if we were to have any hope against the remaining guard, then Damon needed to gain some strength.

I crossed my arms and glanced across at the outside doorway, half expecting the other guard to burst in and catch us. He didn't, but that didn't stop the nerves or the crawling need to be gone.

"Okay," Damon said eventually. He pushed to his feet and stepped across the prone guard, who had a distinctly ashen cast to his features now. He'd be weak when he came to, and I couldn't be unhappy about that, not when our escaping could depend on it.

Damon caught my hand, his fingers wrapping around mine. His flesh was far warmer than before, his grip firm. Part of me wanted to steal some of that heat for myself, but I resisted the temptation. He needed it. I didn't.

We moved quickly through the rest of the kitchen and out a side exit. Stairs ran down into the darkness and small garden lights curved away from the house, their brightness muted by the fog.

We ran down stairs, trying to be as quiet as possible, but the wooden steps rattled and the sound creaked across the foggy silence. We'd barely reached the main path when a flicker of awareness ran across my senses, signaling someone up ahead. Obviously, my dragon senses were slowly coming back online. A heartbeat later, a bright light pierced the darkness, sweeping across the trees and the stony path, missing Damon's toes by inches.

He didn't say anything, simply pulled me off the

path and into the trees. I couldn't see the point of hiding. The man ahead was a dragon, which meant he'd sense us in here anyway. Though I guess the trees did give us one advantage—it was harder for the guard to get off a decent shot if he was carrying a weapon.

And he probably was. Full dragons couldn't flame at night, so carrying a gun was probably the next best option, even if it was unusual for a dragon to do so.

Stones crunched softly up ahead. Damon released my arm, then bent and grabbed a fallen branch, hefting it lightly, as if testing its heaviness and maneuverability. The footsteps slowly drew closer. The guard might not know who was in the trees, but he knew someone was.

Damon tossed the limb across the path and into the trees opposite. It landed with a crash, scattering leaves as it fell to the ground.

The footsteps stopped. Damon touched my shoulder, his fingers warm against my skin. As I looked up, he grabbed the nearest tree branch, shaking it lightly but making no noise. Then he raised two fingers. When I nodded, he melted back into the darkness and disappeared.

I couldn't sense him, even though my senses were humming with the presence of the guard up ahead. I shivered. Obviously, the man who'd called himself Death had a few skills up his sleeve the rest of us didn't know about.

But his departure meant I was now alone and feeling rather vulnerable. Which I wasn't, of course—at least, under normal circumstances.

The footsteps resumed, edging up the path toward me. The bright flashlight swept across the darkness, moving ever closer. I raised a hand and gripped the tree branch above my head, my knuckles almost white with tension.

The light pierced the nearby shadows and my heart just about jumped into my throat. I licked dry lips and watched as it moved on, slowly sweeping across the trees, drawing ever closer.

Two minutes seemed to be taking forever.

The beam of light hit my tree and stopped. Tension slithered through me and my legs twitched with the need to move. While I was protected by the width of the trunk and several lilac bushes, he didn't actually have to see me to know I was there. His dragon senses would be screaming with the knowledge. Whether he actually realized it was me, or whether he simply thought I was an intruder, didn't really matter. He'd know I was here, and that meant time had run out, whether or not Damon's two minutes had passed.

I dropped my weight onto the branch, dragging it down and then letting go. The branch sprang upward, creating a whole lot of noisy distraction. The light jumped around the tree, piercing the shadows in which I stood. I ducked down behind the bush and held my breath, waiting.

For a moment, nothing happened, but my awareness of the guard was so strong it was painful. Then a hand reached over the green leaves of the lilac bush and grabbed at my shirt. "Got you," the man with the silky voice said.

There was a whoosh of air and the guard released me so suddenly that my butt hit the ground, jarring my side and sending pain shooting through the rest of my body. I ignored it, trying to watch the two men fight, but the darkness and the lilac bushes made it all but impossible. So I shifted position, getting ready to run should Damon go down again, my breath catching in my throat and tension winding through me.

After several more grunts, silence fell, silence that seemed to stretch on and on, sawing at my nerves.

Then the bush moved and I jumped, half turning to run before I realized it was Damon. His shirt was in shreds and he was covered in dirt and smears of blood, but he was still on his feet and his skin had a warmer glow than before. But heat wasn't all he'd stolen from the guard. He'd also taken his coat and sweater.

He held the sweater out to me. "You need to keep warm."

I hesitated, then somewhat reluctantly took it. It smelled of musk and sweat, and had my nose wrinkling in distaste. But with my internal fires barely even embers, the sweater would at least keep the night's chill at bay.

"You took your time taking care of that guard," I said, as I pulled the sweater on. "I would have thought Death would be a little more efficient."

He raised an eyebrow as he dragged on the coat, his expression an odd mix of amusement and disdain. "It's better to take your time and do something properly than rush and end up with a half-assed job."

I was tempted to point out that a half-assed job was better than remaining here any longer than necessary, but I resisted. "Just because you can't sense any other guards out there doesn't mean there aren't any."

His dark eyes glinted dangerously. "Trust me; I'm trained to know these things. There's no one else nearby, and the guard beyond that bush is currently fighting hibernation."

He held out his hand. I hesitated, then placed my fingers in his, noticing that not only was his skin far warmer, but the underlying tremor that had been evident the last time he'd stolen heat was absent.

It made me wonder just *how* much he'd stolen and whether hibernation was the worst of the guard's problems right now—made me wonder just what the man called Death was really capable of.

But if these men *had* been involved in Rainey's death, they certainly deserved whatever Damon had dished out to them. And even if they hadn't, I very much doubted whether compassion or kindness was what they'd planned for me tomorrow. The welts on Damon's body were evidence enough of that.

We walked on through the garden until an archway covered by some sort of vine loomed. Damon led me though the green gateway then turned left, following the footpath with long, sure strides. Trees lined either side of the street, their leafy tops lost to the ever-moving fog. The houses were little more than large, somewhat vague, outlines, but even so, I recognized where we were. I'd done a write-up on one of the homes in this area last year.

"We're in the St. Francis Wood area, near Terrace Park," I said softly. I'd been right—Angus *hadn't* driven very far at all. We hadn't even left San Francisco.

"Have you got somewhere safe to go?" Damon asked. "You can't go home. That's the first place they'll look."

Fear twisted through me. I hadn't gotten as far as thinking what I would do now that I was free. Hadn't gotten as far as thinking what *they* might do.

"Do you really think they'll come after me?" Even as I asked the question, I knew the answer. I had firsthand experience of how far they were willing to go. But I was hoping he'd deny the truth, give me false hope, if only for a moment or two.

I should have known a trained assassin would never do something like that.

"They kidnapped you for a reason. I doubt they're going to just give up."

My gaze flicked around, searching the foggy shadows for assailants I knew weren't there. Not yet, anyway.

"But I don't know anything." That probably wasn't the point. They knew I was trying to track down the culprits behind the cleansings—and given the lengths to which they'd already gone to keep their secrets, that would surely be more than enough reason for them to do whatever it took to stop me.

Although again, it begged the question, why kidnap me rather than just kill me?

What was so different now than two days ago, when they'd tried to kill both Rainey and me?

"Understanding the motives of evil men is often a difficult thing," Damon said, philosophically.

I looked up at him. His prominent nose gave his face a sharpness that should have been less than appealing. Instead, his features suggested strength and courage—much like the character of the man himself, I suspected. "We could go to the police. Tell them that those men kidnapped us."

It might work—might being the operative word. And really, could I afford to waste the time? Even if the cops caught our kidnappers, that still left at large the man in charge and the man who'd driven the truck, and it was them I needed caught.

No, not just caught. Dead.

A shiver ran through me. I rubbed my arms, raising static and causing sparks to fly from my fingertips. They spun across the darkness—bright chips of fire that were all too quickly snuffed out.

Much like Rainey.

"You could try," he said, "but I very much doubt our captors would still be at the house by the time the cops got there."

"I could give them the name of the man who drugged me."

"His word against yours. And I bet he'll have a watertight alibi."

That was almost funny, given we were talking about a sea dragon. "So we're just going to do nothing?"

"What you'll be doing is keeping out of their way." His voice held the whip of command. "I'll sort out the problem of our kidnappers."

Anger rose and I clenched my free hand against it. I should have been used to dragon men bossing the rest of us around, yet it still irritated the hell out of me. But then, I guess it was something of a family trait to defy authority. My brother didn't exactly take to being told what to do, either.

"Considering how well you were doing on your escape plan before I got there," I said, voice dry and holding little to hint at the annoyance, "that might not be such a good idea."

"If you have so little faith in me, then why are you still here?"

His tone was amused, though there was little to be

seen in his expression, which was as forbidding as ever.

"We're not out of the woods yet," I said. "You might still come in handy."

Besides, I *did* trust him. To an extent, anyway. That was odd, considering I very rarely trusted anyone—and especially not strangers. But there was something about this man—something about his calm, dark strength that sparked a hint of faith.

"Despite the heat I stole, I may not be up to the task if we get hit again." He slanted me a glance that said our kidnappers had better *not* be on our trail—not if they valued their lives. "And you didn't answer my question."

I must have looked confused, because he added, "About somewhere safe to go."

"Oh. I can go to my brother's." He probably wouldn't be there, but I knew the security code and could get past the additional deadlock easily enough.

Damon didn't look happy with my answer. "That might not be the wisest move. It's not hard to look in the phone book for his address."

"He's my half-brother. And he's not listed."

"Then that's a little better." He contemplated the fog ahead for a moment, and though there seemed to be little to threaten us, his tension was a living thing, filling the soupy darkness with a dangerous energy.

But I really hoped no one else came after us. I'd had enough excitement for one day.

"Where does your brother live?" he added, his gaze coming back to me.

"Parkside. Twenty-ninth Avenue, near Taraval."

"Then we can get you home easily?"

"We can," I said. "But don't feel obliged to escort me. I can look after myself."

"Consider it payback for getting me out of that place," he said, a smile playing around the corners of his lips.

My pulse did a happy little dance at the sight and I dragged my gaze away. It had to be a leftover effect of the drugs, combined with the fact that I hadn't eaten much. Nothing else.

I didn't *want* it to be anything else.

We headed toward the shell-like construction that was West Portal Station and waited for the next train. It wasn't empty; they never were. We sat in silence and were left alone—not surprising, given that his stolen coat couldn't quite cover the bruised and bloody state of his body.

But even on the train, where there was little threat to either of us, his tense alertness never dissipated. By the time we reached my brother's building, I was beginning to jump at shadows myself.

Damon stopped at the bottom of the steps and looked up at the mustard-colored building. "No one appears to be home."

"No. But I'll be all right."

"Are you sure?" His gaze met mine, and though there was nothing to see but distant coldness in those dark depths, there was an edge of concern in his voice. Or maybe it was my imagination, and sudden unwillingness to be left alone.

Which was stupid. Those men couldn't possibly track me down so quickly. They might have my driver's license and press card, but I didn't even keep a photo of my brother in my wallet, so how would they know about him, let alone suspect I'd come here?

If they got your phone number, an inner voice whispered, *then they can get your brother's address.*

Fear swirled, but I stomped on it firmly. Even if they *did* have a hotline to my mom, I doubted she'd give them Trae's address, which meant I was safe enough here for the moment. But the thought of losing my defender still filled me with an odd sort of fear.

"I'll be fine," I said, more to myself than Damon.

He studied me for a moment, and the tension I'd sensed in him earlier sharpened to an awareness that was all sexual. It thrummed through the night, and burned through me. Gleamed in his dark eyes.

I couldn't ignore that awareness, no matter how much I might have wanted to.

He leaned forward until his face was near mine and his mouth was so close I could taste his breath against my lips. It was warm and dry and it drew me even closer, until our lips were almost touching.

"Thank you," he said softly, and then he kissed me. Lightly, sweetly.

I closed my eyes, gently moving into the kiss. Savoring the contact. Wanting more and yet, at the same time, fearing it.

And oh, it was *so* good. So delicious that my body hummed in response and my legs felt weak.

But it ended all too soon. By the time I'd opened my eyes again, Death had disappeared into the foggy darkness.

Chapter Five

The first thing I did when I got upstairs was to phone work to tell them I'd need a new ID card when I got back in another week or so. I couldn't do much about my driver's license—I'd have to show up at the DMV office to fix that, and right now I couldn't take that risk.

With that done, I headed to the kitchen to grab something to eat. Food might not help fuel the fires, but I hadn't eaten since breakfast and I was hungry enough to eat a horse. *Not* that I would have unless really pushed. Their meat tended to be too gamey for me, although many dragons consider them a delicacy.

Luckily for my stomach, my brother kept a far better stock of food than I usually did, so the fridge was full of the good stuff. Several thick beef sandwiches later, I had finally settled the uneasy rumblings in my belly. After rechecking that all the doors were locked, I headed to bed and slept the sleep of the semidrugged—although even the remnants of the drugs had not been strong enough to stop me reliving the moments of the crash, over and over.

It was well after ten when I woke. I dragged myself into the shower, washing away the grit of sleep and the last vestiges of the dreams, then grabbed some coffee and headed over to my brother's desk and laptop.

I found the card Angus had given me and googled his business. His website came up straight away. I clicked on the link and was confronted by a smiling picture of my kidnapper.

I picked up my coffee cup and leaned back in the chair, sipping the steaming liquid as I contemplated his image. Damon had warned me off going after our kidnappers, but I wasn't going to get the answers I needed by doing that. And I very much doubted he was going to return and explain what was going on— especially given he'd been more than a little recalcitrant about the reasons he was there in the first place.

Besides, I had a friend to avenge and a soul to save. And while sitting here in my brother's house might be safer, it wasn't what I *needed* to do.

Angus had known about the accident—he'd obviously been sent information about me *before* our meeting—and he'd been talking to the man who had driven the truck, so he obviously knew a whole lot more than I did. I just needed to find out what.

It would probably be a good idea to find out more about Damon, too—just in case our paths crossed again. I reached for the phone and quickly dialed Leith's direct number.

"Phoenix Investigations, Leith Nichols speaking."

His usually mellow speech had taken on a formal note, and I couldn't help smiling. "And don't you sound mighty professional today, my friend."

"Hey, babe, how you doing?" His voice relaxed into the easygoing tones I was used to.

"I'm doing fine," I said, as I opened the glass door to the small side balcony and stepped outside. The sunlight wrapped around me, warming me, fueling me. I closed my eyes and resisted the urge to hum with pleasure. "But I was wondering if you could do a few favors for me."

"You already owe me dinner. This could bring breakfast into the equation as well."

I grinned. I'd known Leith for nine years, and he'd been trying to get into my bed for eight and a half of those. Trouble was, he wasn't serious, and we both knew it. I think if I ever *did* say yes, he'd actually run a mile the other way rather than risk ruining a wonderful friendship.

Mind you, I had no doubt he'd be a damn fine lover. He just wasn't the right lover for me.

"I don't mind buying you breakfast, but there won't be bed before it."

"Damn, woman, you spoil all my fun."

"Oh, I think you're doing just fine."

He chuckled softly. "What can I do for you, Mercy?"

"You remember that sea dragon I told you about?"

"The one you asked me to do the background check on?"

"That's the one. We had our meet, during which he drugged me, then kidnapped me, then dumped me in a metal-lined cellar over in St. Francis Wood."

"Shit, are you all right?"

"I'm talking to you, aren't I?"

"Thankfully, from the sound of it. You want me to go beat him up for you?"

I laughed at the enthusiasm in his voice. Leith might be the boy-next-door type, but he liked a fight. It got the blood moving, apparently. I guess that's why he'd become a private investigator rather than the lawyer he'd studied to be.

"No, I do not want you to beat him up." Not yet, anyway. "I need to talk to him again."

"You want me along this time?"

I hesitated. To be honest—and despite the fact that he'd drugged me—I didn't fear Angus. But I certainly didn't trust him.

"No, but I need to know if you've uncovered anything about him."

"Mercy, meeting your kidnapper alone is not the brightest idea you've ever had—and you've done a few dumb things in your time."

"Yeah, mostly with either Rainey or you standing right beside me."

"Well, some damn fool has to protect you."

"I'll be fine, Leith. Really."

He grunted, but it didn't sound like he believed me. "We haven't been able to find out much about him. He's been running the bay cruises for about ten years and living here for about as long. He's been a model citizen, is hardworking, and is socking away the cash, from what we saw of his bank records. We haven't been able to uncover much about him before he came here, though."

"He's got a bit of a Scottish accent, so he may have come from there originally."

"We're running overseas checks, but it's going to take time."

"Which I don't have," I snapped. He didn't say anything, and I took a deep, calming breath before adding, "Sorry, Leith."

"It's okay. I know the anger isn't aimed at me." He hesitated, and I heard a soft, feminine voice say something in the background. "Janelle says don't be tempted to go to Whale Point this morning. Angus won't be there, but they will have men watching the area, just in case you show up. You don't want to go anywhere near them."

Janelle was the psychic who worked with Leith, and a sweet old woman who had to be at least eighty. She'd been with Phoenix Investigations for as long as anyone could remember. According to Leith, the place would fall apart without her.

Though I hadn't actually been planning to go anywhere near Whale Point, I still said, "But if those men are the ones who killed Rainey—"

Another murmur in the background, then Leith said, "They're hired muscles, not the brains. They won't give you answers, just more bruises and pain."

All of which confirmed my decision to avoid the place like a plague. "What about Angus? Can I find him at his boat?"

Leith passed the question on to Janelle. "She says no, but to try the *Heron* on Pier 39. He should be back there at about seven. And she says to watch your back. He could be a marked man, and anyone with him could meet the same fate."

Especially if that someone had already escaped from the very people who might now be after him.

I drew in a deep breath, sucking in the morning's heat, feeling it flush the sudden chill from my body. But it was harder to ignore the notion that I was getting in way over my head.

It wasn't like I had a choice. Not if I wanted to save Rainey's soul. I had four days left.

"Tell Janelle I'll be fine and to stop worrying."

There was more murmured conversation, then Leith said, "She says it's her job to worry. She also says not to play games with Death. He's dangerous."

I couldn't help smiling. I might not work for Phoenix, but I hung out with many of its employees, and I'd known Janelle almost as long as I'd known Leith. It was nice to know I was one of the ones she kept a psychic eye on.

"Tell her Death has been met and conquered. He holds no fears for me."

He passed on the message and a second later, the cackle of her laughter came over the line.

"I guess that means she doesn't believe me," I said wryly.

"I guess," Leith said. "So what are these other favors you want?"

"What can you tell me about the muerte?"

"The who?"

"It's what my kidnappers called the dragon who was being held in the cellar with me. Apparently it means he's an assassin of some sort, but he wouldn't explain it any more than that."

"I'm guessing this is the man Janelle just warned you about?"

"Probably. But he escorted me home and then disappeared, so I don't think he's going to be a problem."

Though I was probably tempting fate even thinking that.

"I'll hunt around and see what I can dig up," Leith said. "And I'd tell you to be careful, but we both know that would be a waste. You're the most foolhardy cautious person I've ever known."

"That's a contradiction."

"So are you."

I grinned. "The other thing I want you to do is run a check on a Seth Knightly, from the Jamieson clique. He's a dragon, and his father is our king." Meaning the bastard was my brother's half brother, but two men had never been so different. If Trae was warmth and sunshine, then Seth was everything that was dark and horrid in the world. "I heard he died in a car accident several years ago. I need to know whether that's true, and if it's not, where the hell he is now."

"You know, it'd be nice if you actually asked me to do something easy for a change."

I laughed. "You get everything I've requested, and I'll feed you for a week."

"I'll hold you to that."

He would, too. Not that I minded—not if he came through with the information. And I had no doubt that he would. Phoenix Investigations had a reputation for getting the job done quickly and efficiently, and a lot of that was due not only to the psychics in its employ, but to Leith's ability to source the most innocuous details. "I'm at Trae's for the moment, but I may be in and out, so I'll give you a call later in the day."

"I'll wait with bated breath."

I snorted and hung up, then leaned back against the wooden wall of the apartment and let the sunlight soak through me just a little longer. After a few minutes, I sighed and headed back inside to google Whale Point, the town that had given Angus his scars. I didn't expect to find anything, and I got precisely what I expected—nothing. Of course, that didn't mean the town hadn't existed or that he'd been lying. It just meant that the truth had been so obscured by his lies that it was hard to tell one from the other. Part of me still wanted to go there today, if only to source out who and what might be waiting for me. But that was a risk I couldn't take—not after Janelle's warning.

It meant my only choice now was Angus. And while I wasn't sure if talking to him again would clarify the situation, I had to try. He was the closest I'd come to getting some answers so far.

I looked at my watch and saw it was barely one. Obviously, time was intent on crawling by.

I switched on the TV, then headed into the kitchen to make myself another sandwich. After grabbing a soda from the fridge, I headed back into the living room—arriving just in time to see a local news report about a fire at a bar on Fillmore Street.

It took me only a second to realize it was the same bar I'd met Angus in. I grabbed the remote and turned up the sound.

"Police are treating the fire and deaths as suspicious," the reporter said. "Several survivors have been interviewed, and one man is currently being questioned by the police."

On the screen they showed the back of a dark-haired man whose gait was all too familiar. He walked beside several police officers, and while he wasn't handcuffed or anything, they were heading in the general direction of a police car.

I just about choked on my sandwich. What the hell had Damon been doing at the bar? Had he caused the fire and the subsequent deaths? Part of me wanted to think he hadn't, but there was no escaping the fact that he'd described himself as a killer.

Still, if they'd had any actual evidence against him, surely he would have been arrested rather than merely taken in to be interviewed. I didn't know a whole lot about the workings of the police and the law, but that seemed the logical route.

Maybe I should go down there and provide him with an alibi. I'd been with him a good part of the night, after all, and even though he'd stolen heat from both the guards, he was a full dragon and restricted by the rule of night. He couldn't flame, even if he had been at full strength.

Hell, even daylight might not have helped him. It could take days to get back the sort of strength needed to set a fire that large. At least, it would for an ordinary dragon.

But there were other ways of lighting fires, and surely a dragon trained as an assassin would not be above using them.

In truth, the part of me that wanted to help him was undoubtedly the same part that remembered the feel of his lips on mine, and the way the merest hint of a smile had sent my pulse racing like a mad thing.

I *hated* that reaction. Or rather, hated the fact that it was aimed yet again at the wrong sort of man. Why couldn't my hormones pick some kind, gentle, *normal* man for a change?

Of course, the *sane* part of me—the part that actually remembered the pain of trusting too easily and that had sworn never to trust like that again—was reluctant to go anywhere near him.

After all, there was a very real possibility that he *was* responsible. I had no idea when the fire had started. No idea where he'd gone after he'd left me.

And yet I felt like I owed him. While I might have gotten us out of that cellar, he'd gotten us free of the house and made sure I'd arrived at Trae's safely.

I gulped down my sandwich, then jumped off the sofa and headed for the phone once again. Before I decided what to do, I needed to find out where he'd be. The bar was on Fillmore Street, so it seemed logical he would have been taken to Northern Station, but I wanted to be sure before I wasted cash on cab fare.

Robyn would know that sort of information. She was one of the crime reporters at the *Chronicle* and had been a friend since journalism school. She was also very human—and didn't know that I wasn't.

"Hey, chickie," she said, voice its ever-cheery self when I phoned. "How you doing?"

"Not bad, considering that in the last twenty-four hours I've been run off the road, drugged, and then kidnapped."

"No! Seriously? Are you okay?"

"Yeah." I hesitated. "I was told the *Chronicle* ran a story on the accident?"

"Not that I know of. I'm sure Frankie would have mentioned one of our own being in an accident, and he knows we're friends."

"That's what I thought." So Angus *had* been lying.

"Listen, I need some help with a story I'm tracking down."

"And here I was thinking you were off on a vacation with that mad friend of yours."

"I was. Am." *Only the mad friend is dead and I need to save her soul.* "But I caught a whiff of something that may or may not amount to anything."

"If it amounts to anything, I want the details. In full and over coffee. And cake."

"Done deal." Although the details would be highly modified, given she had no idea what I was. "What can you tell me about the fire on Fillmore Street last night?"

"Nothing much more than what's been said on TV. Why?"

"Because I know the man arrested for it, and I don't think he did it."

"No one was arrested." Confusion darkened her tone. "Although a Damon Rey was taken in for questioning."

Well, at least he'd given me his correct name. "What station is he at?"

"None of them. I think they released him about an hour ago."

"Damn." Why I was disappointed I couldn't entirely say. At least it solved the problem of me having to provide an alibi for the man. "What time did the fire start?"

"Witnesses say about three, but the arson investigators have only just started sifting through the ruins."

Which meant he *could* have been responsible. Damn, damn, and damn.

"He's staying at the Ritz-Carlton, if that's of any use," Robyn said.

Who'd have guessed Death was a five-star sort of guy? "How do you know all this shit?"

"It's my job," she said drily. "And I'm good at what I do. So you're not even going to give me the slightest hint as to how this fire is connected to what happened to you?"

"Not yet. But we *will* have that cake."

"I'll hold you to it."

I smiled and hung up. Now what? It was still too early to go find Angus—Janelle said he wouldn't be at the boat until this evening, and she wasn't often wrong.

So, what next?

I knew what I *wanted* to do. It might be stupid, but I wanted to see Damon again. I had a feeling he could answer more than a few of my questions—not that he actually *would*.

I bit my bottom lip for a moment, then thought: *What the hell?* I had nothing to lose by at least trying.

I grabbed a sweater, raided the cash my brother kept in his so-called secret spot, then headed out. I caught a cab, but the traffic was its usual chaotic self, so I got out near the Fairmont and walked the rest of the way. The Ritz looked as impressive as ever, its grand façade almost seeming to belong to another century, one more suited to horse-drawn vehicles and ladies in fine silks.

I crossed the road and headed into the foyer. After a moment of admiring the lush surroundings, I headed over to the reception desk. A pleasant-looking woman gave me a friendly smile and said, "May I help you?"

"I'm looking for Damon Rey. He's a guest here."

"I can give him a call and let him know you wish to see him, if you like."

"That would be great." Even if it wasn't. He was just as likely to send me away as see me.

"Who shall I say is calling?"

I hesitated. "Just tell him Mercy Reynolds is downstairs waiting for him."

She nodded and made the call. She didn't say anything, which meant he wasn't answering, a fact she confirmed minutes later. "I'm sorry, but he doesn't appear to be in. Would you like to leave him a message?"

"Sure. Thanks."

She handed me a notepad. I scrawled down my name and my brother's phone number, then pushed it back.

"Will that be all?" she asked.

"Yes. Thank you."

I walked away. So much for *that* great idea. Maybe I should just head down to Angus's place, and hang around on the off chance he would get there earlier than Janelle predicted.

I exited the hotel, smiling at the doorman as he wished me a good day, and headed toward California Street. But I'd barely taken a dozen steps when my heart just about leaped into my throat and I froze. In the shadows of the trees lining the curb was one of the men Damon had knocked out last night—the guard with the silky voice.

God, I was stupid. *Stupid*.

If I could trace Damon to the Ritz, it stood to reason his kidnappers could, too. Hell, for all I knew, this could have been where they'd captured him in the first place.

I needed to get out of here—and *fast*.

But even as the thought crossed my mind, he looked up. I didn't have to see his expression to know his anger and his sense of triumph. The feel of it rode across the breeze.

He pushed away from the tree.

I turned and ran down the street and right onto Pine Street, scattering pedestrians as I went. I swung right again, keeping to the shadows of the trees and hoping against hope that I was faster.

A quick glance over my shoulder proved that I wasn't.

Fear slipped through me. I thought about stopping, about asking for help, but I just couldn't risk anyone else's safety. Besides, I *could* protect myself if I really needed to, and other people—especially if they were human—would just get in the way. Even with the tight control I had over my flames, things could very easily get out of hand in a street filled with cars and people. I didn't want anyone getting hurt. I couldn't live with that guilt.

So I kept on running.

My pulse was racing as fast as my feet and sweat was beginning to trickle down my spine. I'd let my fitness slip since leaving my clique, and I might just pay the price for that slackness now, because the footsteps of my pursuer were getting closer and closer.

Panic rolled through me, sending a surge of energy through my legs. Somehow, my speed increased, and the footsteps seemed just a shade farther behind.

I couldn't let them catch me again. I just *couldn't*. There'd be no second escape, of that I was sure.

I turned left onto California Street. More people,

more parked cars, trees, and lots of big tall buildings. And nowhere to hide that wouldn't endanger others, leaving me with little option but to keep going. I ran across the street, heard the screech of brakes from behind, and jumped sideways. The hood of a green car slid past my side, missing me by inches. It came to a halt between me and my pursuer, but instead of the irate driver flinging abuse, he reached backward and flung the door open. A familiar voice said, "Get in."

I didn't hesitate, just dived into the backseat and slammed the door shut. With a squeal of rubber, Damon took off. My pursuer quickly became a speck lost to the distance, then disappeared altogether as we sped down another street.

I collapsed back into the seat and let out a relieved breath. "Thank you," I said, wiping the sweat from my forehead with a shaking hand.

"What the hell were you doing at the Ritz?" he said, voice not in the least bit friendly.

"Looking for you."

"And it didn't occur to you that our kidnappers might well be doing the same thing?"

"Not until I saw that guy waiting outside, no."

He shook his head, his dark gaze meeting mine briefly at the edge of the rearview mirror. "Stupid."

Heat burned into my cheeks and sparks flickered briefly across my fingertips. I clenched my hand and tried to calm the annoyance. "I realize that now. I don't need your admonishment on top of it."

He grunted slightly, swung the car onto another street, then said, "What did you want to see me about?"

"I saw on the news that you'd been arrested—"

"Not arrested," he corrected, and I swear there was

humor in his voice, even though there was little emotion to be tasted on the air. " Just answering a few questions."

"We both know that's only one step from being arrested." I paused. " Did you set that blaze?"

He contemplated me through the rearview mirror for a moment. "What do you think?"

"I think you're crazy enough to set a bar alight." I studied his back and wondered if anyone could ever accurately tell what this man was thinking. I certainly couldn't. Not at the moment, anyway. " But I don't think you actually did."

A smile tugged at his lips. "Nice to know my fellow prisoner has a little faith in me."

"I don't have faith in anyone but my brother and Rainey." And she was dead. I looked briefly out the window, wondering where we were going and realizing I didn't really care, then added, "It's a simple matter of facts. You were locked up for thirteen days without sunlight. Even with the heat you stole, I doubt you'd have been able to maintain enough fire to set that building alight."

"There are other ways to light a fire, you know. Even dragons can use them."

"Yeah, but you seem the type to want to do your own dirty work, right down to the flame that kills."

His gaze met mine again, the dark depths of his eyes contemplative. "You seem to have formed a very quick opinion of someone you don't really know."

My smile held a bitter edge. "You have to where I come from. It can be the difference between gaining new scars or not."

One dark eyebrow winged upward. "Surely a pretty woman like you wouldn't have that many scars."

I snorted softly. Death obviously needed glasses. I might be many things, but pretty wasn't one of them. *Not* that I considered myself ugly. Just plain. Very plain. A brown dragon who couldn't shift shape in a world filled with beasts who could shimmer and fly. "I've more scars than I have fingers."

He frowned. "I saw the one on your forehead. What happened there?"

I reached up and touched the rapidly fading scar. "That one was courtesy of a recent run-in with a truck. The others were courtesy of my clique."

"What in the hell goes on in your clique?"

There was an edge to his voice that had my eyebrows rising. It wasn't concern, but it seemed very close to it, which was odd.

"Nothing much different from many others, I suspect." I crossed my arms and looked out the window again. "Where the hell are we going?"

"Back to your brother's place. You need to get some things together, then get the hell away from there."

"I don't really think—"

"Yeah, we discovered that."

Annoyance flowed through me again. "You have a smart mouth for someone who was close to hibernation last night."

"Good point." He slowed the car as the lights ahead changed to red, then said, "Why were you coming to see me?"

I don't really know. But I couldn't admit that—or rather, I wouldn't. I didn't want to appear indecisive. Why, I had no idea. I mean, he was a stranger, and a rather odd one at that. "I want to know who those men were. I want to know who is pulling their strings."

"And why would you think I'd know?"

"You know a hell of a lot more than you're admitting, so enough of the games, Damon. I need to know what's going on."

He considered me briefly, then said, "Why is knowing so important to you?"

I hesitated, torn between the need to trust someone and a past that suggested men like him could never be counted on. "I'm a reporter."

I didn't need to see his grimace to feel the sweep of his disdain. "And you think you're on the trail of an award-winning story? Lady, you have no idea."

"If you keep saying that, I just might think you mean it." I kept my voice deliberately light, masking both my growing irritation and perhaps a little hurt, which was stupid. Why should the opinion of this man carry so much weight? Why would I even let it?

"This is not something you should be sticking your pretty little nose into." His voice was as cold as the look he cast my way. "These men are dangerous. *I'm* dangerous. You'd best get well away from us all."

"Thanks for the warning but I'm afraid I can't oblige." I hesitated, then added softly, "There's someone I need to save. To do that, I need answers."

He didn't reply, but his disapproval continued to sting the air. I stared out the windows. Obviously, this man had no intention of helping me out. I was stupid to think he ever would.

He turned right onto another street, slowing down as he slotted into the unusually heavy traffic. I realized we were about to pass *my* apartment and shifted to look out the window. Would any of the guards from last night be lurking around the front of the building? They had my driver's license, after all, so they knew where I lived.

I didn't see the guards. What I *did* see was flashing lights and dark plumes of smoke.

My apartment building was on fire.

Fire engines blocked the road ahead, and thick sprays of water were being directed up high. People huddled farther down the road, some crying, some wrapped in blankets, all of them looking shocked. Some of those faces I knew—my elderly neighbors. At least they'd gotten out. I hoped everyone else had, too.

My gaze went back to the flames leaping out high above from the top-floor windows.

My floor.

And it was a big fire—maybe too big. Had I been there, I might have been dead. I wasn't, so I guess I had to be grateful for that. But everything would be gone.

Everything.

All the photos, all the little bits and pieces that I'd gathered over the years. Little things that had no value and wouldn't mean much to anyone else, but to me they were reminders of good times—and there'd been few enough of those in my childhood.

Tears stung my eyes, and I clenched my fists against the urge to jump out of the car and race to the fire, to save something, anything, of my life and my past. But the flames were just too fierce and there were far too many firemen and cops. I'd never even get near the building, let alone close enough to suck in all that heat and fire in an attempt to quell it.

God, these bastards just kept destroying things I

loved. It had to stop—and *before* I didn't have any-thing left to destroy.

Of course, it was always possible the fire might have been accidental, but even as the thought crossed my mind, I dismissed it. What were the odds of an accidental fire happening days after Rainey being killed and me being kidnapped?

I swiped at my eyes, then muttered, "I think I need cake. Thick, gooey chocolate cake."

"What, now? Why?" Damon said, confusion evident in his voice as he eased the car's speed.

"Because chocolate cake is a perfect pick-me-up when life decides to deal you one of those nasty little surprises." My voice broke a little, and I took a deep, shuddering breath before adding, "That's my building on fire."

He didn't say anything for a moment, then shook his head. "It's probably not a coincidence," he said softly. "First the bar, and now your place. It would seem one of our kidnappers is something of an arsonist."

"So you think it was one of the guards who set the bar on fire?" My gaze was dragged from the blaze as a police officer directed us down a side street. In some ways it was a relief. If I couldn't see the flames, maybe I wouldn't think about the destruction they'd wreaked on my life. Not until I lay down to sleep, anyway.

"The bartender was one of the men who questioned me when they had me locked up. I recognized his voice."

"Well, that explains how I got snatched." And proved my instincts had been right. Shame I hadn't listened to them and got the hell out of there while I still could. "I was in that bar meeting Angus when I was drugged. He was the one who took me to that house."

"Angus?"

"A sea dragon." I hesitated. "I got a feeling he's working for them unwillingly."

"You do make the oddest judgments about people you've barely met, don't you?"

"You learn to judge very quickly when it means avoiding another scar."

He frowned. "That's the second time you've said that. Why on earth would anyone want to scar you?"

"Because of what I am." Because they could. "So you *did* go back to the bar last night?"

Damon's sudden smile was something I felt rather than saw, but it was a cold thing that sent goose bumps across my skin.

"Yes."

"How? I mean, you might have stolen heat, but you weren't exactly a powerhouse of energy when you left me."

"Perhaps not, but like the other two guards, the bartender kindly decided to loan me his heat."

"And did he survive the encounter?"

"He was weak, but alive—and the bar intact—when I left." Damon shrugged, a movement that was surprisingly eloquent. "I was hoping he'd lead me back to his master's lair sometime over the next few days."

"So you merely put the fear of God into him while firing up the furnaces?"

"More like the fear of death." He met my gaze in the mirror again, a slight frown creasing his brow. "The only one who doesn't seem to be afraid of me is you."

"That's because I have no sense."

A smile twitched his lips again. I pulled my gaze away and tried to think sensible thoughts rather than what I'd really like to do to those lips. "The cops must have found you pretty quickly—which means those men could have, too."

"I'm a little smarter than that." The look he cast my way reminded me that *I* hadn't been. "When I heard on the news that the cops were looking for a man fitting my description, I turned myself in. We talked, then they let me go." He paused, and swung the car around another corner. "You don't give up until you get your answers, do you?"

"It's the reporter in me."

"Or your naturally stubborn nature."

"That, too."

He swung onto another street. "With the bar torched, and the bartender dead, I had intended to keep an eye on my hotel and follow any watchers to their source. That plan got a little sidetracked."

"Yeah, sorry about that." Though I wasn't. Not entirely. At least I'd gotten to talk to him again, even if he hadn't provided any real information.

He turned right again, and my brother's apartment came into sight.

Only it was on fire as well.

Chapter Six

_A_nything else I can help you with?" the waiter said, a too-cheery smile plastered on his face as he placed the rich-looking cake on the table.

"No, thanks," Damon said, a touch impatiently. When the waiter left, he looked at me. His dark eyes were filled with a sympathy that was just about my undoing. "Are you okay?"

I nodded and wrapped my hands around my coffee. It didn't do a lot to ease the chill.

"It's losing all the little things that hurts the most," I whispered. "All the photos, the knickknacks that wouldn't mean much to anyone else—"

My voice broke, and I stopped. _No thinking_, I told myself fiercely. _No feeling. Shove everything back into its box and deal with it later._

"What I don't get," I added, once I had everything under some semblance of control again, "is why they'd want to burn down both apartments."

Damon's expression suggested he wasn't exactly buying the act, but he didn't say anything, instead grabbing several sugar packets and tearing off their tops before pouring them into his black coffee. "There could be a number of reasons."

"Like what?"

"Like wanting to destroy any evidence you might have collected. Or ensuring you had nowhere to run." He shrugged and picked up his mug. "Or maybe it's simply a warning."

"What, stay away or they'll burn me to death?"

Even half-breeds like me were hard to destroy with flames alone. Fire was part of our soul, and it was in our nature to be able to control it—whatever the source. This wasn't to say mistakes didn't happen, or that we could control every single fire we came across—especially if they were as large as the one currently destroying my apartment—but such things were rare.

His gaze met mine, dark eyes somber. "I think you'll find it's more a 'Stay away, or we'll completely destroy everything in your life.'"

I steeled my mind against the thought that they already had, and tried to ignore the cold tremor that ran deep through my soul. "There isn't a whole lot more in my life that these men *can* destroy."

I hoped that by saying that, I hadn't jinxed myself—or the people I cared about.

"At least you still have your *life*. As does your brother." He hesitated. "Where is he? Perhaps you should warn him."

"He's away on business. But trust me, they wouldn't want to tackle him anyway." Unlike me, he wouldn't be an easy target.

"These men have killed to keep their secrets, Mercy. Don't doubt that they will kill you, or your brother, or anyone else who happens to get in their way."

He wasn't telling me anything I didn't already know. I took a sip of coffee, but it didn't do a whole lot to chase off the chill. "So why didn't they kill you?"

He raised an eyebrow. "For the same reason they didn't kill you. They wanted information."

"The difference between us is the fact I don't know anything." And yet I'd recognized the voice talking to Angus on the phone, and if his comment about the steel room bringing back delicious memories was anything to go by, he'd obviously known me. So, was this more than what it seemed? Was a grudge behind the initial attack? Or was the chance to make good on a grudge just a bonus?

Maybe the information I needed was somewhere in the mists of my mind—I just had to remember it. Which was easier said than done when I'd spent the last ten years trying to *forget*. "You, on the other hand, know a whole lot of something."

"If I knew as much as you seem to think, those men wouldn't still be out there."

Because he would have killed them. I shivered, then reached for a fork. Maybe some chocolate cake would help make the situation feel less dire.

"So what's our next step?" I said around a mouthful of the deliciously gooey cake.

"*Your* next step is to be sensible and get the hell out of here."

I didn't answer immediately, concentrating on the chocolaty goodness instead. "You're a smart man, so you can probably guess my response to *that* particular suggestion."

He leaned back in his chair, his expression so cold the chill of it ran down my spine. *Scary* didn't even begin to describe his countenance right now. "You really *don't* have any common sense, do you?"

Anger swirled again—a firestorm that rippled across my skin, making the shadows in which we sat briefly flame to life.

His gaze flickered to my arms then swept past me, studying the half-empty restaurant.

"Careful," he murmured. "We don't need to be attracting attention right now."

"I realize that," I snapped, drawing the heat back in, letting it burn deep in my soul instead. "I'm not stupid, no matter what you might think."

"I didn't—"

"No, you just figure I'm a silly little reporter who has no idea what she's really getting into."

"And do you?"

"I've seen the towns and I've talked to Angus. I *know*." My voice burned with a fury that wasn't particularly aimed at him, but at fate itself. Just this once, I'd have liked to break through one of those damn walls between me and any useful information. Just once, I'd have liked to *learn* something rather than ending up empty-handed again. Damn it, I didn't have the time to be running around in useless circles. "I'm not going to let you browbeat me into walking away, Damon. I *can't*."

He studied me for a moment, then said softly, "Because you need to save someone."

I looked away, fighting the sting of tears. "Yes."

"And is saving this person really worth the possible cost?"

I briefly closed my eyes. "Yes."

"Then you must really love them."

"I do." I took a deep, somewhat shuddery breath and met his dark gaze. It was compassion and steel combined, and it was almost my undoing. "They killed her three days ago, Damon. I'm all she had, which means I'm the only one who can save her soul. And no matter what it takes, I *will* find and kill the bastards responsible for her death. No matter what you—or anyone else—says or does."

The steel in his expression faded. He leaned forward and gathered my hands in his, his touch so warm, so comforting, that the tears spilled down my cheeks. God, it felt good to have someone to talk to. Someone who seemed to understand exactly what I was going through.

"How did she die?" he asked softly.

I closed my eyes against the rush of memories—the force of the impact that sent us flying, the crunch of metal, the high-pitched scream of the tires that was almost drowned out by our own, the bitter taste of fear as we realized there was nothing we could do to save ourselves. I'd relived those moments over and over in the hospital and would no doubt catch them in my dreams for years to come. While I doubted time would make them any easier to take, I hoped it would at least make the pain fade.

I took a deep breath, and said, "We were looking for clues in Nevada, but a phone call had us heading back to San Francisco. A truck ran us off the road before we got anywhere near here, and Rainey . . . went through the windshield." I paused, swallowing heavily. "It was no accident."

He shifted his grip so that his fingers were laced through mine. It was comforting and yet, at the same time, very intimate. The heat of his flesh chased the chill from mine and made me feel safer than I had ever thought possible.

"What makes you think it wasn't an accident?"

"The truck accelerated as it came toward us. The driver never applied his brakes and, in fact, gunned the engine to hit us a second time. The police found the truck abandoned—and wiped of prints—two hours later."

"Did you see the driver at all?"

I shook my head. "We were too busy trying to get out of his way."

"Maybe the driver simply panicked—"

"No." I raised my gaze to his. "They killed her, and they tried to kill me. I need to know why." I needed answers if I was to have any hope of saving Rainey.

I breathed deep, trying to control the turmoil within me, trying to keep calm. It didn't work. The tears continued to trickle down my cheeks regardless.

"The worst of it is, no one prayed for her, Damon. They ran us off the road and left us to die in the night and the cold, and I wasn't aware enough to pray for her soul at sunrise."

And that was the worst of it. I wasn't there for her when she needed me the most.

"Her death was not your fault."

"But if I don't get my answers and claim my vengeance, then her soul will be forced to roam this earth forever. And that *will* be my fault."

He didn't say anything, just continued to hold my hands, and it offered more comfort than mere words ever could. Yet I could sense the conflict in him—the need for information warring with the need to be sympathetic. "Say it," I said quietly.

He gave me a lopsided smile that warmed me more than his touch. "You must have found something to make them nervous."

"We made a ton of notes, but I can't remember anything that specifically points a finger at anyone." I hesitated, then added, "But the man who gave us the tip . . . His voice was familiar."

"You can't place it?"

"No." I hesitated again. "I have a friend doing a check on the whereabouts of a Seth Knightly, although the voice was too elegant to be his."

"Then why do you suspect him?"

"Because he made a reference to something that happened to me in the past—something that only a few people were aware of. And running us off the road like that, and then leaving us to die, is the sort of thing he'd do."

He frowned slightly. "And there was nothing in the town that you were investigating before the accident?"

"Nothing at all." I hesitated. "Though I did wonder how they got my cell number."

He frowned. "Cell phones are digital and hard to pick up on scanners, although that doesn't mean it can't have happened. But it's more than likely someone would have given them your number."

"I've only got a couple of friends who have my number, and none of them would have given it out without telling me."

"What about your mother?"

"It's possible, if the king ordered it." But that man didn't even know I existed, so I couldn't imagine he was the source. "I'd like to think she didn't, though."

If only because that would mean they knew altogether *too* much about me.

Damon's frown deepened. "Did you phone anyone unusual in the few days before the accident?"

"No." I hesitated. "Well, I did phone the council about the cleansed towns, but they, of course, could not have cared less. I can't imagine they'd attempt to destroy us when they didn't even give a damn about two towns that had been destroyed."

He didn't comment on that, but I felt his quick flash of interest anyway. "You think someone on the council is working with the people behind the cleansings?"

I shrugged. "Right now, I think anything is possible."

"It's a shame those notes all burned along with your apartment. They might have been useful."

"They're not much more than a listing of what we've found, who we know is missing, stuff like that."

"Which may not mean a lot to you, but could be the difference between me finding these people and not."

"Meaning, of course, that you *do* know a whole lot more than you're admitting."

"I'm a muerte. I always know more than I admit."

His tone was gently mocking, and I resisted the urge to flick some cake in his direction. But only because it would have meant taking my hands from his.

"If Death is all-knowing, then why doesn't he know that the notes are actually on a netbook that wasn't in either apartment?"

His dark gaze scanned mine, as if searching for lies. "So it's safe?"

"More than likely." If no one had stolen the thing out of the desk. "I'd been writing up the latest batch of notes at work and left them there." Rainey had been in such a hurry to get back to Nevada that I'd forgotten to pick up the netbook on the way out.

"So we can still get to it?"

"If you can figure out a way to enter the building without being seen. Those men have my license and press card, so they'll know where I work and will probably be on the lookout."

His sudden smile was full and rich, and crinkled the corners of his eyes. And I'd been right before—it was absolutely heart-stopping.

"I'm a dragon *and* a muerte. Trust me when I say that I know a thing or two about sneaking into places unseen."

It took a moment to ignore the glow of that smile and to think like the calm and rational person I supposedly was. To remember *why* I was here, doing this.

"I won't help you retrieve the netbook unless you stop insisting that I walk away and let me help."

His smile faded and I mourned its loss. "I understand why you need to do this, but that could be tantamount to condoning murder. *Your* murder, if these men get hold of you."

"I'm going to keep investigating regardless of whether I have your help or not. And it seems to me that if we're investigating the same thing, we'd be better off pooling resources."

He pulled his hands from mine. "You'd be better off. I'd be landed with a complication I don't really need."

"Kindly remember the complication rescued your butt from hibernation and might yet have some information you need." I picked up the coffee mug. It really didn't provide the same sort of comfort as his touch, but it was better than nothing. I studied him for a moment longer, then added softly, "If you had the chance of saving a friend's soul, wouldn't you take it?"

"Yes."

There was something in the way he said it that made me say, "I'm thinking your reason for tracking these people isn't all that dissimilar to my own."

His gaze met mine again. "You might be right."

"Then don't expect anything less from me."

"I don't expect *anything* of you—or from you—simply because I don't know you."

"That hasn't stopped you from trying to boss me around."

"I'm only trying to keep you safe, Mercy. I'd hate to see you end up like your friend and mine."

It was on the tip of my tongue to ask why my death even mattered to him when we were strangers, but I resisted the temptation. Most people didn't like to see lives thrown away needlessly, and though Damon was far from most people, it wasn't fair to think he wouldn't feel the same.

"I'd hate to see me end up like Rainey, too. But you're investigating the same thing, so you're just as much at risk as me."

He smiled again, but this time it held a bittersweet edge that tore at something deep inside. He reached for the other fork and scooped up some chocolate cake, and I knew in that moment I'd won.

But I didn't feel victorious. I just felt even more

afraid. Because I knew, without a doubt, that this whole quest had just gotten a lot more dangerous. Because of this man, and because of the world he appeared to walk in.

"The difference between you and me," he said, "is the fact that I'm as deadly as they are."

"I can protect myself," I said softly.

He didn't say anything to that, but he didn't have to. I could taste his disbelief in the air. "Tell me about this Angus you keep mentioning," he said instead.

I shrugged again and picked up my fork, scooping up some more cake. It wasn't doing a lot to ease the ache of losing all I'd held dear, but at least it stopped my stomach from rumbling. "We were going to meet him when the truck hit us. I contacted him again after I got out of the hospital and arranged another meeting. You saw the end result of that encounter."

"How much did you tell him before you met him?"

"He knew we were investigating the cleansed towns."

"If he was involved in the death of your friend, then meeting him alone was a pretty stupid move."

According to him, my life was full of stupid moves. I squashed down my irritation and forked up more cake. If he didn't hurry, he was going to miss out on his share—and given the barbed comments he kept flinging my way, maybe he deserved to.

"He's a sea dragon. Rainey was killed in the middle of nowhere. My guess is that there was no direct involvement."

"You can't be sure of that."

No, I couldn't. But in this case, I trusted my instincts. Angus might be peripherally involved with whatever was happening, but I didn't think it went as deep as murder—I'd overheard him say as much in the van. "I'm going to interview him tonight."

"We should go get the netbook first. Just in case those men decide to do a little desk investigation of their own."

"It won't do them any good. I wasn't using my desk." I hesitated, but couldn't help adding, "I'm not *that* stupid."

Amusement twinkled in his eyes. "So there's hope for you yet?"

"Apparently," I muttered, unable to keep up with this man's sudden mood changes. Although I couldn't be annoyed by this one. Or that half smile. I glanced at my watch. "We've hours to spare."

"But good disguises take time. Finish the cake, then I'll show you some magic."

I looked up into his dark eyes and saw the devilry there. I felt myself smiling. "Are you sure you're capable of magic after being locked up for so long?"

"Why don't you come back to my car and find out?"

Anytime, I thought, and I threw the fork down on the table. "Consider the cake finished."

He rose and took my hand, pulling me gently upward. "Then let's go."

As I followed him out the door, I let my gaze wander up the length of him—admiring the way his jeans clung to his butt and emphasized the long, lean power of his legs. The silent, easy-flowing way he moved. The shoulders that hinted at the strength of the man, both within and without.

He reminded me of a predator, and I guess in many ways he was.

But however dangerous Death might be, however moody he might be, there was one inescapable fact.

He was also damn *hot*.

A wig, some artfully applied makeup, and a change of clothes later, and Damon did indeed look like someone else. He now looked and walked like a man twenty years older, and if I hadn't seen the transformation myself, I wouldn't have believed it. I certainly wouldn't have looked twice at him on the street.

I watched him disappear into my office building, then glanced up and down the street. I couldn't see anyone acting suspiciously, let alone anyone who seemed to be watching the entrance, but that didn't mean anything. I hadn't seen the watcher at the Ritz until it was almost too late.

Of course, Damon had insisted that I also undergo a change of appearance, which is why I was sitting at the bus stop with blond hair, a low-cut top that exposed way too much breast, and a miniskirt that bordered on indecent—all courtesy of a recent shopping spree. Damon's theory was that if they were looking at my body they weren't looking at my face, but the twinkle in his eyes as he'd said it suggested the bad guys might not be the only ones enjoying the look.

That was the sole reason I'd actually agreed to wear the outfit. Janelle might have warned me not to play with Death, but the inner dragon just wasn't listening.

Not that I really expected anything to develop between us, because Damon seemed to be the ultimate loner. Besides, I knew from experience that dragons of his caliber didn't consider half-breeds like me to be anything more than playthings.

I turned the page of the newspaper I'd been pretending to read and tried to ignore the rising chill in the air. I might have a dragon's fire, but that didn't mean I was immune to the cold. Especially when—like now—I couldn't actually use my flame to warm myself.

Sharp music cut through the roar of passing traffic and it took me a moment to realize it was the cell phone Damon had given me.

Why Damon actually had spare cell phones sitting in his vehicle I couldn't say—although it did seem to be packed with all sorts of useful items. Like spare clothes for himself, phones, the makeup that disguised us both, and a variety of guns and other weapons—although I'm not sure I was supposed to see the latter. Death might be a dragon, but he wasn't beyond using human firepower.

I reached into the oversized red purse at my feet and grabbed the phone.

"Damon?" I said, without actually looking at the number.

"Wrong man," Leith said. "And what the hell have you been getting involved in, woman?"

"Ah. You heard about the fires." I didn't bother asking Leith how he'd gotten the number. Janelle's psychic abilities ran to the oddest bits of information sometimes. Like telling me that Angus wouldn't be at his friend's boat until tonight, but not telling me where he actually was this afternoon.

"Yeah, I heard about the fires," Leith said, his voice dry. "Kinda hard to miss when it's all over the news. You need help?"

"I've got help. Although don't be surprised if I call you back in a day or so to take you up on your offer."

"We're always here." He paused, and the sound of shuffling papers came down the line for several seconds before he added, "Haven't been able to find out much more on that Angus fellow, but I've got some information on muertes."

"And?"

"They're trained assassins who work under the direction of the Council of Dragons."

"To what aim, do you know?"

"According to my source, it's the muertes' role to enforce the council's edicts and punish those who break the rules."

Enforce being a more pleasant word for *kill.* "I wonder if that also includes rogue draman towns?"

"From what I understand, the muerte don't leave evidence. If they had destroyed any of those towns, we wouldn't even know about them."

It didn't mean the council *hadn't* destroyed the towns, just that there was no evidence of it. And yet, if the council was behind the cleansings, why would Damon now be investigating them? Then I frowned, remembering the words of the oddly familiar-sounding stranger who'd talked to Angus in the van. He'd said something about Damon's presence *not* being the result of direct council orders, meaning that this was either a private investigation or something else entirely was going on.

"Anything else?"

"Yeah, my source said don't fuck with them. If the man you call Death is one of them, you might be wise to get the hell away while you can."

"Leith, he's investigating the cleansings just like I am. Right now, I need him. Or at least I need the information he's holding."

"And are you sure it's worth the risk? We already know these bastards will do whatever it takes to get the job done, no matter what—or who—gets in the way. I'd hate to see you follow the same path as Rainey."

I'd hate to see me going the way of Rainey, too, but it wasn't like I could walk away. I wouldn't be able to live with myself if I didn't do everything I could to save her soul. And if that meant endangering my own life, then so be it. I owed her that, and more, for all the years she'd protected me from the worst of our clique's ravages.

"But with the muerte by my side, there's less chance of me ending up like that, isn't there?"

"Being with him didn't stop your apartment—or your brother's—from being torched."

"At least I wasn't in them, Leith."

"But you could have been."

A point I couldn't argue, so I simply said, "Did you uncover anything on Seth Knightly?"

"I've found several people who swear he died in a car accident, but there's nothing official. I don't suppose you know where the accident happened? It might make hunting the death certificate easier."

"Sorry, I can't help you there. I was too busy dancing in celebration to actually listen to details." I glanced across the road, just to check whether Damon had reappeared yet, and found myself staring into the blue-eyed gaze of the stranger who'd chased me from the Ritz not three hours before.

My heart leaped to the vicinity of my throat, and it took every ounce of control to keep meeting his gaze, and to *not* react to his presence. To trust that the subtle changes Damon had made would make the difference between that man recognizing me and not.

"Leith, I have to go."

There must have been a touch of panic in my voice, because he said, very quickly, "Problem?"

"I've just spotted someone I need to talk to." The man was still staring, and sweat was beginning to trickle down my spine. So much for the chill in the air. "I'll ring you back later."

"Make sure you do, or we're coming after you."

I hung up then crossed my legs. The miniskirt rode up my thigh even farther and the guard's gaze slipped downward. A smile touched his thin lips and, for one panicked moment, I thought he was going to cross the street to talk to me.

But he turned away and moved to the bus stop near the Fifth Street intersection, leaning against the outside wall of the shelter and taking a newspaper from his coat pocket. He'd positioned himself in such a way that he could see both the building entrance and me.

It might not mean he suspected my identity, but it sure as hell made things awkward. I dialed my phone's twin and listened to it ring.

"Hello?" The urbane voice that answered was Damon's and yet not. Like his looks, it could easily have belonged to someone older. In the background, I could hear Robyn talking and other phones ringing. Our office was never quiet, even on slow news days. With the recent spate of fires, today wouldn't have been one of them.

"Our Ritz watcher has just turned up. He's standing at the bus stop near the entrance, reading a paper."

"Has he spotted you?"

"He saw me before he moved to the bus stop. He hasn't made a move toward me, so he may not have recognized me."

"Or he's just waiting to see if I turn up or if you'll lead him to me."

"Could be." He had more chance of understanding the motives of the bad guys than I did. He played in their world, after all. "So what do we do?"

"You need to move. If he follows, we know he's recognized you."

"And if he does follow, what will you do? Take him out?"

"It's what I do, Mercy."

A shiver went through me at the matter-of-fact way he said that. And he *would* do it—without thought, without remorse. But knowing someone was a killer and actually standing by and watching them do it were two entirely different things.

"It's broad daylight and rush hour. You can't risk that." I wasn't sure whether the slight edge in my voice was fear or anger, or even a touch of both. "And it makes *you* no better than them."

He snorted softly. "I don't attack innocents. That makes me a whole lot different."

"It's only a matter of degree. And I won't be a party to it."

"I didn't ask you to join my investigation, remember?"

"No, I asked you to join mine. For the moment, I'm the one with all the information—information you apparently need."

"Which I now have, thanks to your pretty friend."

I smiled grimly. "The information is coded. Just try and read it without me."

His voice was oddly weary as he said, "Letting the bad guys live almost never works out, Mercy."

"I don't care."

"You will if they get hold of you later on."

Maybe I would. No, I *definitely* would. But I'd regret standing by and watching Damon ruthlessly get rid of the guard even more. Killing might be an accepted part of dragon mentality, but murder was very different to killing in self-defense. It left a stain on the soul that was hard to erase. My brother had spent the last few years of his life living close to the edge in an effort to escape it. He might not have any remorse for his part in helping hunt down the men responsible for killing his half-brother's soul mate, but the guilt of taking a life lay deep all the same—even if he refused to acknowledge it to himself or to others. I didn't want that weight, didn't want the regret. I had enough problems in my life as it was.

"Question him, restrain him, do what it takes to stop him from following us. But don't kill him." I hesitated, then added softly, "Please."

He didn't answer immediately, but when he finally did, his voice was flat and filled with steel. "This once, and against my better judgment. Walk down to Fifth Street and head right. When you come to Minna Street take another right and head through to Mary. Just keep walking. If he's following you, you'll spot him."

I nodded, remembered he was on the phone, not in front of me, and said, "Then what?"

"Keep walking. I'll go out the side entrance and take care of our problem a few streets away."

I drew in a deep breath and let it out slowly. It didn't do a whole lot to calm the sudden rush of nerves. "Okay."

"Give me five minutes to find the exit to Minna Street."

"Will do."

I hung up, popped the phone back into my bag, then continued to read the paper. Or at least, I tried to. But every nerve was tingling with the awareness of the man across the road. It was hard to curb the instinct to run, and yet that was the one thing I couldn't do. When five minutes had passed, I made a show of glancing at my watch and making a face, then grabbed my bag and left, forcing myself to saunter down the street as if I didn't have a care in the world. Or a madman on my tail. Unfortunately for me, this part of town was either populated by office buildings or parking lots, so I couldn't pretend to stare into storefront windows and use the glass to check for pursuit. And yet he *was* following me. I could feel him. Could feel the heat of him, and smell his cindery scent.

I strolled down Fifth Street, matching my pace to the couple in front of me, not wanting to feel so alone. A lazy sea breeze swirled around us, and though I shivered I wasn't entirely sure it was due to the chill in the wind. I needed to warm up, and that was the one thing I *couldn't* do right now. Even if that guard didn't recognize me, he was close enough to know I wasn't human, and that just might be enough to have him paying a lot more attention to everything I did. Besides, a dragon's flame was as individual as its scent.

I came to the Minna Street intersection and hesitated. The couple I'd been following continued down

Fifth Street, leaving me feeling suddenly bereft. Ahead, Minna Street tunneled through my paper's building, becoming dominated by shadows and artificial lighting, with a bright patch of sunshine beckoning on the other side. It was the perfect place for an ambush, but it certainly *wasn't* where Damon was planning his.

I swallowed heavily, my nerves crawling and sweat tracking down my back. I glanced back at the traffic, using the moment to see not only what the traffic was doing, but where my follower was.

The road was clear and the guard had paused near the parking garage's exit. I crossed the road quickly. The minute I was out of my follower's line of sight, I broke into a run, bolting for that patch of sunshine and the false sense of security it offered.

When the sun hit my face, I slowed, my breathing ragged more from fear than the short run. I was so tempted to look behind me, but that would warn him that I was on to to him. Although, if he'd witnessed my mad dash through the tunnel, he'd probably have guessed anyway.

I passed two doorways and walked under the fire escape. I had no sense of Damon, but he'd had more than enough time to find these exits. For a moment I wondered if he'd simply taken the netbook and left, but something inside me said no. He wanted to stop the people wiping out the draman towns as much as I did, and I was currently his quickest way of doing that.

I flexed my fingers and tried to relax as I came to another cross street. I paused, looking right and left, not really wanting to continue down this lonely-looking street. Not until I knew for sure whether my pursuer was following. I bit my lip then crossed to the sidewalk on the other side of Minna Street. In the process, I casually glanced sideways. The street was empty. The guard hadn't followed me.

Relief washed over me, leaving me shaking. I took a deep breath and released it slowly, then continued down Minna Street as I'd been instructed.

I wasn't alone for long. A familiar warmth crept over my skin, chasing the chill from my flesh as quickly as an inner fire. I smiled slightly as Damon fell into step beside me, and felt any remaining tension slide away. He might be just as dangerous as the men who were hunting us, but he made me feel a whole lot safer.

"He's not following," he said, stating the obvious as he glanced sideways at me. "I'll accept your apology for saying the disguise wouldn't work."

I smiled. "I don't think it's fair to penalize me for *not* remembering men can be sidetracked by a small pair of breasts and a whole lot of leg."

"An apology is not a penalty. And the breasts may be small, but the legs are magnificent."

The compliment had heat flushing my cheeks. God, anyone would think I was a giddy virgin—and that hadn't been the case for more years than I cared to remember. "Well, I'm glad I have *one* good feature."

His gaze met mine, the dark depths serious despite his faint smile. "You have lots of good features. Unfortunately, your stubborn refusal to see good sense *isn't* one of them."

My smile faded. So much for the compliment. "You were going to murder him, Damon. I can't be a part of that."

"And do you think they'll show any such restraint if they catch you again?"

Fear rose like a ghost—half-formed, insubstantial, but mind-numbing nonetheless. "I realize that." My voice was sharp with the panic threatening to bubble over. "But if I somehow manage to survive all this, I then have to live with my actions. And I won't take someone's life just because it's expedient. Life of any kind deserves more respect than that."

At least until I knew for sure who was responsible for Rainey's death. Then I wouldn't restrain him.

And I wouldn't restrain myself.

Deep down, though, I wondered if I was really ready to claim the revenge Rainey needed.

"Expedience is taking care of problems *before* they take care of you," he snapped, then raked a hand through his hair. "This is a mistake, trust me on that."

"So you've said." Repeatedly. "And if I pay the price, then so be it. You've got the netbook?"

"Yes." He pulled the little computer out from under his coat and handed it to me. "What sort of code is it?"

I shrugged as I shoved it into my bag. "Just one we made up when we were kids. It was safer sending notes no one else could read—there was less likelihood of offending someone and getting punished."

He gave me a look that bordered on disbelief. "Why on earth would someone want to punish a couple of kids for sending each other notes?"

"Because it was outside guidelines." I hesitated, then reluctantly added, "Draman never got the same sort of consideration as full-blooded dragons."

"Ah," he said, in a voice that suddenly seemed cooler. "I understand."

His reaction had disappointment swirling, but with it came a lifetime of annoyance.

"How can you possibly understand? You're a full-blood, and a dragon of rank and privilege besides. You could never, *ever* understand just how it is for those of us who sit in two worlds, but are never really considered a true part of either. You use us, abuse us—but heaven forbid you ever think us worthy of any sort of consideration."

He looked a little startled, and I wasn't sure whether it was my words or the anger so evident in my voice. "I have to admit, I've never really thought much about the draman's lot in life," he said.

I snorted softly. "Few full-bloods do."

He slanted me a sideways glance. "We don't have draman in our clique. We never have had."

"Meaning your clique refuses to sully dragon blood with the human taint?" God, how often had I heard such a phrase from the bastard who ruled our clique? Which was ironic when *he* was one of the biggest transgressors. Half his get—my brother included—were draman.

"Meaning my clique is mostly where the muerte come from," he said softly. "It's hard to create potential problems yourself when you are constantly cleaning them up."

"Meaning draman are the first and only source of dragon problems?" I snorted again. "You have to be kidding me."

Hell, I *knew* from experience just how far off the mark *that* statement was.

"You're right; they're not the sole source of our problems." He slanted me another glance, his expression grim. "But trust me when I say that you lot are a major problem when it comes to keeping the existence of dragons secret."

"And of course the full-bloods are perfect little angels, and would never do anything to jeopardize the security of the cliques." I shook my head in disbelief. "I expected better of you, Damon."

He quirked an eyebrow at that and, just for a moment, humor warmed his dark eyes. "As I've mentioned before, you barely know me. And yet here you stand berating my ideals and beliefs."

"And yet you've called me stupid multiple times, and would deny me existence if you could."

"I didn't mean to imply—"

"I saw your reaction when I mentioned I was draman. Hell, I *felt* it. So don't try to bullshit me about what you did and didn't mean."

"I won't deny I reacted to the fact you were draman, Mercy, but it's not for the reasons you seem to think."

"So explain it to me, seeing I so *stupidly* got it wrong."

I stopped at another street and crossed my arms, waiting for the flow of traffic to ease so that we could cross. The sea breeze was getting stronger, and the heat of Damon's presence was no longer enough to keep me warm. I reached down inside myself and called forth the fire, feeling it ripple through my muscles, warming me from the inside out. It wasn't enough to make my skin glow with heat, but at least it kept the bite of the wind at bay. And that bite would get worse the closer we got to the sea.

"I've never seen a *dragon* with your fire control, let alone a draman." He began shrugging off his coat. "It's unusual for draman to even get dragon skills, let alone have them so refined."

I frowned, more than a little confused by his statement. While it was true that there were few enough draman who had my control of fire, there were plenty of us who had most or all of the dragon skills. "Why would you think it's unusual?"

"Because it is." His tone edged toward mocking, and annoyance rose again.

"No, it's *not*. Just about every draman born at Jamieson has full dragon skills." I shivered again and stoked the fires a little bit higher, trying to chase away the growing chill.

"Interesting," he said softly, then offered me the coat. "Here, take this and cool the furnace. If this Angus is a sea dragon, he'll sense your fire and run long before we get to him."

"Thanks." I handed him my red bag and slipped my arms into the coat sleeves. It was quite a bit longer on me than on him, swallowing my hands and dropping past my knees. But it was thick and warm, and filled with the raw scent of him. I flared my nostrils, drawing in the aroma, letting it slide across my senses.

Then I took back my bag, and said, "When you say 'interesting,' does that mean you didn't know about it?"

"The council knew it was happening. I don't believe they're aware it's occurring in such numbers."

I frowned. "But I was under the impression it was happening in all the cliques."

"No, it's not. It seems to be just the seaside cliques."

"But why? And how did the council find out about it? I doubt our king would offer such information." He wasn't the caring-and-sharing type—especially when breeding too many draman was forbidden by council law.

"He didn't. But thirty-one years ago, there was an unapproved cleansing of a small seaside town. Your king denied any knowledge, but the council heard whispers that the town had been filled with his draman—many of whom had the skills of full dragons. They have been watching the seaside cliques ever since."

A chill ran through me. Whale Point. It had to be. "So why would our king tell us that draman in all cliques were gaining dragon powers when he knows it's not true?"

"I don't know." He hesitated, looking down at me, his expression no warmer than before, but maybe that was merely the face of a muerte rather than the man I was occasionally getting glimpses of. "But the Jamieson clique has always been something of a headache for the council."

"Why?"

His expression didn't alter, but I felt his contempt. It wrapped around me, as dark and as deep as the man. "Your king believes the cliques should be autonomous."

I frowned. "But they basically are, aren't they? I thought the council only ruled over decisions that affected all the cliques as a whole."

"Yes and no. Securing our position in this human world is the council's number-one priority, and everything the cliques do affects this."

"So how often are the kings supposed to report to the council?"

"Daily, but the Jamieson clique is somewhat remiss.

Your king hasn't done enough to warrant a reprimand, but he skirts the edge."

"But that doesn't explain why the council wouldn't know the full truth about us draman."

His smile was cold—though its harshness was not aimed at me. "Your king wouldn't tell the council about the draman gaining full dragon powers simply because it is against council edicts to produce too many draman."

"But if the council was watching the clique, they surely would have been aware of our numbers. Why not make a ruling that draman were not to be produced until numbers fell?" After all, in the air-dragon world, it was the male dragons who decided whether a female got pregnant or not. If they didn't want all of us little half-breeds hanging about, then it was simply a matter of choosing *not* to be fertile with their human lovers.

When I actually thought about it, this suggested our king was breeding draman deliberately. But *why,* when he supposedly hated us?

"As I said, I doubt the council is aware of the true extent of draman numbers, although they know that the number of full dragons being born in the seaside cliques is falling. Maybe there's a correlation." He hesitated, then added, "But draman are answerable to the kings and council. Humans are not. Maybe they deemed it safer to allow higher draman numbers than human."

If he thought humans weren't answerable to the kings, then he *hadn't* been to our clique. There wasn't one human living there who would look sideways at our king without fearing some sort of reprisal, although most of them—my mother included—had been with the clique so long they saw nothing wrong with this. We stopped at a set of lights and I punched the button with more force than necessary. "So what is the council considering doing about the draman in the seaside cliques?"

He hesitated. "It's an abnormality that should be explored—"

"And destroyed? Isn't that the council's usual modus operandi when it comes to anything threatening dragon culture?"

"Draman *are* a part of that culture—"

"We've *never* been a part of the culture," I spat back. "And it's people like *you* who have enforced it."

The walk light flashed. I strode out ahead of him, suddenly not wanting to be near him. My fury was just too great—and while it wasn't particularly aimed at him, he was a part of the mentality that had made growing up such hell for me.

The roar of an engine broke through the anger. It was loud and close. Too close. My heart skipped a beat and my breathing was momentarily frozen as I looked up. I saw the white car and the man inside. A man with blue eyes and an almost dreamy smile touching his thin lips.

And I knew, without a doubt, that he *had* recognized me—despite the skirt and the wig.

We hadn't lost him. We'd just given him time to find a weapon.

And he was driving it right at me.

Chapter Seven

A hand wrapped around my waist and dragged me backward, into a body that was hard, strong, and burning with heat.

The car roared past inches from my toes, the tires squealing as the driver hit the gas, sending debris thudding into my bare legs and leaving a thick cloud of black fumes in his wake. The white car quickly disappeared into the traffic, leaving me shaking in shock and disbelief.

"Move," Damon said, his grip sliding down to my elbow as he hustled me away.

He didn't give me time to think or recover, but simply forced me forward, off the street and onto the sidewalk. Three seconds later, we were in a cab and heading God knows where. Which didn't mean he hadn't given the driver a destination, just that I'd been too shaken to hear it.

"Thank you," I said, when I actually found enough air to speak.

He didn't say anything—particularly not "I told you so"—but the anger practically rolled off him in waves. Oddly enough, it didn't really feel as if that anger was aimed at me—which may have been wishful thinking on my part. And I was quite happy to continue the silence. It gave me a chance to settle my nerves and catch my breath more fully.

Eventually the cab stopped, and I realized we were back at the multistory garage where he kept his car.

"How do you think he recognized me?" I said as the cab zoomed off.

"I don't know." He glanced at me then. "Did he ever get close enough to smell you?"

"He was on the other side of the street—"

"Not then," he said impatiently, grabbing my elbow again and hurrying me inside the garage. "In the house."

I remembered Angus carrying me in; remembered the guard touching my hair and drawing in that breath before he'd yanked my head up. "Yes."

Air hissed out between clenched teeth. "You could have mentioned it."

"Why on earth would I think to mention something like that?"

"Because dragons have olfactory senses as sharp as any bloodhound. He might not have recognized you by sight, but he would have recognized your *scent*."

"Well, no one ever thought to mention that to me."

"But you grew up in a clique. It's something you should damn well *know*!"

"I'm a fucking *draman*. I don't know *anything*."

He gave me a disbelieving look and marched on toward the elevator. I ripped my elbow free of his grip, but continued to walk beside him. It wasn't like I had a lot of other options right now. If I called Leith, he'd come running all right, but he'd probably tie me up and start investigating by himself. I'd already lost one good friend to these thugs. I didn't plan to lose another.

"Stay behind me," Damon said as the elevator came to a bumpy stop on the fifth and the doors swished open.

I did as ordered, following his long strides across the oil-stained concrete. His car was parked on the opposite side of the garage from the elevators and the stairs, in a position that wasn't immediately visible from either. There were no other cars parked near it and no one around.

He relaxed a little, then glanced over his shoulder at me. "Lose the wig. We need to give you a new look."

I placed the handbag beside me, then pulled off the wig and tossed it into the trunk once he'd opened it. "What's the point if that guard has my scent and can track me down regardless of the disguise I'm wearing?"

"There are ways around the scent problem." He ferreted through several bags, then pulled one free with a grunt of satisfaction. "Get undressed."

"What?"

He glanced at me, and even in the dusky confines of the garage, the devilish glint in his dark eyes was all too evident. "Suddenly bashful?"

"No." Though I was. Dragons normally weren't, of course, but then, I wasn't full dragon and I really didn't want to expose my body—and my scars—to this man's critical gaze. It might have been different if it was night and I had the illusion of privacy, but in this dusky daylight, everything was far too visible. "I just want to know what you plan to do."

"I plan to temporarily get rid of your scent. Now, strip." He pulled out a plastic spray bottle filled with a lemony-looking liquid, then tossed the bag back into the trunk. After glancing rather pointedly at his watch, he added, "We haven't got all day. Not if you want to catch this Angus person."

"This isn't exactly a private area," I said, the heat of embarrassment growing in my cheeks. "And stripping could definitely attract the wrong kind of attention."

"The cameras can't see us here, and we're also out of visual range of anyone who comes out of the elevators or stairs—facts you're more than aware of." Then he gave me the ghost of a smile that had my face flaming hotter. "What if I promise to turn around until you're naked?"

"Fine. Turn around," I muttered, wondering how the hell I was going to stop the blush from rolling right down to my toes.

He turned, although his amusement spun all around me, heating my skin more than his gaze ever could.

I hurriedly undressed, stacking my clothes on the car's roof before crossing my arms across my breasts and turning my back to him. "Okay, I'm naked."

A heartbeat later I realized just how wrong I'd been before. His gaze *could* warm me far more than any emotion riding the air. The weight of it burned by skin, making my spine tingle and my pulse flutter.

"You weren't kidding about the scars, were you?" His voice was cool and controlled, and it jarred against the hint of anger that stirred the air.

It was almost as if he were fighting for control.

But if Death didn't like the scars, then why didn't he—and the council he worked for—do something to make the situation for draman more bearable? Yet even as that thought crossed my mind, I dismissed it. We were draman. In the scheme of things, we didn't matter.

I shivered a little, and knew it didn't have a whole lot to do with the gathering coolness. "Why would you think I'd joke about something like that?"

Though I heard no sound of movement, his finger suddenly touched my skin, trailing heat as he traced the S-shaped scar along my right side. "This one's nasty."

His finger stalled at the knotty end of the scar, and the heat of it spread across my butt, making me ache. I fought the urge to press back into his touch and said, in a voice that sounded amazingly calm, "It's retribution from someone I wouldn't sleep with."

"The man who did this wanted to sleep with you?" A note of incredulity had crept into his otherwise controlled tone. "That's not exactly the most convincing way to seduce a reluctant partner."

I smiled, though it belied the anger that still burned somewhere inside. But it was an anger aimed just as much at myself as the man who'd given me the scar. I'd been stupid that day. Stupid enough to put myself into that situation, and to believe that a dragon could ever change his colors. "Apparently there was a bet between Seth—the man who gave me the scar—and his bisexual mate. The object was to bed as many draman as possible in a day. I refused to be one of many, and he lost the bet by one draman."

To say he'd been unhappy would be the understatement of the century. And if I'd thought his tormenting had been bad up until then, afterward it became ten times worse.

Damon's finger was moving again, tracing a line down my back. He reached the junction of my legs and my breath hitched. For a moment, neither of us moved. My awareness of that finger—and of him—was so acute that every little hair on my body felt like it was standing on end, and my heart was going a million miles an hour. Wanting, needing—and yet fearing it at the same time.

How many times had I been in a situation like this, wanting someone I shouldn't?

And how many more times did I need to get hurt before I learned my lesson? Before I stopped hoping that not all dragons were tarred with the same brutal brush? That there *was* one out there who *could* accept me?

That man *wasn't* Damon. He was a hit man for the council, for God's sake, and a man who believed draman shouldn't exist.

I should be running as far and as fast as I could.

And yet here I stood. Hoping. Needing.

"What about the scar that cuts across the middle of your stain?" he said softly, his touch shifting. Up to the snakelike skin that twined around my spine. Not downward. Not to where it ached.

Disappointment mingled with relief, but both were quickly washed away as his caress slid across my hip.

"The result of fighting off yet another would-be suitor who wouldn't take no for an answer."

"And this?" he said softly, his fingers tracing the jagged scar that cut across my shoulder blades, slicing into the tip of my stain.

I shivered, as much from his caress as the memories. "A gift from a flight lesson gone wrong."

His hand slid around my waist, and suddenly there was no space between us. All I could feel was the heat of him pressed up against me. The hardness of his erection nestled against my butt. The warmth of his breath flowed past my ear as he said, "Draman can fly?"

I could barely breathe, let alone think, but somehow managed to say, "Most can."

"Can you?"

His lips brushed my ear as he spoke. I shivered, the memories of past hurt crowding present pleasure, the need for caution warring with the simple desire to feel and enjoy the touch of another. "I've never been able to fly."

It was the truth in more ways than one.

"Then perhaps that is something we should fix when we have a little more time."

His lips brushed the junction of my neck and shoulders, and for a moment it felt like he were branding me.

Then he stepped back and cold air washed between us, cooling my skin but not my reaction. I ached, and there was no simple remedy for something like that. Not here, and not now, anyway.

"Raise your arms so I can spray you down," he said, his tone calm and unperturbed. Which was annoying, to say the least. Death could at least have the decency to sound a *little* hot and bothered.

I raised my arms as ordered, and moisture hit my skin, its scent slightly acidic but not unpleasant. He sprayed my back, arms, and legs, then ordered me to turn around. I did, and he repeated the process, all in a very cool, calm, and collected way.

Highly annoying indeed.

When he'd finished, I reached for my clothes again, but he'd already grabbed them and tossed them into the trunk. "They've seen that outfit. You'll need something else."

While he scavenged through his trunk, I reached for my flames and used them to cover my nakedness. They lapped across my body gently—a fiery blanket that neither burned nor smoked, and one that had the bonus of keeping the chill from my skin. I just had to hope that no one came out of the elevator—although standing there naked was as likely to catch as much attention as standing there on fire.

Not that Damon seemed to notice either way, despite the powerful erection I'd felt only moments before. My gaze slipped downward. It was still there, and that made me feel a little better. At least Death wasn't in control of *absolutely* everything.

"I thought you didn't carry female clothing around with you?"

"I don't, and we can't risk going out to buy more, so this time you'll have to make do with male."

"Oh. Great." Just what I needed when in the company of a dynamic and sexy man—to look like a kid dressing up in her daddy's clothes. "It's going to look ridiculous. And certainly not very manlike."

He glanced up from the confines of the trunk, the glimmer of amusement evident in his eyes. "At least you have rather small breasts, so they're not going to be a problem."

"There's nothing wrong with small breasts," I said, a little defensively.

"I didn't say there was."

"You didn't say there wasn't, either."

He began pulling clothes out of a bag. "Your breasts are perfect, just like the rest of you."

"It'd be more believable if you didn't say it in such a sardonic tone," I said drily.

He raised an eyebrow. "You wouldn't believe I meant it no matter what tone I used."

He had a point. I wouldn't. I had a good figure, a reasonable face, brown hair, and brown eyes. Nothing out of the ordinary. Nothing that would make anyone look twice. But in a clique where the shimmering golds and fiery reds of a sunset dominated, being born a boring brown had meant I'd stood out in an altogether unwelcome way.

At least it had taught me to fight.

Damon tossed me a pair of jeans and a sweatshirt, and the scent of smoke and musky male teased my nostrils. It wasn't *his* scent, though.

"They're a friend's brother's," he said, obviously noting my expression, "He's smaller than me, so they should fit you."

I slipped on the gray sweatshirt and wished it smelled more of him than of a stranger—though I guess a stranger's scent made more sense if dragons did have such keen senses. The sleeves covered my hands and the shoulders slid halfway down my arms, and it was even bulky enough to hide the fact that I had breasts. The jeans had similar problems in length and were a little tight in the butt, but otherwise they fit okay.

I began rolling up the sleeves as he pulled out a small backpack and transferred the netbook and the other bits and pieces from the red handbag to it before handing it to me. He dumped the now-empty handbag into the trunk and slammed down the lid.

"Why are you carrying his clothes around?" I asked.

"Because I didn't have a chance to return his effects to his parents before I was kidnapped." He walked around and opened the passenger side door for me.

"So this friend's brother—he's the victim you mentioned before?"

"Yes." His answer was controlled, but I felt the anger in him regardless.

"I'm sorry—"

"So will they be, trust me." He handed me a multicolored woolen cap. "Tuck your hair up in that."

Once I'd done it, he brushed my back lightly, guiding me into the car. I was still so attuned to him that I couldn't help a tremor of delight.

But the casualness of his threat against those men seemed to hang in the air, sending another shiver through my soul. And while half of me questioned the wisdom of hanging around such a man, the other half—undoubtedly the insane part that was so attracted to him—knew he was still my best chance of getting the answers I so desperately needed.

I waited until he climbed into the driver's seat and had reversed out of the parking bay before asking, "So, did they kill him because he was too close to finding answers?"

"No, he was a victim of one of the cleansings."

I raised my eyebrows. "He was draman? I thought you didn't like draman."

"I never said that," he replied, his voice holding an edge. "What I *said* was that draman cause us a lot of problems."

"Well, your tone certainly didn't imply affection, so what else am I to think? And you never did bother to explain *how* we cause you problems."

The look he gave me was wintry, to say the least. "Most draman are stronger and faster than ordinary humans, and there are many who seem to delight in using this advantage."

"History is full of the strong taking advantage of the weak. It's not just a draman trait." And I had the scars to prove it.

"True. But it is the draman who seem to most delight in risking exposure to us all."

I raised an eyebrow. "I wonder why that might be? Surely it couldn't have anything to do with the treatment dished out to most draman?"

"Not all cliques treat draman the way Jamieson does." The winter hadn't lifted from his eyes. In fact, it had probably gotten deeper. "And my friend was not draman. He was merely having a liaison with one."

Was that liaison Chaylee? Rainey had told me that her sister had met someone, but surely if she'd known that someone was full dragon, she would have mentioned it. "In the draman town of Stillwater?"

He flicked me a glance. "Yes. And before you ask your next question, I neither approved or disapproved of the relationship. It was not my place to do either."

That didn't stop him from having an opinion about it—though it was one he obviously wasn't going to share with me. "How do you know for sure that your friend is dead when no bodies have been found?"

"Because his kin felt his passing. His brother—who had a broken wing and couldn't fly out himself—phoned me and asked me to investigate what had happened."

Though his voice was flat, his anger seared the air, rolling across my senses as sharply as an axe and making it difficult to breathe. "Damon," I panted, "control it."

He glanced at me sharply, surprise in his eyes. Then the anger disappeared as if sucked away into a vacuum, and suddenly I was able to breathe again.

"You didn't say you were sensitive to emotion."

"You didn't ask." I tucked a sweaty strand of hair behind my ear and thought about admitting that I didn't often get *so* attuned to the emotion of others that it affected me physically. That, in fact, I didn't usually get a whole lot from him, either. But that might lead to him controlling himself even more, and I actually liked feeling the occasional flashes from him. So I simply said, "You flew straight out?"

"Yeah." He was silent for a minute, and though the force of it was muted, his anger and guilt still touched the air. Those were emotions I was all too familiar with.

And the only thing that would help either of us feel better would be stopping the bastards behind this destruction. And in my case, saving my friend from an eternity stuck in between worlds, never able to move on and be reborn, but never able to participate again in this one.

He added, "I *did* get there in time to stop the fires from destroying every building. His belongings were in one of the remaining ones."

I took a deep, shuddering breath that did little to

shake the residual pain, and said, "So if you were there in time to stop the fires from destroying the town, do you know what happened to the inhabitants?"

"No. The place was empty and there were no remains. I suspect they were all taken elsewhere to be killed and buried."

"But how would that be possible? I mean, you must have gotten there quickly if the place was still ablaze. Surely they couldn't have gotten rid of that many bodies so fast?"

"If the attackers were dragons or draman with full powers, and the majority of the town were draman *without* dragon powers, then it would be very easy to herd them into trucks and ship them somewhere else to kill them."

"But your friend's brother was a full dragon, and Rainey's sister had full dragon powers." And if they'd fought and somehow escaped—only to be caught and killed near dawn—then that would explain how both Rainey and his friend had felt their kin's passing.

Damon looked at me, his expression grim. "Two against God knows how many? That's not good odds in anyone's book."

"Meaning you think dragons *are* behind these attacks?"

"Well, it can hardly be humans. While most draman haven't got dragon powers, they are, as I mentioned, stronger and faster. There's no way humans could have wiped out a whole town so quickly and efficiently. And why would they bother? They're more likely to want to stick us in a lab and study us."

He had a point, but I couldn't help adding, "Humans

have a history of killing things they don't understand, and even draman can't outrun bullets."

"But there were no shots fired at Stillwater. I would have found evidence of it."

"Which doesn't mean they weren't shot somewhere else."

"No."

I closed my eyes against the images that arose. I didn't need to think about all those other people. I had the chance to save Rainey's soul, but it wasn't within my power to save anyone else who'd been in that town. Not even Rainey's sister.

"Would the council have ordered the cleansings?" The urbane man who'd talked to Angus in the van had claimed that it hadn't, but he'd also mentioned that muerte didn't move without orders from one of the kings.

"No. If they had, the muerte would have been informed. We were not."

I guess that was *something*. "So if not the council, then who? Could this be the result of several kings plotting?"

"It's possible, though I don't see what it would achieve."

"Maybe they wanted nothing more than a reduction in draman numbers." But if that was the case, why would they go to such lengths to keep their secrets?

There had to be more than that behind all of it. There had to be.

"So tell me," I said, my voice suddenly holding a slight edge, "if a full-blooded dragon hadn't been killed in these cleansings, would you have been investigating them?"

He pulled out into the traffic then glanced at me, his expression still cool. "He wasn't *just* a full-blood. He was a king's son."

"And of course, his life was *far* more important than all the draman who have perished." The bitterness was more evident this time. "After all, if draman aren't doing the dirty work around the cliques or providing sexual services, what earthly use are they?"

"I never said that."

"You didn't have to. It's a common thread in dragon thinking." I shifted a little to study him better. "If it was a king's son that was killed, why *isn't* the council investigating?"

"Because the king prefers to keep the investigation private. This sort of news would spread wildly through the cliques, and might just drive the culprits underground."

"And *that* was a lie." Or rather, a fudging of the truth. While it might very well be a consideration for not getting the council involved, that wasn't the major reason.

He glanced at me sharply. "And why would you say that?"

"Because I can taste it." I paused, then added, "So what's the real reason?"

He considered the question for several minutes, and eventually said, "Julio has heard whispers of a plot against the kings. He fears his son's death might be the start of it, but he does not want to raise the alarm until he has something concrete."

That raised my eyebrows. "Surely warning the council should be his first priority?" After all, the council was made up of the thirteen kings themselves.

Damon glanced at me sideways. "His son was killed in a draman town. How do you think the council might react?"

"Badly." Meaning draman blood would be shed. Especially given they already considered us a major cause of their problems. It was surprising that a dragon king actually seemed *concerned* about shedding draman blood unnecessarily, but maybe they *weren't* all tarred with the same brush. "I see your point."

"Finally."

I ignored the barb. "Well, our kidnappers appear to know that your actions are a result of *someone's* orders. They kept you alive to try and find out who."

"At least that explains their refusal to do the sensible thing and get rid of me when they had the chance." His smile was grim. "Hopefully, it'll be a mistake they'll live to regret."

That was my hope, too. We continued in silence, and eventually he drove into the parking garage near Pier 39, once again finding a dark and gloomy spot in one of the corners. I slipped my arms into the backpack, settling it across my back before following him to the elevator. Once we were at street level, we joined the dwindling crowds of tourists looking at the stores and enjoying the carnival atmosphere. Eventually we made our way toward the marina and leaned against the railing to look at the small group of sea lions.

Damon glanced at his watch. "It's twenty past six. What time was this guy supposed to be at the boat?"

"Seven."

"We'll stay here for another thirty minutes, then move across."

I nodded and crossed my arms on the old wooden

rail, watching the snoozing sea lions. The setting sun began to streak the sky with red and gold—bright banners that heralded the onset of night. The air burned with energy, the music of it so sweet and strong that I felt like singing right along with it. I raised my face to the flag-covered sky and drew in a deep breath. The energy of it flowed through me, renewing and revitalizing.

"You're practically humming with pleasure," Damon said softly.

"I'm a dragon," I said without opening my eyes. "I'm just not as much dragon as you."

"You're draman. You shouldn't be able to *feel* the energy raised by the dusk, let alone thrive on it."

I opened my eyes and looked at him. "Can I ask you a question?"

A somewhat sardonic smile touched his lips. "You've been asking me nothing *but* questions. Why stop now?"

"Why did you kiss me last night?"

He blinked. "Your thought processes really don't follow any logical path, do they?"

"No. Are you going to answer the question?"

He leaned forward and crossed his arms on the railing. He was so close that my skin tingled with awareness. "I kissed you because I wanted to."

Part of me wanted to do a happy little dance, but I resisted the urge. "And now that you know I'm draman?"

He glanced at me, eyebrow raised. "You being draman doesn't alter the enjoyment of that kiss, however brief it might have been."

"So you don't regret the action?"

"No."

"Then why keep bringing up the fact I'm draman like it's some kind of problem?"

"It's just that you're constantly surprising me, Mercy." He hesitated and raised a hand, his fingertips lightly touching my cheek. "My reaction has nothing to do with you personally."

His caress sparked the fires deep inside and a shudder that was all pleasure ran through me. But I stepped away from him, even though it was the last thing I really wanted to do. I needed to make him understand. Needed him to see *me*. Not just the draman. Not just the woman. *Me*.

Why, I don't really know. It wasn't like we had the possibility of a future.

Maybe it was just some perverse idea that if a man who didn't believe draman should exist could see *me*—the person rather than the draman—then maybe there *was* some hope of a better future for us all.

"But it *does*, Damon," I said softly. "It makes me feel like I'm a second-class citizen. Like I'm never going to be good enough, no matter what I do."

He frowned and clasped his hands together on the railing again. "Draman are *not* dragons, and that is something you're never going to change."

"No, but we can change the attitudes that go with it." I waited until a young couple had walked past, then added, "Because what you're saying now is that despite the fact that some of us can do exactly the same things as full-blood dragons, we don't deserve an equal footing. That we indeed *deserve* the punishments and death."

"I'm not saying that at all, but—"

"There *are* no buts here, Damon. We live and breathe fire just like you full-bloods, and we deserve the same sort of respect."

"You're never going to get that respect easily, Mercy. The old ones are too set in their ways."

"But I'm not standing here talking to an old one, am I?"

He studied me for a moment, his dark eyes as unreadable as his expression, then he glanced away again.

I sighed. "If you can't respect me, what's the point of kissing me?"

Still he didn't say anything.

Way to go, Mercy. Open your big mouth, make your point, and lose any chance of getting down and dirty with Mr. Dark and Dangerous. Maybe one of these days I'd learn to shut the above-mentioned mouth.

But then again, maybe not.

Because really, it needed to be said. I was sick to death of full-bloods thinking I was a quick and easy lay just because I was draman. Granted, I enjoyed sex as much as any other dragon—or draman, for that matter—but there had to be *something* there. And that something *wasn't* disdain for what I was.

Unfortunately, full-bloods could be great deceivers, and sometimes not even those of us who had spent our whole lives around them could tell truth from lie. I wasn't even sure *they* knew the difference, sometimes.

And I was fervently hoping Damon wasn't one of those deceivers, because I had a feeling he could cause me a whole lot more heartbreak than any of the full-bloods in my past.

I dropped my gaze back to the sea lions, who were doing little more than lying on their blubbery bellies, soaking up the last few embers of sunlight.

As the last of dusk's energy and music faded, I pushed away from the railing and said, "Let's walk toward the boat, just in case he gets there early." Anything was better than standing in that depressing silence.

"Do you know the mooring number?" he said, walking close enough that the heat of him washed over me, chasing away the growing chill of the night.

It was nice, sharing someone else's heat, although it probably wouldn't last too much longer, because he'd have to flame down once we got near the boats.

"I wasn't given that information, but the boat's name is the *Heron*. We should be able to walk along and find it."

"I think it'll be quicker and easier to ask."

"So we'll ask. It's not like it's a major problem."

"Except if we ask the wrong person, and we end up notifying our kidnappers that we're down here."

I frowned. "But we know what our kidnappers look like."

He glanced at me. "We may have beaten two of them, but there are more henchmen than that in this little gang, I assure you."

I supposed he was right. The truth was, I hadn't actually thought about it, even though I knew it must have taken more than the four men I was aware of to destroy the draman towns. "We're not going to Angus's boat, though, but his friend's, so as long as we're careful, we should be all right. After all, neither of us resembles our usual self."

He raised an eyebrow. "You say that like it's a bad thing."

"It is when you look like a kid wearing your much-older brother's clothes."

A smile touched his lips. "I think you look rather cute."

"And I think you're insane."

"You wouldn't be the first person to think that," he mused. "I can see the *Heron* from here. She's the white-and-blue motor yacht."

I followed the line of his gaze and saw the boat he was talking about. It was large and long, and had at least three decks. It also looked damn expensive. But I saw something else, as well. Or rather, *someone* else.

Angus.

His sea-colored head was visible for only a few moments, before he ducked down into the lower decks, but I had no doubt it was him.

"Our quarry is on the boat," I said softly.

"Good." Damon flexed his arms, reminding me of a fighter getting ready for the next bout. "You go straight to the boat. I'll board via the rear of the yacht in the next berth. Between the two of us, we should be able to prevent an escape."

"He's a sea dragon. He won't need to escape. He can just call the sea and drown us."

He gave me a cool, calm smile that sent a chill racing down my spine. Death had reentered the building.

"Even the canniest sea dragon isn't faster than a bullet."

Goose bumps joined the chill. "And just when does a dragon need a gun?"

"Since I became a muerte." He shrugged, and it was a surprisingly eloquent movement. "Burning is not a pleasant way to die, and I'd rather a quick kill before I burn."

"So Death *does* have a soft side?"

"There's nothing soft about mercy." He smiled suddenly, and it was like sunshine breaking through rain: brief but glorious. "Although, if we're talking about you, I suspect you have *lots* of lovely soft spots."

"Which you're never going to uncover unless you work on that attitude of yours."

His smile faded. "I can't change the attitude of a lifetime in a matter of minutes, no matter how much I might want to kiss you again. You ready?"

I nodded, too struck by the knowledge that he *did* want to kiss me again to say anything intelligent. We walked on. That, at least, I could manage—although part of me wanted to dance.

There were locked gates between us and the boats, but it didn't take much of an effort on Damon's part to get past. We slipped inside and parted ways—he moving into the first slip area and me stepping on board the *Heron*.

The minute I set foot on the boat, Angus's familiar voice said, "Is that you, Mikey?"

I saw Damon leap across to the stern, then said, "I'm afraid not, Angus."

"Jesus, girl, what the fuck are you doing here?" He appeared in the main cabin area, then just as quickly disappeared as a black-haired blur grabbed him and pushed him back down.

I scrambled along the railing and into the upper cabin. Damon stood behind Angus, one arm wrapped around the sea dragon's neck and holding a silver gun to his head with the other.

He glanced up as I entered, and with a slight movement of his head motioned me toward the plush leather couch that half wrapped around a teak coffee table. I slipped the backpack off, dumping it on the floor and out of the way before sitting down on the end of the couch, avoiding the large window.

Damon's attention returned to Angus. "I'll put a bullet in your brain the minute the sea does anything untoward."

The other man held up his hands. "No trouble, I promise."

Damon released his grip on Angus's neck and pushed him unceremoniously onto the smaller couch opposite mine. Angus looked at me somewhat reproachfully. "There was no need for this, lass."

I snorted softly. "I trusted you the first time, and ended up drugged and held captive by psychos. Why wouldn't we show a little more caution this time around?"

"Because if I'd meant you any real harm, I would have ensured you got a full dose of the drug. You wouldn't be free now if I'd done that."

I couldn't sense a lie in his words, and yet I couldn't help retorting, "Why even dose me at all if you wanted to ensure I'd escape?"

"Because I needed you to be out of it when I carried you in. These boys aren't fools, and neither am I. I'm not about to risk my neck needlessly."

"And this is supposed to make me grateful? Those men burned down my *apartment*."

"At least you weren't in it, and you could have been. They don't care who they hurt in order to protect themselves." He hesitated, then glanced up at the man standing so watchfully behind him. "I saw what they did to you. I wanted no part of that when it came to the lass."

"Then why get involved in Mercy's kidnapping at all?" Damon asked, the tension emanating from his body reminding me of a rattlesnake ready to strike. "Why stay here, when you could so easily disappear into the sea and never be seen again?"

"Because they have Coral." Angus's voice was an odd mix of anger and defeat.

"Who is?"

"My mate. They're holding her hostage against my good behavior." He hesitated, glancing at me with a grimace. "And they'll kill us all the moment they're sure there's no widespread interest in the cleansed towns."

My sudden smile felt brittle. "So the real truth is that you eased up on the drug dosage to save your own skin rather than mine."

"Well, yes. But I didn't want anyone else to suffer the same fate as your friend, either."

Something inside me went still. Cold. "So you *did* set us up that night."

He hesitated. "I had no choice. Not with Coral being held hostage. But I did call the cops and report the accident as soon as I knew that's what they intended."

"Which would have been useless if they'd both been dead," Damon pointed out, voice harsh.

"I know." Angus glanced at me. "I'm sorry, lass."

The apology was sincere enough, but something inside me remained cold. He'd basically signed Rainey's death warrant by setting us up like that, and even if he *had* done it to save the life of his lover and himself, it was something I could never forgive.

"So why didn't they just kill you both the minute they ran Rainey and me off the road?" I asked, voice sounding amazingly calm considering part of me really did want to jump up and hit him. Repeatedly. "And why the hell didn't they check that we were both dead?"

"Have you any idea how far that car fell? You really shouldn't have survived." He studied me for a second, as if contemplating how the hell I actually *had*. "Of course, they realized a little later that they had no idea how many other people you might have told about the towns. Given they'd made me your original point of contact, they released me to see if any other fish would take the bait."

"And that fish was me again."

"Yeah. You should have just walked away when you had the chance."

I flicked a somewhat dark glance Damon's way. "People keep telling me that. So why didn't they kill me the second time?"

"Oh, they intended to. They just decided to do it right this time, and question you first."

Which is why he'd made such a point of saying when we'd met in the bar that these men weren't going to be scared of one lone draman. If I'd answered any other way, if I'd mentioned there wasn't anyone else, then I might now be a dead and lost soul, just like Rainey.

"But how could you be so sure that I'd come out of

the drug quickly enough to escape?" I asked. "I'm draman. A drug meant for dragons could do anything to us."

"It was a human drug, and most of them don't affect dragons. Draman are, of course, half human, so it *does* affect you, though to a lesser degree. But I still only gave you half a dose to be sure."

"You couldn't have been sure I'd escape the cell."

"No, but I figured you'd wake the muerte, and that he'd work something out." Angus glanced at the gun, still pointed in his direction. "They're tricky bastards, these muerte."

Damon's smile was cold. "What makes you think those men are any different from me?"

"Oh, I have no illusions about the men I'm working with. It's part of the reason I changed boats."

"You're still in the same general area. If they want to kill you, changing location won't stop them."

"No, but it'll delay them a little. Right now, I just need time."

"For what?" Damon asked, one eyebrow raised.

"I've called Coral's family in to help, but it'll take them a little while to get here. The sea never hurries herself, even for a message that's urgent, and it's a long way from here to where they're currently vacationing."

"Tell us about the men," Damon said flatly.

Angus blew out a breath. "There's not a whole lot to tell. I only got into this a few weeks ago, after I recognized one of the men from the attack on Whale Point."

"Whale Point?" Damon raised an eyebrow. "You were in that town when it was destroyed?"

Angus's smile was grim. "I was barely fifteen, but yes. I think it was one of the first."

"So why did you lie about not recognizing the people behind it?" I asked.

"I'm hardly likely to admit to something that might get Coral killed, am I?" He scrubbed a hand across his face, and there was an edge of frustration in the sharp movement. "As it turned out, my memory played me for a fool. The man I attacked wasn't one of the ones who destroyed Whale Point. He sounded just like him, but he's far too young. But he *was* involved in the more recent cleansings."

If he heard the voice of the Jamieson king, would he recognize it? Somehow, I suspected he might. And Seth did sound a whole lot like our king.

He also hated draman—and he'd take great pleasure in erasing us. But there had to be more behind it than just that.

There had to be.

"Why didn't you just call the sea once you got into trouble?" Damon asked. "It's not like we're far from water in San Francisco."

"You're not the only one who knows holding a gun to someone's head is a good way to prevent trouble," Angus said wryly. "And they were holding it to Coral's. If it had been just me, I might have tried anyway. Any form of revenge would have been worth the price, even if these bastards weren't involved in the Whale Point massacre."

"So who *was* involved?" I asked.

"I don't know."

"Name the people you *do* know, Angus," Damon said softly. "Stop avoiding it."

He sighed. "I only know some. You met Evan—he

owned and ran the bar you were both caught in. They killed him last night."

"Do you know why?" Damon asked. "Seems a strange move, seeing as the place was proving useful."

Angus shrugged. "Maybe he wanted more money. He was greedy like that."

Damon didn't look convinced, but all he said was "Keep going."

"Albert and Jay were the men you knocked out to escape. They're just muscle. As are the four men who alternate minding Coral. They're draman, though."

"Draman shouldn't be able to restrain a full-blood dragon, whether they're of the sea or the air," Damon said with a frown.

Angus snorted softly. "How out of touch are you? Many of the draman around here are more than capable of standing up to full-bloods, simply because many have the same capabilities."

"Having them, and using them, are two entirely different things."

"Draman aren't dumb. It seems to me that you and your much vaunted council might be, though. Or at the very least, behind the times." Angus sniffed disdainfully, and I couldn't help smiling. It was nice to know that I wasn't the only one who had a less-than-stellar opinion of the council. "But Coral's also got one of those home-detention devices on her, and it's combined with a boundary fence alarm set to a frequency that'll just about fry her brain if she attempts to break it. She did try to push past the pain of the thing, but to no avail."

"Which those men undoubtedly delighted in telling you about," I murmured.

Anger flared in his eyes, deep and bright, and suddenly this sea dragon seemed a whole lot more dangerous. "Oh, Vincent and Harry delighted in telling me lots of things. And they will die for that alone, if I have my way."

I believed him. You couldn't look into his eyes and not believe it. And just for that brief second, he was every bit as scary as the man standing so vigilantly behind him. I licked my lips and said, "Who was the elegant-sounding man you were talking to in the van?"

Angus raised his eyebrows. "You heard that?"

"Some of it."

"Then you've more dragon blood in you than I figured. I gave you enough to knock you out for a good hour or so." He hesitated, then glanced up at Damon. "Can I get a drink? No tricks."

"The moment I suspect anything untoward, you die." Damon's voice was flat and deadly, and left no one in any doubt that he meant what he said.

Angus's answering smile was bitter, but he rose and walked over to the bar, pouring himself a bourbon without offering either of us one. Can't say I really blamed him.

"Tell you what," he said, turning around to face us again. "I'll do a trade. The name of that man for your help in rescuing Coral."

"We're not here to do a deal, Angus." Damon's voice was still flat. "We intend to stop these men, and we intend to get the answers we need from you. It's your choice as to whether we do that nicely or not."

Angus downed his bourbon in one gulp then poured another. "Then you might as well kill me now, because I'm not helping you unless you help me to save Coral."

Damon shifted and the tension in the air sharpened abruptly.

"Don't," I said, half pushing to my feet. I wasn't entirely sure what I intended to do, but I couldn't just sit here and let him kill Angus. I might not entirely trust him, I might never be able to forgive him for his part in killing Rainey, but I didn't want to see his brains splattered across the boat decks, either. He didn't deserve that any more than Rainey had deserved what happened to her.

Damon glanced at me, jaw clenched and eyes as harsh as stone. He was going to do it, I thought, and I added hurriedly, "Please, Damon."

He continued to study me, then said sharply, "For you, not for him. But don't ask for any more favors, Mercy. You've had more than your fair share."

I relaxed back into the seat and blew out a breath. Danger averted, but for how long? Death might have been restrained this time, but not for long. If Damon believed it was for the best, then he *would* kill, regardless of what I thought or did. It was his job, after all.

And I was insane to be so attracted to the man.

"I'll take that as a yes," Angus said, the tension in him as sharp as that still riding Damon. His gaze met mine. "If I can get her out before her family arrives, we can all just flee, without her family putting themselves in danger."

"Meaning you're endangering our lives rather than theirs," Damon said in an annoyed sort of voice.

"You're more than capable of taking care of yourself, *muerte*."

"Mercy's not."

"Mercy *is,* and she won't be left behind, so don't even think it," I said, before Angus could even open his mouth.

Damon gave me a dark sort of look. "Where are they keeping your mate?"

"Santa Rosa," Angus said, then grimaced. "It's far enough away from me—and far enough from the ocean—that neither of us can be of much help to the other."

"So why call in reinforcements from the sea?" I asked, confused.

He glanced at me. "Because there are at least two men guarding her at the one time, and only one of me. I need the additional muscle." He glanced at Damon, and a hint of mischief touched his lips. "You'll do just fine in that department, lad."

Angus shifted a little, moving from one foot to the other, and in that moment, the window exploded inward. He jerked sideways and blood splattered the mirror behind him.

Then he fell to the floor in a heap.

Chapter Eight

Damon moved so quickly he was little more than a blur. He hit me low and fast, dragging me facedown onto the wraparound couch while he knelt beside me on the floor.

"They shot him!" I said, voice half muffled by the leather and more than a little shaky. "Why the hell would they shoot him?"

"Maybe they've figured he's outlasted his usefulness." His attention was on the window above us rather than me, and his body hummed with an energy that seemed dangerously ready to explode. "Keep your head down until we know if they're still out there."

The warning made my heart race even harder, and I hadn't thought that was possible. "But why would they risk shooting him with so many people around?"

"With rifles these days, you don't have to be anywhere near your target to be certain of a kill."

"It just seems wrong for dragons to be using

weapons," I muttered, and looked up at the middle of the three windows that lined the side of the boat. The thick glass was shattered, the pebblelike shards littering the top of the couch, glittering like diamonds in the cabin's bright light.

"A gun is anonymous," Damon said, his face so close to mine that his breath washed across my cheek. "Dragon fire isn't."

"It's still wrong," I said, wishing he weren't so close, that he didn't smell so good. Wishing I could just snuggle up a little closer to all his heat and strength and confidence.

"It's not the weapon," he refuted. "Weapons have their place in the world. It's the reasoning of the man behind it that's wrong."

I shifted to stare at him. "Says the man who kills for a living."

"What I do, and what these people do, are two different things."

"Both of you have reasons and both of you think they're good ones. But that doesn't make either of you right."

On the floor, Angus made a whispery noise.

"Shit, he's alive," I said, and scrambled toward him, away from Damon's grasp. I grabbed the sea dragon's hand and stared into the blue of his eyes. His flesh was like ice against mine. I tried not to see the blood soaking into the carpet behind his head, and tried to ignore the sensation of death gathering close. "Angus? We're here. We'll get help. Just hang on."

His mouth opened, and although no words came out, he struggled on, trying to speak. I glanced up at Damon. "We need to get a doctor here."

"It won't do any good, Mercy."

"But we just can't sit here and watch him die!" Although I didn't raise my voice, the desperate need to do something—*anything*—to help this man filled it with a hard edge.

"There's no dragon medic close by, and we can't risk human intervention. *That* could lead to complications with the council neither of us would enjoy." His voice was as stony as his face. "But even if we *did* bring in human help, they wouldn't be able to save him. Look at him. Half his head is gone."

"But—"

"I'm *not* arguing about this. We'll wait to see if the shooter comes to investigate his kill, and then we leave."

"But someone has to stay here until dawn." Disbelief and anger ran through me. "Someone needs to be here to guide his soul on. You can't just leave—"

"We *can,* and we *must.*"

It was said so coldly that I could only shake my head. "God, you're an unfeeling bastard."

"Death often is." He said it almost gently, like he was speaking to a child.

"But you're *not* death," I snapped back. "It's just your job. It's not what you are."

"Then you see things that no one else does." Humor touched his tone, but it held an edge that was lightly mocking. "Including me."

I didn't know what to say to that, so I simply glanced back down at Angus. His face was etched with pain and the knowledge of death, but when his gaze met mine, the blue depths were aware and desperate.

"Coral," he said, his words slurred and voice hoarse. "You must—"

"Shhh," I said, squeezing his fingers. "Just rest. We'll help her. I promise."

"Go to her now. Save her. They'll kill her."

"If they haven't already," Damon murmured.

"No, she lives. I'd know." Angus gulped down air and his fingers clenched against mine, squeezing them hard enough to hurt. "Moraga Drive. Blue house—"

His voice faded, and a heartbeat later his eyes rolled back into his head and his grip against my hand suddenly loosened.

He was dead.

I blinked back tears as I leaned forward and closed his eyes. This man might have betrayed both Rainey and me, but he didn't deserve this sort of death, didn't deserve to be alone when his soul moved on.

"Damon—"

"We are *not* staying here to pray for his soul, Mercy."

"If you'd just shut up and let me finish a sentence," I snapped back, "you'd learn that I was about to ask how quickly we can get to Santa Rosa."

Because if we could get Coral free soon enough, then Angus would not be alone come dawn.

He looked at me like I was crazy. "You're not actually going to attempt this rescue?"

"I promised—"

"That's neither here nor there. By the time we get there, the woman will be dead. They're obviously getting rid of all possible complications. It's your own safety you should be worried about."

"Except that Santa Rosa is the *last* place they'd expect me to go, so it's probably the safest place to be.

Besides, she might know something that could help us, and that alone makes it worth trying." I stared at him mutinously. "I'll do this alone if I have to."

"You're crazy enough to do it, too," he muttered, and ran a hand through his hair. "Okay, we'll rescue this woman. But if she doesn't have any information, we start doing things my way."

"I don't like your way. It involves killing people."

"If I kill them, I can't get information out of them," he snapped back. "If we want to get there quickly, the best way to do so is to fly."

My heart began to race. Not from excitement but rather from fear. Flying and me weren't exactly compatible. And I had the scars to prove it.

"We can't—"

"We can take the boat out to sea and fly from there. It's going to be a cloudy night, so the chances of being seen are low. Especially given we're black and brown respectively."

"That's not the problem."

He raised an eyebrow. "Then what is? Are you afraid of the sea?"

"No. But as I told you before, I can't fly. I'm a draman without wings."

Confusion touched his expression. "But you have every other dragon skill imaginable."

"Well, as you keep noting, I'm strange. And I didn't get the wings."

"I said you're crazy, not strange. Totally different things." He made a frustrated sound. "And this makes things more difficult."

"You could carry me."

He raised an eyebrow. "You say that like it's easy."

"Well, isn't it? There'd hardly be all those myths of dragons carrying off virginal women if it wasn't possible."

Humor brightened his eyes. "Ah, but virgins have always held a special place in a dragon's heart. Something to do with the meat tasting sweeter."

And he wasn't talking about *actually* eating them, if that smile was anything to go by. I slapped his leg. "I'm trying to be serious here."

"Okay, serious question. How much do you weigh and are you a virgin?"

I raised my eyebrow. "That's two questions, and why would you need to know the second one?"

"Because I make a point of not seducing virgins."

Meaning he had every intention of seducing me if I wasn't? My pulse rate danced joyously at the thought.

"Then you'd be the first dragon in history to do so." I shifted back from Angus and sat on my heels. "Or is it a muerte thing? The bringer of death not taking innocence, or something like that?"

"It's a personal thing." He glanced up at the window, and frowned. "I don't want to seduce anyone who might expect more than just a good time, and virgins tend to get a little clingy with their first lover."

"Speaking from experience, are we?"

My voice was dry, and he looked back at me briefly. "No. Just consider it a warning."

I snorted softly. "As if any draman actually *needs* a warning when it comes to dragons, sex, and emotion." Hell, we learned all too quickly that the latter just didn't come into the picture when you were a half-breed. "And you're getting a little ahead of yourself. The whole respect thing I was mentioning before has to be addressed before the whole seduction thing even comes into play."

He didn't answer, and something in the way he was holding himself—a mix of intentness and alert readiness—had tension crawling down my spine. I lowered my voice a little as I asked, "What's wrong?"

"Footsteps, coming this way."

"Could it be the guy Angus referred to when I first stepped onto the boat?"

He was shaking his head before I'd finished. "There's at least two men, and their steps are cautious." He glanced back at me again. "Slip down the stairs to the lower deck. Don't come up until I say its okay."

"Damon, I can help—"

"This is what I do," he said coldly. "Please let me do it without having to worry about you."

Annoyance flared, but I held it in check, scooting across the floor to the stairs before heading downward. There were four bedrooms here, as well as a large storage area toward the stern. I opened several doors, looking for something I could use as a weapon and finding nothing but wetsuits, flippers, and life jackets. But in the final locker there were several air tanks and a large tool kit. I opened that up, grabbed a heavy-looking wrench, then walked across to the door that led out to a small platform at the back of the boat. I tested the door handle to ensure it was locked, then stepped back into the confines of another locker and waited.

For too long, nothing happened. But the awareness that someone was close began to grow, sending goose bumps crawling across my flesh. The dragon within stirred, her flame surging through my muscles and causing little sparks to leap across my fingertips. I toned it down, trying not to let whoever was outside know that I was here—although if they were full dragon, they'd probably already know. It was only us draman who couldn't always sense these things.

After a few more minutes, the door handle moved. My heart caught in my throat and my breath came in hitches. The handle inched downward then stopped, and the door rattled softly. It was locked, but I had to wonder if that would stop whomever was on the other side.

A second later I had my answer, with the sound of something jiggling around in the lock. I flexed my fingers then wrapped them tighter around my improvised weapon and waited.

The door began to move, pushed by fingers that were long, brown, and oddly elegant. When the door was fully open, they withdrew. The silence stretched, tearing at my nerves. My heart was beating a million miles an hour and sweat trickled down my spine. I licked my lips and tried to ignore the fact that my hands were shaking.

The nose of a gun appeared. My breath caught again and I briefly closed my eyes, fighting the desire to lash out. It was too soon. I needed to see *him*, not just the weapon.

Upstairs, there was a thump, and then a curse, the voice dark and dangerous. A stranger's voice, not Damon's.

The hand that held the gun appeared. Whoever this man was, he wasn't about to be rushed by whatever was happening upstairs.

I waited, still not daring to breathe, hoping he had

as little sense of me as I was getting of him. An arm appeared. My fingers twitched, my palms sweating against the steel of the wrench. He stepped forward, began to turn around, and I knew I'd run out of time, that at any second he'd realize I was hiding there in the shadows.

I swung the wrench upward rather than down, smashing it into the underside of his wrist, the force of the blow sending the weapon and his arm flying backward. I followed through even as he moved to face me more fully, smacking the wrench into his face. Bone crunched and blood splattered across the walls and my hands. Bile rose but I swallowed hard and swung again, this time hitting him under the chin. His legs collapsed from under him, and he fell face-first onto the floor. I stood back, keeping out of grabbing range even though he was obviously unconscious. My breathing was harsh and tension rippled through me as I waited to see if someone else would come through the door.

No one did, but that didn't make it any better. I had no idea what was going on above me—or whether there was someone else waiting outside to pounce.

So I continued to stand there, my breathing rapid and my fingers bloody, the knuckles almost white with the force of my grip on the wrench.

No one came. After a few more minutes, my skin began to crawl with awareness, and although I'd heard no sound and could see no one coming down the teak-lined hallway, I knew Damon was near.

"Mercy?"

His voice sounded so close that I jumped. "Where the hell are you?"

"On the platform outside the door. I'm coming in. Don't hit me."

"Okay." But I didn't relax, keeping the wrench at the ready until he was through the door and it was obvious he was alone. Only then did I lower my weapon. "You okay?"

He half smiled. "There were only three of them, and they were draman rather than dragon. You?"

"Just the one, thank God." I looked down at the man at my feet. "Should we tie him or something?"

"I'll need to question them, so yeah. But if they are draman who can flame, then we'll need to find something a little harder to burn than rope."

He stepped over the man and walked across to the storage lockers. I dropped my weapon and pressed two fingers against the man's neck. His pulse was a little rapid, but it was strong enough, and his nose had already stopped bleeding. If there was one good thing about being draman, it was having a dragon's healing capabilities.

I wiped his blood off my hands, using the ends of his shirt as a towel, then rose and stepped away from him again. Damon came back with what looked like a fishing reel.

"That's not fireproof," I commented.

"No." He raised the man's hands so that they were behind his head, then tied them together with the fishing line. Then he looped more around the man's neck and tied it back to his hands. which meant if the stranger struggled in any way, or tried to slip the line, he'd probably end up garroting himself. "You'll have to keep an eye on our captives until we get out of the harbor."

"You know how to drive a boat this size?"

"I've got one," he said, and grabbed the man under the shoulders, hauling him as easily as a sack of grain up and over his shoulders. "The sea is a vast place, and sometimes it's the only way you can get peaceful flying time."

I followed him up the stairs. He dumped the man he was carrying on the sofa then tied up the other three, all of whom looked a whole lot less bloody than the man I'd confronted. But then, if Death didn't know how to drop someone without effort, who would?

He turned and faced me. "Stay next to the stairs. Don't go near any of them. If they start flaming in *any* way, call me."

I nodded. "Can we get the boat out of the harbor without someone coming after us?"

"We'll find out soon." His voice was grim. Then he smiled and touched my cheek lightly. "I doubt there are any more henchmen out there right now. Four men to check a dead sea dragon could be considered overkill as it is."

I resisted the urge to lean into his caress, and stared into his dark eyes instead. It wasn't hard to find strength in those black depths. "What happens if someone realizes we're stealing the boat?"

"We deal with it when it happens." He glanced at his watch. "The moon doesn't actually rise for another half hour, so it's not going to be light enough for anyone to see who's in the boat."

Unless it was the owner himself. But I held the words in check and nodded. I wanted to keep my promise to rescue Coral, and this seemed to be the best way to achieve that.

He disappeared up to the bridge and I sat down on the stairs to watch the men. A deep rumble soon filled the silence, then lights flared across the stern and we began backing out of the slipway.

Tension slithered through me, and I half held my breath, expecting at any moment to hear someone shouting at us to stop. But we continued to back out, turning as we did, then the boat was moving forward slowly.

No one shouted. No one stopped us. And all too soon we were motoring under the Golden Gate Bridge and heading for open water.

I blew out a relieved breath and glanced at the four men. They were still and silent, yet heat was beginning to caress the air, meaning one of them was surreptitiously attempting to use his flames.

I rose and walked a little closer. Slow waves of heat lapped at my skin, and they were coming off the man lying on the curved end of the couch. Though his eyes were closed and his jaw slack, it was obviously an act. A draman—or a dragon, for that matter—couldn't flame when unconscious.

His legs had been tied as securely as his arms, so I stopped next to him and touched two fingers to his shoulders. Waves of heat rose, flushing through my fingers and running up my arm, waking my inner dragon and making her hungry.

"Keep flaming," I said softly, "and I will suck up every ounce of heat you have."

For a moment he didn't respond, then carefully he turned his head and looked at me. His neck was red from the tautness of the fishing wire, but wasn't yet bloody, and his blue eyes were bright with anger.

"You're draman. I can smell it. Only fucking dragons can do that sort of shit."

I smiled mirthlessly. "No, some of us draman can, too. Now stop flaming, or I *will* steal your heat."

"You're lying, bitch."

I raised an eyebrow, then let the dragon loose. She surged forward—an invisible being that was all fire and hunger, twining through my muscles and down into my fingertips, then into him. He jerked when her energy hit him, and his eyes widened in horror as she began to wrap around his inner dragon. But as much as I wanted to revel in the intensity of his flames and draw them back into my body, I didn't.

"Last warning," I said softly.

"Okay, okay, I won't flame." He said it almost desperately, and I let my fingers drop away. He closed his eyes and let out a breath. Then he muttered. "Fucking bitch."

"Don't try it again," I said, and turned away from him, to find Damon standing on the bottom of the steps, staring at me.

"What's wrong?" I asked immediately. "And who's driving the boat?"

"I jammed the steering into place." He stepped off the stairs and walked toward me, a creature of darkness. The instinctive need to retreat hit, and I actually stepped back a little before I stopped myself. I might not *want* to be afraid of this man, but he sure could be intimidating at times.

"That's dangerous—"

"So was your being down here alone." He stopped in front of me and crossed his arms, his otherwise stony expression touched with the slightest hint of amusement. "However, I didn't actually realize it would be dangerous for *them* rather than you."

"I keep telling you I can take care of myself."

"Yeah, but those scars tend to say otherwise."

"Hey, I'm alive, and that takes a whole lot of skill in my clique, believe me." I could almost taste his disbelief, and I wasn't really surprised. If he didn't have much to do with draman, then he really wouldn't have any idea just how badly some of us were treated. "Hadn't you better go back up and steer the boat before we plow into something? Or someone?"

"I will. But it's odd that you can do everything a dragon can do except fly. Even your fire control is stronger than that of most dragons I know."

I shrugged. "I guess I just lucked out on the good stuff."

He frowned, suggesting again that he didn't really believe me, but all he did was turn and head back up the stairs. I walked to the small galley, making myself some coffee while keeping my senses tuned for the caress of energy that would indicate one of our captives was again trying to escape. Thankfully, they restrained themselves.

With the coffee made, I headed back to my perch on the stairs and contemplated the sanity of making a promise to a man who had basically betrayed both me and my best friend. Yet I couldn't regret it. These men had taken too many lives already, and while Angus might not be lily-white himself, his mate didn't deserve to die for his sins.

Besides, she just might hold some much needed answers. I didn't think our captives would end up being very useful in the information game. Dragons tend not to tell draman the greater details of whatever operation they are involved in. We are only the grunts—fine for the dirty work and highly expendable, but never deemed suitable for anything more. Of course, that could be my personal bias speaking—I really had as little to do with other cliques as Damon had with draman.

The boat surged on through the night. I finished my coffee, then rummaged through the cupboards for something to eat. I ended up munching on some health bars while three of the four men on the couch glared at me balefully. All three had bloody slashes around their necks—testament to the fact that they'd tried escaping their bonds. None of them had tried to flame and escape, though. Maybe the other two hadn't been as unconscious as I'd presumed.

Eventually, the boat stopped and the engines fell silent. Chains clinked softly and the boat began to rise and fall gently with the waves. I glanced up, then shifted, as Damon began to make his way down the stairs.

"Where are we?"

"Far enough away from civilization that swimming would be unwise." He touched my shoulder lightly as he passed, and gave me a look that was all warning. *Don't interfere*, it said. *Or else*.

I swallowed heavily but nodded, and watched as he walked toward the man who'd tried to flame earlier. With little effort, Damon dragged him upright and bunny-hopped him toward the door. After opening it, he forced the man out onto the aft deck. I took a step forward, then stopped. We needed to know what information these men held, and we needed to know it fast if we were to be of any use to Coral. And Damon couldn't actually get those answers if he killed them first.

But if he killed one, the others might just open up.

I shoved the thought away and hoped like hell it was wrong. I hoped that somewhere within that deep, dark, and dangerous interior there was a person who wasn't *just* a killer.

Damon hopped his prisoner to the railing, then switched his grip, holding on to his hands while leaning him out over the sea. In that position, the fishing line had to be cutting into the draman's neck, and although I couldn't see any blood from where I stood, the tang of it touched the air.

"Start talking," Damon said softly, his voice devoid of anything but ice, "or we'll see just how long a man whose hands and feet are tied can remain afloat."

The man made a few odd noises that seemed little more than expressions of pain. Damon eased up on his grip a little, meaning the wire wasn't so tight.

"What?" he said.

"I don't know nothing!" the man said, the words so rushed they practically ran together. "He just phones me, gives me the job, and I do it."

"Who phones you?"

"I don't know his real name."

"What do you call him, then?"

"Sir!"

Damon pushed him out over the railing again. "Really?"

"Really. For fuck's sake, I've no reason to lie!"

"Then how are you paid?"

"Something called Frederick Enterprises pays it directly into my account."

Damon glanced at me. "What do you think?"

"He's not lying." He was too scared to lie.

So was I. My heart seemed to be pounding somewhere in my throat and my fingers were twitchy. Although in my case, it wasn't so much fear of the man but fear of what he might do.

Damon raised an eyebrow, but pulled the man back from the edge again. "What clique do you come from?"

"Jamieson. Jesus, man, I was just hired for the hit, you know?" Blood was staining the collar of his pale shirt.

Then his answer sank in and my stomach lurched. These men were from my clique? I'd never seen them before, but I guess that didn't mean anything. Not only did Jamieson have a huge population of draman, but many of them left well before adulthood, either to escape the abuse or to find something better. And this man looked several years older than me, so he would have been in a different crèche.

"So you've worked for these people before?" Damon asked.

"Shit, yeah. Been getting work off and on for two months now."

Two months. The first cleansing had happened about two months ago. Coincidence? I suspected not.

"Doing what?"

The man shrugged, then winced as the movement forced the wire deeper into his already bleeding neck. "Whatever they wanted. Shooting, burning, whatever."

I closed my eyes. So he *was* involved.

And the truth was, he probably *did* deserve whatever Damon decided to dish out to him. And yet

I knew if he decided to drop the man into the ocean, *I'd* try to rescue him. Not because he deserved to be saved, but simply because, if he was offering no threat, killing him was nothing more than murder. And that still wasn't something I wanted on my conscience, no matter how right the reason.

Did that make me weak in Damon's eyes? More than likely.

"How do you make contact once the job is done?" Damon asked.

"There's a card in my wallet. Take it."

With his free hand, Damon pulled the wallet out of the man's back pocket and tossed it to me. I caught then opened it. There were tons of business cards inside. This guy obviously had a moneymaking business. "Which one?"

"Black one. Red writing. Jesus, ease up on the wire! I'm being honest here."

"If you were an honest man," Damon said, "you wouldn't have been involved in mass slaughters."

Our captive didn't say anything. But then, the dangerous edge in Damon's voice would have scared even the strongest soul.

I flicked through the cards until I found a black one with red writing. "It says—in somewhat pretentious gothic print, I might add—Deca Dent. Under that is a number." I looked up at him. "What the hell is Deca Dent? A name or a place? And how is that related to the guy who pays you?"

Damon gave his captive a shake, and he stammered, "Deca Dent is a bar. I have no idea how the bar and the man are related to the money or my jobs. I get paid, and that's all that matters."

I shoved the card in my pocket and resisted the urge to ask about all his victims, and whether they'd mattered. It was obvious that they hadn't.

Which made me study Damon and wonder if there was anything that mattered to him. Or whether I was looking at two sides of the same coin. One light, one dark, and both intent on doing the job and caring for little else.

"Is the man at the bar draman or dragon?" Damon asked.

"Dragon."

"And is he the man in charge of the whole operation?"

"I told you, I don't know. He just gives me my orders and I report to him when I'm done. I swear, that's it."

"And has he got an elegant-sounding voice?" I asked.

Damon glanced at me, then shook the man when he didn't immediately answer. "Not really. It's more gruff than elegant. Please, the wire is fucking hurting."

"You can thank my lovely assistant for the fact that that's *all* it's doing," Damon said, and frog-hopped him back to the lounge.

He repeated the process with the other three men, but none of them had anything else to add. The first man was obviously the brains of this outfit. Or at least, the one who made contact.

"What are we going to do with them?" I said as Damon pushed the last man back into place.

"We stop them from escaping."

I frowned. "The minute we leave, they're going to flame themselves loose."

"Not if they haven't got any flame to begin with," he

answered, and then touched the last man lightly on his forehead.

Damon closed his eyes and power began to crawl through the air. It was dark, that power—as dark and as dangerous as the man wielding it.

The man he was touching screamed—a short, sharp sound that was filled with pain and fear. I swallowed heavily, my gaze jumping between the two men, wondering what the hell Damon was actually doing. The man was alive—I could see him breathing—but he looked as if someone had ripped his heart out.

What the hell was Damon doing to him?

He moved on to the next man. I frowned and stepped forward, touching the first man lightly on the shoulder. His flesh was icy, even through the thickness of his shirt. But it was more than just the chill of stolen fire, and my stomach did an odd flip-flop.

No, I thought, *he couldn't have.* I reached down inside myself and unleashed the dragon, letting her energy swirl into the stranger. But instead of fire, she found nothing. Not even the broken, scattered ashes where once the soul of a dragon had lived.

He hadn't just stolen his heat, as I'd threatened to do. He'd completely *erased* it.

"How is that possible?" I murmured as I glanced at Damon, feeling sick. "How can you extinguish someone's very essence?"

He didn't open his eyes. "Any fire can be put out, Mercy. You just have to know how."

I swallowed heavily, but it didn't ease the dryness in my throat. "Can you do that to full dragons as well?"

"It's harder, but yes." He dropped his fingers from

the last man and looked at me. "It beats killing them, doesn't it?"

"But—"

"They're alive, Mercy. They just can't flame."

"For now, or forever?"

He hesitated. "Draman do *not* need flames or wings."

"Of course not. After all, what right have we got to be able to protect ourselves against you lot?" I snorted softly. "You really have no understanding of what goes on in cliques, do you?"

"And you have no idea just how close the cliques are to being exposed," he snapped, then made a visible effort to control himself before adding, "Let's not get into this argument again. If you want to rescue this woman, we need to get moving."

He went back out onto the deck without waiting for me. I grabbed the backpack, checked that the netbook was still in one piece, then followed. It was a large space, but there wasn't enough room for a dragon to stand, let alone unfurl his wings.

"You can't shift shape here," I commented.

"I know." His voice was almost absent as he studied the darkness off to our left. The breeze ruffled his dark hair and a half smile touched his lips. "The wind is strong tonight. It'll help me lift you."

"Just promise not to drop me."

I couldn't help the edge of fear in my voice and he looked at me, his smile growing, once again lending his otherwise arrogant features a delicious warmth. "There may be a lot of things I want to do to you, but dropping you isn't one of them."

His gaze burned with sudden desire, and warmth

crept into my cheeks even as part of me basked in the heat of that look. "Oh, I've seen some looks thrown my way that suggest you'd love to do that very thing. Drop me from a height, that is."

"Only when you're being so frustratingly stubborn."

I smiled. "Which is a lot, according to you."

"That's true." He gripped the railing of the ladder leading up to the steering deck. "Once I take off, climb to the nose of the boat. I'll swoop down and grab you."

"Just you watch where you put those claws," I said, crossing my arms and trying not to think about all the things that could go wrong. "I do not need any more scars, thank you very much."

"If I pierce you with one of my claws, you'll be dead." He grabbed the rail and climbed up to the next level.

I moved to the back of the boat, leaning my butt against the railing in hopes I could see what was happening above. The roof made that impossible, but the burn of energy across my skin told me he was shifting shape. I closed my eyes, enjoying the sensation while trying to ignore the longing that welled up from within. I might have learned long ago that I would never experience the freedom of shifting shape and skimming the wide-open skies, but that never eased the desire for it.

There was a whoosh of air as wings unfurled and began to sweep across the night. A second later, an inky shape appeared in the starlit sky.

And oh, he was *so* beautiful.

The moonlight glinted off his dark scales, making it seem as if his sleek, powerful body was covered in a million stars. His wings were black gossamer, almost invisible against the sky except for the shimmer that ran down the edges with every stroke as he powered upward. And he was big for a dragon—a big, powerful beast who looked as deadly as the man.

I sighed—a sound that was part admiration and part frustration at not being able to join him in flight— then walked to the ladder and began to climb.

After moving as far forward as I could and ensuring I was clear of anything that would obstruct his wings, I closed my eyes and waited. While part of me wanted to watch Damon swoop in, part of me feared it, too. I'd seen the damage claws could do to a human body and I doubted I could force myself to stand still while such a large dragon swept down toward me.

The air began to stir, softly at first, barely even teasing my hair. But the nearer he got, the more tumultuous it became, until I felt like there was a maelstrom swirling around me.

Then, as gently as a first-time kiss, his claws wrapped around me, encasing me securely as his wings swept us upward again.

At first I was too frozen by fear to even open my eyes. *Any minute now he's going to drop me.* Any minute now, I was going to crash down on the rocks like before. And while there might not actually be rocks below us, the ocean gained the consistency of concrete when you plunged into it from any great height.

The air howled past my ears—a sound that should have been all-encompassing but wasn't. I could hear the ocean far below, feel the chill wash of moonlight across my skin, smell the leathery, musky aroma of dragon—sounds and scents that sang to my soul and made me want to smile.

As the minutes ticked by and his grip didn't loosen—and I didn't drop—the fear eased enough to open my eyes.

Far below us, the ocean raced for the shore, thin strips of white foam breaking across a blacker expanse. On the fast-approaching land, multicolored lights twinkled like stars in the night. The howl of the air became a sound that was sweeter than any I could have imagined, and the sweep of wings filled my soul.

And suddenly it wasn't scary anymore. It was beautiful and exhilarating and I spread my arms wide, imagining that I was a dragon, that it was me flying on gauzy, glittering wings, sweeping through the night so swiftly and so elegantly.

It was a glorious sensation. A dream fulfilled—even if it wasn't my wings or my shape. Laughter rose, bubbling through my body—a sound that was as free and as happy as I felt.

But it ended far too soon. We were barely even over land when we were sweeping downward again. The starlight twinkle of lights separated and grew, becoming long sweeps of roads along which the occasional car traveled. Rooftops and trees became visible, along with brightly lit shopping malls and office districts.

Damon banked and headed to the right. Ahead was a vast blot of darkness. As we drew closer, I realized it was a golf course. The perfect spot for a dragon to land unseen.

As the ground grew closer, our speed dropped until it almost felt like we were hovering. Damon released me, and I dropped the last two feet. I hit the ground running and kept going, getting out of his way.

He landed with unusual grace for such a large dragon, quickly furling his wings as the blue shape-shifting fire began to crawl across his body, giving his black scales an unearthly glow until it encased him completely. Not only did it hide his form, it hid the transformation from dragon body to fully clothed human.

Then the blue fire began to fade and I walked toward him. He turned around, his gaze sweeping my body before returning to meet mine. A small smile teased the corners of his mouth and creased the corners of his dark eyes.

"It sounded like you enjoyed that."

I stopped in front of him, drawing in the delightful musk of man and dragon that lingered on the air, then leaned forward and dropped a kiss on a cheek still slightly chilled by our flight. "I did. And thank you."

I would have stepped back, but he lightly cupped the back of my neck with his hand and stopped me. "For what?"

"For not dropping me." His fingers were barely touching my skin, but it was a weight I felt all the way down to my toes. The heat of his body caressed mine, chasing the last remnants of ice from my flesh. I might not like this man's attitude to my kind, but that wasn't stopping my reaction to his closeness.

"Oh, I can think of better ways to thank me than a mere peck on the cheek," he said, his tone as teasing as his expression.

I raised an eyebrow, even as excitement began to thrum through me. "Can you?"

"Yes," he murmured, not appearing to move and yet somehow close enough that his body pressed against mine, heating me in ways I couldn't even begin to describe.

I licked suddenly dry lips, torn between the desire to seize the moment and the knowledge that it just *wasn't* the right time. And that this man wasn't the type of dragon I should ever play with. Even if Janelle hadn't already given me that warning, every sense screamed with the knowledge that he was dangerous in more ways than I could imagine. And his lack of respect for my kind wasn't even the worst of it.

But it didn't seem to matter. I wanted him. Wanted to kiss him, to feel his lips against mine again, to explore and taste and enjoy.

And the hunger in his dark eyes suggested that he wanted the same thing.

"Damon, we really need to get moving."

The words came out breathy and barely audible, and my gaze was drawn to his lips as another smile curved them so deliciously.

"Yes, we do," he agreed.

Then those delicious lips met mine, and there was no more time for thought, no more time for words. No more time for anything but this kiss. I wrapped my arms around his neck, drawing him closer, tasting him fully even as he tasted and explored me. And though it began as something very sweet, it quickly evolved into something that was raw and powerful and so very erotic.

For too many minutes there was nothing but the hunger of this kiss and the passion that rose between us. Then reality intruded in the form of a gruff voice.

"Hey, you two. This ain't no lovers' lane."

Damon released me and stepped away. Just for a moment, everything around me spun, the abrupt ending to our kiss like a splash of cold water.

I ran a tongue across kiss-bruised lips, drawing in a final taste of him, then turned toward the owner of the voice. He was little more than a gruff-sounding shadow within the confines of a golf cart.

"Sorry," Damon said, voice as cool and calm as ever. As if he *hadn't* just experienced a mind-blowing kiss. "I was just showing my girlfriend where I scored the hole-in-one the other day."

The other man snorted, and it was a sound filled with disbelief. "There's a hotel up the road better suited to your purposes. And besides, the course closed several hours ago."

"Sorry, no harm meant." Damon touched my elbow, then headed down a small gravel path.

"Do you know where you're going?" I shoved my hands in my pockets and tried not to think about the man beside me, the way the occasional brush of his arm against mine sent little tingles of desire racing across my skin.

"I have no idea," he said, his gaze on the night ahead. "But I noticed a couple of large buildings in this general direction when we swooped in, so we're probably headed the right way."

"I guess he'd come after us if we weren't." I resisted the urge to look over my shoulder to see just what, exactly, the man *was* doing, and added, "So how are we going to get to Moraga Drive?"

"Simple. We steal a car with navigation."

I raised an eyebrow. "As grand plans go, that's pretty lame."

"You got a better idea?"

Yeah, kiss me senseless again. I pushed the thought away and shrugged lightly. "Death stealing a car just seems wrong."

"Why? It's practically a national pastime."

I smiled wryly. "So my brother says."

"Your brother sounds like a very sensible man."

"Yeah, my brother inherited all the sensible in our family." *Not,* I added silently, with a wry smile. "And when we get there?"

He shrugged. "It depends on what we find."

I glanced at him again. "You don't expect her to be alive, do you?"

"Honestly? I think we'll be extremely lucky to find her breathing, but you never know—they might wait to get confirmation of Angus's death before they move on Coral."

And if we weren't lucky, then she was dead and both she and Angus were destined to join Rainey in roaming the endless plains between this world and the next. And with all the souls lost in the two towns, it had to be getting pretty crowded.

We walked on in silence. He didn't mention the kiss and neither did I, but I knew what we'd started would not end here. The genie was out of the bottle and— respect or not, dangerous or not—I wasn't about to try and push him back.

Ahead, lights began to twinkle through the darkness, and the mellow tones of music rode the air. I frowned. "I didn't think the clubhouse would be open at this hour."

"Usually they're not, but given the chatter I can hear underneath the music, it's probably hosting some sort of function. Hence the guard. Which means there could be good pickings when it comes to stealing a vehicle."

His guess turned out to be correct. The clubhouse was a massive two-story Tuscan-style building with white walls and a pale green roof. We followed a path around the side of the building and headed toward the parking lot. It was huge, but not entirely well lit, brightness pooling in puddles and leaving many areas locked in shadow—which made it almost perfect for thieves, except that there were static security cameras on at least one light pole in each row.

Damon didn't hesitate, moving with certainty toward an older-looking gray Ford parked in one of the more shadowy areas. He touched my back and motioned me toward the passenger side, then said softly, "Keep your back to the camera."

I did as he said, and watched while he moved around to the driver's side. Three seconds, and he was in. He leaned across and opened the door, then reached back and grabbed the street directory from the backseat.

"Not a navigation system, but almost as good," he said, handing it to me once I was in.

I opened the directory and searched street names, looking for Moraga Drive and keeping my head down as he started the car and drove off smoothly. I found it, traced a route back to the golf club, then began issuing directions as we left. Moraga Drive was, naturally enough, on the other side of Santa Rosa, but traffic was scarce and we got there in pretty good time.

Luckily, there was only one blue house on the street, and even in the dark it was obvious that the place was a "major fixer-upper."

Damon pulled to a halt down the street from the darkened house and turned off the lights. The run-down old house was barely visible through the brick-and-iron fencing, not to mention all the trees, but yellow light peeked softly through torn curtains.

"So what's the plan?" I whispered.

"Angus mentioned a boundary alarm, so the first thing I need to do is find and disconnect that." He glanced at me, his expression fierce. Death was clearly gearing up for another fight. "Our friends on the boat said they were only using draman to mind her, but I'll go in hard and fast, just in case they lied."

"What do you want me to do?" I didn't want to sit here and wait. But, by the same token, I wasn't trained for this sort of stuff, and I might only get in his way.

"Come around to the driver's side and keep the engine running. We may need to make a fast getaway."

I nodded and climbed out of the car. The crisp wind spun around me, holding a hint of age and decay. I hoped it wasn't an omen, hoped that the run-down old house held something more than the chill of true death.

Damon had climbed out of the car and was standing beside the door, holding it open for me.

"Be careful in there," I said, pausing beside him.

He smiled and touched my cheek. "I have an unfinished kiss to get back to, so rest assured that I will."

I raised an eyebrow and said, somewhat sardonically, "There you go again—presuming I'll just fall in with your plans."

"There's no presumption about it. You know it, and I know it." He gave me a devilish grin that just about melted my insides. "It's just a matter of when, not if."

I opened my mouth to reply, but just as I did, a soft sound similar to a car backfiring came from the direction of the house.

It had barely even registered as a gunshot before Damon hit me, pushing me down and covering my body with his as the car window above us shattered into a million tiny pieces.

Chapter Nine

I slammed knee-first into the road, but the pain that shot up my legs was nothing compared to the fear. My heart was going a million miles an hour and my throat was so dry, even breathing hurt. We only had the open door as protection, and the metal just didn't seem like adequate armor against a potential rain of bullets.

Only it didn't happen.

From within the house came the sound of screaming—furious, *feminine* screaming—and it was accompanied by the sound of tearing metal and a weird whooshing noise. A second later, the roof of the house exploded upward, propelled by a jet of water. And carried along with it was a man, yelling as he tried to fire a gun back into the house.

A sea dragon's greatest weapon might be the sea, but they can control *any* sort of water. Even the stuff that came through rusting pipes—which made me wonder why she hadn't done that before now, and escaped.

"It appears our sea dragon is still alive," Damon murmured, grabbing my arms and hauling me upright. "Come on."

He hurried me across the road and behind the cover of another car, but the shooters were obviously too occupied by the mayhem within to worry about us.

Another muffled shot rang out and the fountain of water dipped dramatically before rising again.

"Stay here," Damon murmured, then ran, crouched, toward the house.

I shifted position so I could watch him. In the darkness he was little more than a shadow quickly lost to normal sight, and only my odd awareness of the man allowed me to keep track of his progress.

He slipped over the metal gate and ran toward the house. As he did so, an old wooden chair exploded through the front window, hitting the concrete and shattering into a dozen pieces.

A woman with dark hair was briefly silhouetted, running across the shattered remains of the window before disappearing. Several heartbeats later, a blond man appeared, a gun held in front of him as he chased her. More shots rang out. More furniture flew.

In the houses around us, lights were coming on, but no one had come out to see what was happening. I wondered if anyone had called the cops, and how long it would take them to arrive if they *had* been called. I doubted Damon wanted any sort of interaction with the human police, and Coral sure as hell wouldn't. She'd be desperate to get to her mate before dawn—and any delay would be a problem.

All sounds from the house suddenly ceased. Both the crashing of furniture and the gunshots had stopped, though water still cascaded through the shattered remains of the roof, and the guard was no closer to escaping it. I scanned the outside of the building, wondering what the hell was going on in there. I no longer had any sense of Damon—he'd slipped around to the rear of the house, beyond reach of my senses. I bit my lip, hating having to stand here, feeling like a fifth wheel with nothing important to do or contribute.

The front door of a neighboring house opened and an elderly woman peeked out. I shifted back into the shadows to ensure she couldn't see me. She clutched her blue dressing gown close to her chest, peering out at the water, then shook her head and went back inside.

As her door closed, a muffled scream came from inside the shattered blue house, then another window exploded. This time it wasn't broken by a chair, but rather a woman. She hit the ground awkwardly and clambered to her feet, running toward the trees and the metal fence beyond. But the blond man appeared in the window, gun raised and aimed at the woman's back.

"Coral, drop," I shouted, and reached for my fire, feeling it rip through my body—a maelstrom of deadly force that was eager and ready to be used.

As Coral threw herself to the ground, the gun swung my way. I thrust to my feet and flung the fire. The flaming ribbon arced across the night, the force of it all but drowning out the sound of the shot as the guard fired his weapon. I threw myself sideways and felt the burn of the bullet cut through the sleeve of my sweatshirt. Saw my flames hit the guard and wrap around both his arm and the weapon.

Then a black shadow engulfed him, and the guard disappeared from sight. I pushed away from the car and walked toward the fence. The dark-haired woman still lay on the grass where'd she'd fallen, her breath rapid and clothes soaked and bloody. I couldn't see a wound on her back, but that didn't mean there wasn't one.

"Coral? Are you okay?"

She shifted and glanced up at me. Even in the darkness, her eyes seemed to glow with an unearthly sea green fire. "Who are you?" she said, her voice scratchy and holding only the slightest hint of a Scottish accent.

"Angus sent us," I said. "He wanted us to rescue you."

"But no one can rescue him now," she said, her voice breaking a little. She pushed to her knees and tucked a wet strand of hair behind her ear. "You were with him when he died?"

"Yes." I hesitated. "We caught the men who shot him. They're on the boat with his body."

That unearthly glow got brighter. "They're alive?"

"Yes."

"Good."

Though there was little emotion in her voice, it still sent a shiver down my spine. Those men were not long for the world if this sea dragon had anything to do with it.

And while I hadn't actually saved them from Damon just so they could face this woman's wrath, part of me could understand her need for revenge. If anything happened to my brother, I'd shift heaven and hell to find those responsible.

Heck, I was doing that now for Rainey.

The front door of the house opened and Damon appeared. Coral spun, her hand raised and the sensation of power suddenly surging across the night.

"No," I said quickly. "He's with me."

She glanced at me, then lowered her hand. The energy died, and with it went the water that had been jetting through the roof. The guard fell with a scream that ended abruptly as his body snagged on one of the jagged rafters, hanging there like a limp piece of meat.

I tore my gaze away, trying to remember that these men really deserved what they got.

Damon walked toward us, his gaze on me rather than the woman kneeling in the grass. His clothes were wet but otherwise he seemed okay. Some of the tension still filling me slithered away—but not all of it. We still had to get out of here before the cops arrived.

"You okay?" he asked, his nostrils flaring as his dark gaze swept me.

"Yeah." There was blood running down the inside of my sweatshirt, but only a trickle, so obviously I had just been grazed. "We'd better get out of here."

"I can't," Coral said, and pulled down her turtleneck. Around her neck was a band of leather, to which a small black box had been attached. "I'm wired. I can feel the thing now—it's like a dull fire waiting to explode into my brain. If I get any closer to the boundary, it'll set this thing off. And it'll kill me if I go past it."

"Then we need to remove it," Damon said, stopping just behind her.

She was shaking her head even before he'd finished.

"I tried that. Unless you've got the proper key, the thing just goes off."

Damon frowned. "Do you know what sort of signal it is?"

"No, but the radius is a quarter of an acre, which is the size of this property, if that's any help."

"Maybe." He glanced at me. "Meet us in the parking lot near the Bodega Bay marina. There are two, so look for the one with the RVs parked in the lot. It's right near the beach off Highway One, so you shouldn't have any trouble finding it."

"The car is stolen," I reminded him, crossing my arms and wondering what the hell he was up to now. "And the owners will probably be noticing its absence."

"So steal another."

He said that just like my brother would have. But then, a cavalier attitude toward other people's property did seem to infect the dragon population. Even draman weren't immune to it. "Why would I need to? Where are you going?"

"Most of these devices have a horizontal rather than vertical boundary. Rather than trying to break the lock, I think I should just fly her straight up and unlock it once we're free."

"You're going to change form in the middle of a suburban street?" And he thought *I* was crazy?

"We have little choice." He glanced at Coral. "It's your neck. Are you willing to take the risk?"

She took a deep breath then released it slowly. "I need to get to Angus before dawn, so yes."

"And you need to answer some questions first," Damon said, then glanced over his shoulder as the wail of sirens began to shatter the silence. "You'd better go, Mercy."

I didn't move. "You'll wait for me there?"

He hesitated, obviously knowing that I was referring to his questioning Coral, then nodded.

Something inside me relaxed a little. At least he was making an effort to treat me as a partner *some* of the time. As the blue fire began to crawl across his skin, I turned and walked across to the car. The curtains in the house opposite twitched—an obvious sign we were being watched. While the trees hid some of his shape-shift, there was little hiding the explosion of air as he launched skyward. But he was a black dragon surrounded by night, and I doubted the eyes of an old woman would even be able to see him.

And even if she could, who would actually believe her?

I climbed into the car and drove off. I was barely two blocks down the road when a police car screamed past, its flashing lights almost blinding in the darkness. While I knew Damon and Coral had already left, it didn't stop the tension crawling through me. Luck really hadn't been in our corner, and while the old woman probably hadn't seen Damon clearly, she would have been able to see me.

I restrained the impulse to speed up and kept my pace sedate. The quickest way to attract unwanted attention was to do something idiotic—like speed away from an accident.

I switched cars in Sebastopol and continued on, making my way—with the help of the street directory stolen from the first car—to the Bodega highway and toward Bodega Bay.

I couldn't immediately find them when I arrived, so I parked the car, then grabbed the pack and walked down the marina. Both he and Coral were sitting at the very end of the dock. He had his arm wrapped around her shoulders, and even though I knew there would be nothing intimate in the gesture, something inside me still twisted. Which was ridiculous, given I meant as little to the man as Coral did.

I walked down and sat beside her. "Did you get the transmitter off your neck?"

She pulled down her turtleneck. Only a red-raw strip of skin remained. "It took a while, but we managed it." Her bright gaze met mine. "Thank you. Both of you."

I sighed. "We're here for a reason, Coral, and not just because Angus asked us."

"I know. And because I owe you the debt of my life, I've resisted the call of my lover's soul. But you need to ask your questions now, because I cannot stay long."

"Why did those men snatch you and Angus?" Damon asked before I could say anything.

It seemed like a pointless question, because we already had the answer from Angus. But maybe Damon was simply making sure the old sea dragon had been telling the truth.

"You've seen his scars?" Coral asked, picking up a long splinter of wood and twirling it absently in her fingers.

"Yes."

"We found one of the men responsible in a bar. Only it turned out it wasn't him. He just sounded the same." She grimaced, her gaze on the twirling splinter and tears bright in her eyes. "As luck would have it, although he hadn't been involved in Whale Point's destruction, he'd taken part in the more recent ones. So we paid for Angus's mistake by being snatched, beaten, and almost killed. It was only when Angus mentioned he'd been contacted by a reporter about the recent cleansings that they let us live."

"So he'd lied." And convincingly, because Rainey and I hadn't contacted him until the night they'd tried to run us off the road. And that was the contact *they'd* arranged to send us into their trap.

She raised an eyebrow. "Wouldn't you?"

Well, yeah. "But why would Angus even think to give our names to them?"

"Because he'd heard from the friend of a friend that there were some reporters asking about draman from Stillwater." She shrugged. "In the end, the lie didn't really help us."

And it certainly didn't help us, I thought bitterly.

"You were always living on borrowed time," Damon said.

"We knew that. And we did try to escape. But these men are smart, and we were each held accountable for the behavior of the other. Even when they released Angus, they watched him like a hawk. If he even looked like he was manipulating the sea, they would have killed me. It made escape extremely difficult."

"So who is the man Angus thought he'd recognized?"

"I don't know his name, and I don't know whether he's a major player or just another heavy. I've only ever seen him once. He was a tall man, with thinnish features, blue eyes, and reddish hair. He sometimes had a very cultured voice."

"Sometimes?" I asked, eyebrows rising.

She glanced at me. "Yeah. Sometimes it slipped, revealing a more guttural, earthy tone. *That* was the voice Angus recognized."

Seth had a guttural, earthy tone. But then, so did a lot of dragons in our clique, including our king. "Was he draman or dragon?"

"Dragon."

Seth didn't have red hair or blue eyes, but he was at least a dragon. Of course, he might very well be dead, so I had no idea why I kept going back to him as a suspect.

Except that whoever it was knew me, and they'd known about the freezer. And there were only five people who knew about that particular incident—me, Rainey, Seth, and the two thugs he'd used to help lock me in there. And neither of the thugs was bright enough to be in charge of this sort of operation.

Coral flicked the piece of twig from her fingers, watching it spin through the air before adding, "There is another man, but I've never heard his name. He was the one who gave the guards most of their orders."

"Do you have any idea how we can find him?"

"Not really." She paused. "But I think they did most of their business through some sort of club. I heard it mentioned a few times. Decadent, or something like that."

Which jelled nicely with what the draman had already told us.

"And you can't tell us more than that?" Damon asked.

"I wish I could," Coral said. "Now, if you have no further questions, then I really need to go."

"Angus called your family before he was killed," I said. "They won't be far away."

She closed her eyes and whispered, "Then at least I'll have someone with me when his soul moves on."

Unlike Rainey, I thought, with tears suddenly in my eyes. I blinked them away, but the pain would not be so easily pushed aside this time. I hugged my knees close to my chest and tried to ignore the ache.

"I wouldn't suggest hanging around long after dawn," Damon commented. "These men appear to be cleaning up loose ends, and they will come looking for you."

"Oh, have no fear of that. I'll be heading home, and away from these shores." She tucked a strand of multi-colored hair behind her ears and gave us a wan smile. "Thank you again for what you've done. And for what you tried to do."

She pushed to her feet. The sea reacted to her movement, the gentle waves suddenly splashing upward, reaching for her with foamy fingers, like a lover reaching for his mate after a long absence.

I glanced up at her. "Coral, don't kill them."

Her bright gaze met mine, then she nodded once and dived into the water.

Relief spun through me. Though she could do what she wanted to those men and I'd be none the wiser, something suggested that she'd keep her word.

"Those men do not deserve your pity," Damon said, rising to his feet and brushing dust from his rear.

I followed the movement of his hands, admiring the way his jeans clung to the curve of his butt.

"What you've done to them is probably worse than death, Damon." God, the mere thought of someone stealing *my* fire had my stomach churning. "How would you like to live like that? Knowing that the very thing that made you what you are had been snatched away?"

"They deserved the punishment."

"Maybe, but they don't deserve death on top of it."

He studied me for a moment, his expression unreadable, then shook his head. "After all those scars, you can still live up to your name? I think that makes you truly unique."

"Yeah," I said dryly. "So unique you're going to report me to the council and make them deal with me, and everyone like me. Meaning little old unique me will probably end up just like those men on the boat."

"The council isn't likely to steal the fire of every draman capable of it. But if the dragon gene *is* overriding the human one, we need to be aware of it."

"Because we wouldn't want all those half-breeds diluting the glorious bloodlines, now would we?"

"I have never said that," he said, with more than a little exasperation in his tone, "so I'd appreciate it if you'd stop making statements like that."

It was oddly satisfying to discover that Death could be annoyed, and I couldn't help the smirk as I said, "So, what's next?"

"Next, Miss Most Irritating, we find somewhere to stay for the night. It's been a long day, and I need some sleep."

The sudden twinkle in his dark gaze suggested sleep was the last thing he had on his mind right now, and the thought made my stomach clench with excitement. He reached down and offered me a hand. His fingers were warm against mine, his grip like steel and yet somehow gentle as he pulled me upright.

"We can't walk into a hotel looking like something the cat's thrown up," I commented, halfheartedly trying to tug my fingers from his and not succeeding.

"I never said anything about staying in a hotel." He turned around and tugged me alongside him. "There are plenty of vacation homes around, and at this time of year they're not likely to be occupied. We'll just pick one and help ourselves to the amenities."

"And hope the cops don't wander along to arrest our asses." I didn't actually expect an answer to that, and I didn't get one. Normal dragons had an easy disregard for human law at the best of times, and Damon was far from normal. "How does one become a muerte?"

He raised an eyebrow, the beginnings of a smile teasing the corner of his mouth. "You do like asking the unexpected, don't you?"

"It stops me from getting bored."

"I'll bet it annoyed the hell out of your brother when you were growing up."

"That was part of the fun of doing it."

He snorted, then released my fingers and wrapped his arm around my shoulders. Although the action was casual, my reaction was as far from that as you could get. My whole body hummed with anticipation.

"Sometimes it's a family tradition," he said eventually. "Sometimes it's simply talent."

"What sort of talent?"

"My clique has an innate ability to blend with the shadows. Those who become muerte have a higher degree of this skill than most."

His fingers were teasing the top of my arm near where the bullet had clipped me, and it was inevitable that he'd eventually touch the patch sodden with half-dried blood. Sudden concern rippled through the air. "Why didn't you tell me you'd been hit?"

"Because it's barely a scratch, and definitely not worth worrying about." I shifted my shoulder back a little, forcing his hand to drop closer to my breast. "So which one were you? Tradition or talent?"

"Both. And that wound needs cleaning, even if you do have dragon-fast healing."

"So we'll clean it once we find a house for the night," I said, a touch impatiently. The man wasn't going to wriggle out of telling me at least *something* about himself. Not this time. "Your father was a muerte?"

"Yeah. I was his only son, so I've basically been trained for the position since I could walk."

The edge in his voice surprised me. I glanced at him, but his expression was as unreadable as ever. "It almost sounds like it wasn't something you wanted to be."

"I love what I do, but that's not the point. I was never given the choice."

"And if you had been? Would you have chosen to walk this path or not?"

"I don't know." He released me to jump off the marina, then grabbed my waist and lifted me down. We walked in silence through the dark RVs, and it wasn't until we reached the road on the other side of the park that he added, "There was a time I contemplated a life that was more than shadows. A life filled with warmth and family and children of my own, but that foolish-ness vanished years ago."

I raised my eyebrows. "Why would you consider wanting love and a family foolishness?"

"Because such things are not for the muerte."

"Why the hell not? I mean, you exist, so somewhere along the line, love and family must have come into the equation."

"I come from a long line of muerte who breed for necessity, not for love. My father bred three daughters from different women before he produced me. He had nothing further to do with the mothers of his other children. I became his sole focus."

We crossed the road and moved through the trees lining the sandy hill. He obviously had a target in mind, even though we'd passed several perfectly good houses. Of course, they could have been occupied—a dragon's senses were usually keener over long distances than a draman's.

"Why the hell would your father's other partners even put up with that?"

His mouth twisted and became a bitter thing. "Because in our clique, it is considered an honor for a woman to bear the child of a muerte—especially if that child is a male who goes on to become one of the shadow ones."

"And I thought *my* clique had attitude problems." These men were using *dragon* women as little more than incubators—and had them convinced it was a good thing! "But just because you come from a long line of men who refused to settle down doesn't mean you're destined to do the same. You have a choice, you know."

"A muerte's life is nomadic. And it is dangerous."

"So?"

"So," he said, slanting me a glance that sent a chill down my spine—and not because it was his usual scary, death-in-residence glance, but rather one that was briefly filled with a resigned and aching acceptance of a barren future. It was a familiar feeling—simply because it haunted the darkest of my dreams, too. "There are those who do not like what we do, and there is an active—if underground—plot to erase us. My father was murdered, as was his father. I have no doubt that will be my fate, too."

"So you live like a monk until then? Why restrict yourself that way?"

His grin was sudden and decidedly wicked. "Oh, monks and I have *nothing* in common. As you'll no doubt discover soon enough."

"There you go again, getting ahead of yourself." I let my hand slide across his butt until it slipped into the back pocket of his jeans. Even through the material I could feel the heat of him, the ripple of muscle as he moved. I wished it was skin-on-skin contact, but it was probably better that it wasn't. Things might have gotten heated a little too quickly if it had been, and we still had to find somewhere decent to stay. Sandy soil was *not* a good bed, no matter how sexy the partner. "And we still haven't gotten to the bottom of that whole respect thing yet."

"Oh, I respect you," he said, his voice a whisper through my soul. "In fact, I intend to respect every single *inch* of you. And more than once."

Heat surged through my limbs at the thought, and I resisted the urge to fan myself. I needed to get this conversation back on track. Otherwise we were going to get down and dirty right here and now—sand or no sand.

"There are lots of men in dangerous jobs—cops, firemen, and soldiers, just to name a few—and they still allow themselves to love, and be loved."

"But part of the power of a muerte is the fact that he has no family—and no loved ones—to fear for. There is no one in his life that can be used as a pawn in whatever game might be in play."

"So what about when you stop being a muerte?"

"You don't ever stop," he said, amusement in his voice even as his fingers lightly brushed my nipple. "Generally, you're just *stopped*."

"Oh, come on, there has to be at least *one* muerte who has lived to a ripe old age." God, it was amazing how normal my voice sounded considering my insides were all quivery and my knees were threatening to give way under the assault of that simple caress.

Time, I thought, to start causing some havoc myself.

I slipped my hand from his pocket, and moved up to the waist of his jeans, finding the edge of the material and slipping my fingers underneath, cupping his butt. And lord, it was a *good* butt—well shaped and firm.

"A good half of those trained don't even live to see their middle years," he commented, his tone warm and laced with amusement. "And you are making it impossible for me to walk."

My gaze skimmed down his body and came to rest on the rather impressive bulge in his jeans. "That," I commented cheekily, "doesn't look large enough to be causing a problem."

"Maybe not, but the fact that your arm is down the rear of my jeans and is tightening the material everywhere else *is*."

"So are you saying I need to remove my hand?"

"No, I'm saying the house in the trees just ahead is looking mighty perfect for a break-in."

I laughed. "And suddenly Death is sounding a little harried."

"Death is as horny as hell." The smile teasing his lips did all sorts of happy things to my body. "Shall we move along a little quicker?"

"Well, you can hurry all you like, but I need a bath first."

"And a good hair-washing. It's looking a little frazzled after being under that hat." He glanced at me over his shoulder, his grin all cheek. "I'll do that, if you like. I'm very good at it."

I didn't doubt that he was. And at other things, as well.

I let him tug me the rest of the way up the hill, our footsteps leaving sandy indentations behind.

But despite my eagerness to experience what this man had to offer, part of me wanted to delay that moment as long as possible. Maybe it was simply an urge to savor something I knew would be very intense, and yet very brief. There might be a strong attraction between Damon and me, but he'd already made it clear he wasn't going to stick around for long.

But if that was long enough to find and stop the people behind the cleansings, then that would be enough. For Rainey and for me.

I ignored the mocking voice deep inside that called me a liar and studied the house looming through the trees. There weren't any cars sitting in the driveway and there were no lights on. There was no sound or movement, either, but given the time of night, that wasn't entirely surprising.

"Can you sense anyone?" I asked.

"Nope. But I want you to wait here while I go check the place out."

"Damon, I can—"

"Yeah, yeah, heard it all before. Just humor me." He removed his hand from my shoulder, then cupped my cheeks and dropped a gentle kiss on my lips. "Consider that a down payment for later."

"Maybe. But only after the promised bath and hair-washing."

"Deal," he said, then turned and disappeared quickly into the night and shadows.

I shifted my weight from one foot to the other. Except for the occasional purr of an engine going past on the nearby highway and the haunting hoot of an owl, the night was quiet. I couldn't see any other houses and there were none of the usual suburban sounds— no dogs barking, cats squawking, the rattle of street sweepers or garbage trucks doing their rounds. It would have been easy to believe that we were alone— and safe—but I knew better than that. These men— whoever they were—were dangerous, and they'd be more pissed off than ever now that we'd helped Coral escape. And they'd have to know we were involved with that—especially if they questioned the neighbors and learned that a big black dragon had been seen. The cops might dismiss the story, but our hunters wouldn't.

I glanced at my watch and saw that only a few minutes had crept by. I sighed in frustration and shifted my weight again, wanting to feel the warmth and security of having four walls around me. Even if that security was a lie.

Another few minutes crept by, then awareness washed over me and heat prickled my skin. Damon's shape formed out of the darkness, becoming clearer as he approached.

"That's a very neat trick," I said.

"And a handy one." He wrapped his hand around mine and tugged me forward. "The house is ours, and the neighbors are far enough away that we should be able to light the fire and do some cooking. I won't risk turning the lights on, though."

"We don't need lights when we have our own," I commented. "What about my bath?"

The grin that flashed over his shoulder had my blood surging. Labeling it sexy didn't do it justice by half. "All taken care off. I heated the water to boiling, so it should be just right by the time you step into it."

"What about the second of my needs?" I said, then added with a grin, "And that would be food, in case you were wondering."

His grin just grew. "Don't worry, all your needs will be met. And the pantry is well stocked."

Yeah, I thought impishly. *Noticed that before.* Even if I'd said otherwise.

We moved beyond the cover of the trees. The house was a pretty, two-story clapboard, painted a bright blue. I scanned the outside but couldn't see anything resembling security. "Was it hard to break in?"

He shook his head. "They've got deadbolts on the front and back doors, and locks on the windows, but the patio door was just a plain catch. And the screen door didn't have security mesh, just ordinary wire."

He opened the door and ushered me inside. The room beyond was cold, but flickers of warm gold danced across the walls in the next room, providing enough light to see by. We'd entered into a large kitchen and breakfast area. I walked through to the next room and over to the fire. I might be able to create flames of my own, but there was something intrinsically satisfying about standing in front of an old-fashioned fireplace, warming the chill from your bones. I opened the backpack to check the netbook, then dropped it onto a nearby chair and held out my fingers to the flames.

But Damon caught my hand and pulled me away. "Enough with the fire," he said crisply. "You have a carefully prepared bath waiting."

I snorted softly, even though anticipation tightened my insides and made the simple act of breathing seem all the more difficult. "And what's so careful about turning on a tap and heating the water?"

"This," he said, and opened the door.

The bathroom itself was nothing out of the ordinary, but the bath was one of those huge, free-standing claw-foot things, filled almost to overflowing with bubbles. I gave him a grin and a quick kiss, then stripped and walked toward the bath. The moonlight filtering in from the window beyond gave me enough light to see by, but left enough shadows that I wasn't overly self-conscious about my scars.

He followed and caught my hand, holding me steady as I stepped into the bath. The water was just shy of boiling, and I sighed in pleasure as the heat ran from my toes to my legs then spread out through the rest of me, warming my body almost as well as my fire did.

I slid my fingers from his, then dipped into the water, ducking briefly underneath the bubbles before letting my head rest against the bath's end. I waved a hand, splashing water and rainbow bubbles across the tiles as I said, "You may now work your magic on my hair."

He chuckled lightly and moved around behind me. There was a pause, then the whisper of clothes being removed. Though I hungered to see him naked, I wanted to enjoy the sensual experience he was offering more, so I just lay there and waited.

Cold liquid touched my scalp, then his fingers were in my hair, massaging the shampoo into fragrant-smelling foam. I closed my eyes and sighed in pleasure. I loved it when hairdressers massaged my scalp, but *this* experience was on another plane altogether.

Because this experience would ultimately lead to something *much* more satisfying.

He rinsed my hair then repeated the process with the conditioner, the press of his fingers against my head so wonderful that I murmured a protest when he finally stopped. He laughed softly and picked up a comb, gently sweeping away the tangles before rinsing my hair again.

"Kneel," he commanded, his tone one that would brook no arguments.

Not that I was likely to offer any when he had me in such a relaxed state. I knelt, the water lapping at my waist, watching as he squeezed some gel into his large, strong hands. His gaze followed the droplets of water running down my body, then rose to linger on my breasts and puckering nipples. Lust stirred the air, caressing my skin as sweetly as an actual touch. Then his gaze came to mine, and the smile that curved his lips and crinkled the corners of his dark eyes just about sent my senses into overload.

"Beautiful," he murmured. "Totally beautiful."

"No one has ever called me that," I said, blinking rapidly against the sudden, stupid sting of tears. Not just because of the words themselves, but because I *believed* them. It wasn't a compliment thrown out casually for the purpose of lovemaking. I'd heard enough of those over the years to know when someone actually meant it.

"Then they are blind fools," he said. "Now, close your eyes and turn around."

I did, my breath catching as I waited for his touch, my body trembling when it finally arrived. Gently, carefully, he started massaging, beginning at the base of my neck then sweeping down my shoulders, the pressure just enough to ease away any tension that remained from a day of escapes and close calls.

He applied more gel to his hands then continued the sweeping caress, down my spine and sides, and across my butt. I ached for him to touch me more intimately, and yet I wanted to delay that moment for as long as possible. There was something very sweet about the agony of anticipation.

He grabbed a sponge from the basket at the side of the bath and dipped it into the water, then pressed it into my back, working the gel into such a lather that it dribbled down my spine and left me humming in pleasure.

"Turn around," he said eventually.

I was only too happy to comply. He was kneeling in front of me, his body covered with droplets of water and soap that scooted down his well-defined abs and stomach, pooling briefly around the tip of his hard cock before moving on down his legs. I wanted to explore those glistening trails, wanted to linger where they had lingered.

I reached out, but he caught my hands and said, "No touching allowed. I have to finish respecting every inch of you first."

I grinned and let my hand drop. "Then by all means, continue."

He soaped his hands again, then gently spread the lather over my breasts and belly. My nipples hardened almost painfully and a shudder that was all pleasure rolled through me. His soapy caress slid all the way down to my hips, his thumbs gently—and all too briefly—teasing my clit. Then his fingers slipped upward again until his large hands cupped my breasts. I shuddered in enjoyment—a sensation that grew when he pinched my nipples between his thumbs and forefingers and gently began to pull and twist. Desire grew, until I was torn between wanting the delicious torment to go on and the need to feel his *whole* body on me, and in me.

Again his caress slid downward. My breath hitched, expectation thrumming, as his fingers teased the inside of my thighs. I spread my legs wider and softly, tantalizingly, his caress brushed me. I groaned, arching into the press of his hand, wanting more than just teasing. He laughed softly, his lips brushing mine as his fingers delved deeper, pushing into me, sending waves of pleasure lapping across my body. I wrapped my arms around his neck and deepened the kiss, exploring his mouth hungrily as his fingers probed and teased and delighted.

Then he pulled away so suddenly it left me dizzy. "Stand and face the wall," he ordered, voice harsh with the rawness of desire.

I stood, trembling with anticipation and need. He rinsed the soap from my body then stepped into the bath behind me, the hardness of his erection nestled firmly against my butt. I pushed against him, loving the feel of him, but wanting more. His hands slid up my back then around to my breasts, cupping them, squeezing them, caressing them, until every inch of me was shuddering and the ache was a fire that burned through every fiber of my being.

"Enough," I muttered, the words little more than a pant of air. "I need you. *Now.*"

"Good," he growled, and touched the back of my feet with his toes.

I shifted, widening my stance and bracing my hands against the wall. He gripped my hips then thrust inside me, the heat of him piercing and delicious and oh-so-right. A sharp mix of longing and need ran through me as we began to move in rhythm—slowly at first, then gradually faster. Pleasure spiraled, until every muscle felt ready to shatter and I couldn't even breathe, the intensity was so great.

His breathing became harsh, his tempo more urgent. His fierceness pushed me into a place where only sensation existed, and then he pushed me beyond it.

My orgasm hit, and I couldn't think, only feel. And what I felt was unlike anything I'd ever felt before, because what I felt was a connection that went beyond flesh and pleasure. Far beyond it.

And that scared the hell out of me. But it also made me hungry for more.

Well, no one had ever accused me of being sensible.

For several minutes neither of us moved, our panting breaths filling the silence and our bodies still gloriously locked together. When he finally withdrew, I turned around and wrapped my arms around his neck, kissing him tenderly.

"How do you think I did on the whole respect thing?" he said, his lazy smile that of a man who knows full well that he's done a good job.

I pretended to consider the question, then pressed up against him a little harder, delighted to feel he was already half erect again. "Well, as these things go, it wasn't half bad."

"Not half bad? Woman, you *are* crazy!"

I grinned. "No, I just remember a promise to respect the *whole* of my body, and it seems to me that half of me missed out."

"Ah yes. The toes and legs," he murmured. "Well, I guess we'd better go find a bed and tend to that problem immediately."

We did, and he did.

And it was even better the second time around.

The fading moonlight played across Damon's stain, highlighting the rich blues and deep purples in the black leathery strip that wove down his spine. I traced its journey with my fingertips, loving the cool, almost snakelike feel of the skin, which was such a sharp contrast to the heat of the rest of his body.

My fingertips reached the end of his stain, and I let them rest there at the base of his spine as my gaze followed the curve of his butt and traveled down the long length of his athletic legs to his feet. I'd never considered feet and toes sexy before, but this man was rapidly changing my mind. Like everything else about him, they were long, quietly powerful, and elegant.

"Don't you ever sleep?" Damon said, his voice muffled by the depths of the pillow wrapped around his head.

"I'm not used to sleeping beside someone," I said. "The heat woke me."

"I find that hard to believe."

I traced the curve of his butt with my fingers and gently teased at the junction of his legs. He twitched and heat stirred, bathing me with its warmth. "What? That you got so hot that it woke me?"

"No, not that. Though you have dragon blood, so the heat shouldn't worry you." He shifted his legs a little, allowing my fingers to slide between his thighs. "I meant that I find it hard to believe you're not used to sleeping with someone. Especially given you seem to have an insatiable appetite when it comes to sex."

I grinned. "Consider it a case of making full use of available opportunities before the drought begins again."

"I don't believe that, either."

"A plain brown draman who can't fly isn't much of a catch in a sky filled with rainbow fliers."

He shifted the pillow off his head and fixed me with his dark gaze. "There is nothing plain about you, my girl. Why the hell would you even think something like that?"

"Because it's true." I shifted my gaze from his, a little unsettled—and surprised—by the annoyance so evident there. "So, what's our plan?"

"To sleep until dawn, then get up and have a shower."

I wrapped my fingers around his balls and squeezed lightly. Tension rippled through him and the caress of heat got stronger, fueling the fires deep within me. "I meant, where do we go next? Do we try to find Deca Dent?"

"First, we read those notes of yours. Then we head for the club. Although we'll probably have to scout it first, and see who, exactly, is hanging around."

"Do you think the man with the cultured voice is the brains behind the operation?" I shifted my fingers again, scooting them underneath to tease the base of his penis. It was rock hard, thick with heat, and all I wanted to do was take him inside me again.

"I don't know." He shifted suddenly, grabbing my arms and twisting me around, reversing our positions so that he was lying on top of me. "And there is another major problem we have to worry about."

"And what might that be?" I said, grinning as he nudged my legs wider and settled in between them.

"The fact that you don't seem willing to get out of bed."

The heat of him began to slide inside me, filling me, stretching me. And it felt so good I sighed in sheer pleasure.

He chuckled softly and added, "I do so like a woman who's easily pleased."

"Don't start patting yourself on the back just yet, dragon. There's a whole lot of work to be done before I'm utterly satisfied." I shifted and wrapped my legs around him, driving the thick heat of him deeper. "How are we going to get into the club? They'll be looking out for us now."

He began to move slowly, rocking deep inside, sending ripples of delight flooding across my body. A delight that increased when his hands slid up and cupped my breasts. "We disguise ourselves."

"It didn't work the last time." The words came out slightly breathy as his clever fingers began to pinch and tease my nipples.

"It will this time."

"Why? What do you plan to do?"

"Kiss you senseless so you'll shut up and concentrate on the business at hand."

A grin curved my lips. "That doesn't sound like it'll get us past—"

The rest of the sentence was cut off as his lips captured mine and our kiss deepened into something that was pure and simple yet, at the same time, so very complicated. Because it spoke of possibilities that I didn't dare contemplate for more than a second or two.

So I concentrated on the physical and let the enjoyment flow until it filled me, until *he* filled me, and there was nothing left but contentment.

"Now you can ask your questions," he said, kissing my nose then pushing backward into an upright position. "But I think we need to get moving."

"Says the man who was, until minutes ago, lolling around in bed."

"You woke me up." His grin was insolent. "And most delightfully, I might add."

"Meaning it's your turn to be delightful, and go make breakfast while I shower." I leaped to my knees and gave him a kiss before bouncing off the bed. "Pancakes would be nice."

"So they would, but I can only manage toast and coffee."

Which is exactly what I got. I booted up the netbook as I downed my breakfast, then proceeded to explain the code Rainey and I had used.

"Now that you've explained it, it seems really obvious," he commented, swinging the computer around so he could see it more fully.

"Naturally," I agreed, between mouthfuls. "We were all of seven when we dreamed it up."

He picked up his coffee and studied the screen, occasionally flicking the track pad and shifting to another file.

"You've got a note here about some town called East River in Arizona." He frowned at me. "Never heard of it. Is it another cleansed site?"

I shook my head as I rose to refill my coffee mug. "It was a tip we got a month ago. We went to investigate, but the town—and everyone in it—was alive and well. If a little singed."

He raised his eyebrows. "Singed?"

"Yeah. Wildfires came pretty close, apparently, but the draman were able to suck in enough of the fire's heat to stop it from destroying the town." It was tempting—mighty tempting—to add that if Damon and the council had their way, those people would have had no personal fire, and therefore no fire control, and might well have ended up homeless if not dead. But I didn't want to get into another argument, so I simply added, "Interestingly enough, the person who gave us that tip also gave us Desert Springs. He had a car accident a couple of days later. Apparently he collided with a truck."

And a day later, in another so-called accident, a car had lost traction on the wet roads and had come skidding across at us. Only Rainey's quick thinking had actually saved us from being hurt. That time.

Damon's gaze met mine, sharp and edgy. "And that didn't give you a warning that it might be wise to walk away, while you still could?"

"Rainey needed to find out what happened to her sister, so no, walking away was never a consideration."

"Rainey's sister isn't your sister. You didn't owe her anything."

I snorted softly. "Rainey is—was—the sister of my heart, and I could no more walk away from her kin than I could my own. Besides, it was an accident. The driver didn't run off and abandon the vehicle, not like the man who hit us."

"That doesn't mean it couldn't have been planned."

True. And I guess with the benefit of hindsight, it was all too easy to see the connections to what we were investigating. But back then, it had all seemed pretty coincidental and nonthreatening.

Which was naïve of us, I guess.

I poured some milk into my coffee, then sat back down.

"What's this list of names?" he asked eventually.

I leaned over. "The one on the left is a list of everyone we think went missing in Stillwater." It wasn't a huge list, because the only names we really knew were those we'd met when visiting Rainey's sister. A good half of them, though, had been from Jamieson. Stillwater seemed to have been some sort of refuge for the outcasts from my clique. "The column on the right are the various names mentioned when we were questioning people about the towns. The ones asterisked are the ones we'd intended to follow up."

He glanced at me. "Who did you question?"

I shrugged. "Friends. Family. Anyone we could track down, really. Most of them couldn't have given a damn, but there were one or two who were willing to talk."

"I see you've asterisked Hannish Valorn."

His voice held an edge that made me frown. "His name came up in several conversations. He was seen at Stillwater, from what we could gather. Why?"

"Because Hannish Valorn is the son of the Nevada king."

"Well, considering both cleansed towns were in Nevada, I guess it's not unusual for the king's son to be checking up on them." I paused, and frowned. "You don't think Nevada would have arranged the killings, do you?"

He was shaking his head before I'd even finished the sentence. "Marcus Valorn is considered a moderate. As long as neither Stillwater or Desert Springs caused him any problems, he would have left them alone."

"So why did seeing his name there make you pause?"

"Because Hannish Valorn left after a massive argument with his father ten years ago. As far as I know, he hasn't been near clique grounds since."

"Then your information is out of date."

"Not *that* out of date." But he shrugged and continued reading.

After a few more minutes, I leaned against the table and asked curiously, "Is there any king who is actually considered revolutionary in his thinking?" I hadn't heard of any, but my knowledge of other cliques and their kings was limited. "As in actually supporting equal rights for the draman?"

"No dragon in their right mind would ever consider that." He said it almost absently, then, as if realizing exactly *what* he'd said, glanced at me sharply. His dark eyes, so warm and open only minutes before, were noticeably cooler. The dragon was replacing the lover, and somewhere inside I mourned the loss—even if I wasn't surprised by it. "Dragon civilization has existed successfully for thousands of generations. You won't find many who are willing to upset the balance. Not when it has worked for so long."

"But the world is changing, and draman are becoming what the dragons are. You lot need to face that, or there will be consequences."

His smile was harsh. "It's only the sea cliques who appear to be producing draman with dragon skills. It would be easy to fix that, if the council wishes."

Anger swirled at the cool, calm way he spoke about the destruction of hundreds of draman—because that's exactly what he meant by "fix"—but I somehow managed to keep it in check. "And you can see nothing wrong with that?"

"This isn't personal, Mercy—"

"How can it *not* be personal?" I thrust to my feet, unable to sit there any longer. "Damn it, I'm *draman*. Are you saying that if the council ordered it, you would steal my fire and make me even less than I already am? That you would do it without regret, knowing it is necessary to protect the so-called greater race?"

He frowned. "I would never—"

"Why not?" I snapped, "I'm just another worthless draman, aren't I? Good enough to take to bed or to keep around to do those nasty little tasks, but God forbid we ever be treated as equals, let alone fairly."

He reached for me, but I stepped back, sending the chair clattering backward. He sighed, but there was little in the way of compassion in his expression as he said, "I would never do anything like that to you, Mercy. I wouldn't even let anyone else do it, either. But facts are facts. Draman having dragon skills might be dangerous for us all."

"No more dangerous than rearing young dragons. You said it yourself—draman are a part of the dragon culture. All we're asking is to be a *proper* part of it."

"Which probably won't happen in my lifetime or yours. Old ways are hard to break down."

"That doesn't mean you and I can't be the ones to *try*."

He didn't say anything to that, just dropped his gaze back to the netbook. I wanted to scream in frustration, but what was the point? Death and I might be amazingly compatible in the bedroom, but the truth was, he was an integral part of the machine I'd spent my whole life either fighting or running from, and he was never, ever, going to understand what I was trying to say. I had no idea why I even kept trying.

Because you like him, an inner voice said. *Because you still believe things can change.*

Because I'm an idiot, I added silently.

I picked up my mug and walked across to the window. The golden rays of the rising sun caressed my skin and I breathed deep, drawing in the energy and refueling the inner fires. Though the dawn was bright, pink-tipped clouds were gathering. I hoped it wasn't an omen.

My gaze went to the road. It snaked along the coastline, a band of shiny black that reminded me a little of Damon's stain. A white car cruised past slowly, its occupants obviously enjoying the view.

Only the car looked horribly familiar.

"Damon—"

He was beside me, looking out the window, before I'd finished. Maybe he'd sensed the sudden tension in me, although that would suggest an awareness and a connection he'd certainly never admit to.

He swore softly. "That's the same car that tried to run you down in San Francisco."

"But there have to be thousands—millions—of white cars around." I was reaching for straws, I knew that, but I just didn't want to believe that they'd found us again so quickly. "How can you be sure it's the same one?"

"Because I remember the plate number."

"You can see that from up here?"

"I have very good vision." His attention was still on the car, and his whole body practically thrummed with the tension flowing through him. "Get your stuff together, Mercy; we need to leave. And keep away from the windows. I may not be the only one with good sight."

I ran for the bathroom and grabbed my underclothing from the side of the bath, mighty glad it had dried overnight. The rest of my clothes—which I'd also washed in between our bouts of lovemaking—hadn't, but I had no intention of wearing them anyway. I simply scooped them up, then went into the next bedroom and raided the closet. It took several tries to find a pair of jeans that fit me, but a sweater and T-shirt were less problematic. As was a raincoat.

Damon's gaze slid down my body as I reentered the bedroom, and the smile that touched his lips had my heart doing happy little flip-flops. Then his gaze slid back up to my hair. "I think we'll need to dye that."

"Cool with me, but that means stopping by a store. There's nothing here." I knew because I'd looked, having had much the same thought. Dyeing my hair might not stop the guy who'd gotten the scent of me, but at least it would stop a cursory recognition.

He nodded and glanced back to the window. "The car is cruising back and forth, so he's obviously got some bead on us, but not enough to pinpoint us yet. Keep an eye on him, and if he turns onto this street, or stops, yell."

"How the hell did he even track us here?" I moved to the other side of the window and peered cautiously out. The white car was almost out of sight, cruising around the bend and heading back toward the RV park.

"Given Santa Rosa is inland, it's logical that Coral would have taken the most direct route to the sea, and Bodega Bay is the closest city." He stepped around the window, kissed me lightly on the cheek, and added softly, "I think you're priceless, Mercy. And you're certainly not an idiot."

And then he continued on to the bathroom, leaving

me speechless and staring after him. He'd *heard* my thoughts. He had to have. How else could he have even known I'd silently called myself an idiot only moments before?

It meant the connection I'd felt last night was very real, and very strong. But it was also very useless in the long term. Because I was draman, and that would never change.

Damn it, I thought, blinking back the sting of tears, what had I done to fate to turn her into such a bitch? First she steals Rainey from me, then she throws me into the path of a man who could be everything I ever wanted, and yet who is everything I can never have.

Death was dangerous, all right, but not in the way Janelle had warned. Unless she *had* meant just this.

I crossed my arms and leaned against the window frame, my gaze on the curve of the road and tension thick in my gut. Sure enough, after a few minutes, the white car reappeared. I stepped back a little more behind the cover of the lace curtains, but the car slowed anyway. It didn't stop, but it was just creeping past. I swore softly and opened my mouth to warn Damon, but the car took off before the words could emerge. This time, it didn't disappear up the sea road, but turned left and disappeared into the trees lining the street that ran past the house.

I turned and ran for the bathroom. Damon was toweling himself dry, but stopped the minute I burst in.

"He's stopped?" he asked, voice brusque and body still glistening with moisture.

"Worse. He's turned down this street."

He swore softly, then tossed the towel down on the rim of the bath. "Go out the back door and head down to the trees, following the path we took up here. I'll meet you at the car in ten minutes."

"What will you be doing?" I pressed back against the door as he passed, then followed him back into the bedroom, watching as he, too, went through the closets.

"Taking care of our problem." He glanced at me, his expression like stone. "And do *not* tell me to go easy on the bastard. He tried to kill you once, and he may just succeed the second time."

There wasn't anything I could say to that. He was right. This was the best option open to us, but it still didn't sit right. I didn't *want* to kill, didn't want to be a part of it. Didn't want *him* to be a part of it, even if it was his job.

That was just plain stupid. The man was never going to change who and what he was, especially for someone like me.

Besides, these people had killed Rainey, Angus, and countless others in the draman towns. So why the hell was I giving them such consideration when they'd given absolutely none to anyone else?

Even though my mouth was dry at the thought of what I was condoning, I nodded, then leaned forward and kissed him quickly. "Be careful."

He smiled and cupped his hand to my cheek, his flesh so warm against mine. "I'd offer you the same warning, but I've got a feeling it'll probably fall on deaf ears."

I couldn't help grinning. For a man who didn't really know me very well, he'd sussed out that part of my nature easily enough. "Don't worry about me. I can—"

"Take care of yourself," he finished for me, voice dry.

"Yes, I know. But a little bit of caution never hurts."

"For you, I'll try." I kissed him again, my lips lingering a little longer than necessary, then with a sigh, I turned and made my way down the stairs.

I peered out the side door for a long time, my gaze probing the shadows still lurking among the trees to make sure no dragons were hiding within.

When I was sure it was safe, I scooted out, running across the grass as fast as I could, feeling exposed and vulnerable even though I knew I wasn't. But I'd seen the lengths to which these bastards would go, and deep inside I couldn't escape the notion that sooner or later, my turn would come.

Fear ran through me, but I pushed it aside, concentrating instead on slipping through the trees as quietly as possible. The day might be stirring, but the immediate vicinity was quiet, with little moving except the wind through the leaves. Dawn's energy was fading, leaving a sparkly resonance that tingled across my skin. I slipped down the slope, moving from shadow to shadow, my gaze skimming the path ahead even as I strained to hear if anything was coming up behind me. But everything continued to be silent.

When I neared the road, I slowed, keeping to the protection of the trees until I knew for sure it was safe to cross. I ran into the RV park and remained as close as possible to protection, be it the RVs or the trees, until there was little other choice but to step into the open and walk the rest of the way to the car.

But just as I was about to, one of the shadows moved.

Chapter Ten

$\mathcal{M}$y heart slammed into my throat, and for several seconds I couldn't even breathe.

The white-car guy hadn't come alone.

I had no idea why we'd thought he had, considering these people had a tendency to hunt in packs. But I backed away and leaned against the outside wall of an RV for a moment, closing my eyes and breathing deep.

What now?

Waiting for Damon to take care of the problem was the obvious solution, but I just felt too exposed here in this park—if only because the travelers would be waking soon and would start questioning why I was hanging around. That meant I needed to find somewhere more secure—somewhere downwind and in deeper cover.

I shifted and peered around the corner again. And again, my heart just about stopped.

The shadow had disappeared.

Fear clenched my gut and the litany that ran through my mind was little more than a rambling, panicked, *oh fuck, oh fuck, oh fuck.*

But neither panic nor that litany was going to help me, so I took a deep, calming breath and tried to think sensibly.

Obviously the watcher had moved back through the trees; anything else I would have seen. I had no idea whether he'd seen *me,* but I had to presume he had. Which meant getting out of here.

Fast.

I pushed away from the RV and ran to the next one, dropping to my knees and crawling underneath. The asphalt was cool and smelled of oil—evidence of the number of leaky vehicles that had parked here over the years. Once through, I climbed to my feet and ran to the rocky shoreline, jumping down the slight embankment and keeping low as I ran toward the pier. I was heading away from the car, but right now that was probably the safest option.

I reached the ramp that crossed the water to the pier, then risked taking a peek at my surroundings. Though a nearby RV was blocking the majority of my view, I couldn't see anyone in the immediate vicinity. But people were stirring in the various vehicles, and lights were beginning to flicker on—yellow blooms whose brightness wouldn't last long against the growing light of day. I had to get to the trees before then.

I bit my bottom lip, torn between ducking under the ramp and getting wet, and taking the higher, less secure route through the RVs.

The higher road won. I wasn't about to run around all day in wet shoes.

I pulled myself up the rocks and ran for the back of the nearest vehicle. Murmured conversation rode the air, followed by the buzz of a microwave timer going off. I peered around the RV's corner, saw that the blinds were still shut, and ran for the next vehicle. There were three more RVs and a long stretch of nothingness before I reached the tree line. It seemed a mile away.

I blew out a breath, and once again told myself that Damon would be here soon. All I had to do was stay out of harm's way long enough.

And as much as the thought of relying on someone else to get me out of trouble rankled, it was definitely my best option now.

I ran for the next RV, pressed my back against the metal side and listened intently for any sign that the shadow might be near, then repeated the process.

Then that huge expanse of empty parking lot was upon me. I contemplated it warily, mouth dry and heart racing. Of course, it was always possible I'd seen nothing more than one of the campers out for an early morning stroll, but I did not dare take that chance. Not with the way fate had been playing my cards of late.

Even as that thought crossed my mind, the wind shifted and suddenly I knew I was no longer alone. My gut twisted and with a soft cry of denial I half turned, my fist rising, ready to punch, to fight. But it was already too late. A leather-clad arm snaked around my neck and forced me back against a body that was thick and muscular, and smelled of ash and death.

But he was draman, not dragon.

"Got you at last, my pretty," he whispered, his harsh tones whispering past my ear.

Just for one second, the fear that churned my gut

got the better of me, freezing my limbs and turning my thoughts to mush. But as his arm tightened around my neck and started cutting off my air, adrenaline surged.

I shifted my foot and stomped down on the top of his as hard as I could, then clenched my fist and elbowed him in the gut. His grunt was an explosion of air and his grip released a little, giving me air but not freedom.

I twisted my chin to the side, dropping it down into the pit of his elbow so he couldn't cut off my airway any further, then reached for my flame, dragging it through my body and pushing the explosion of heat back into his.

Such was the force that it wrenched him away from me. His arm tore away from my neck, his watch catching and cutting my skin, but I spun around and kicked him, as hard as I possibly could, in the groin. He might be draman, and therefore tougher than most humans, but he was still a man. He made an odd sort of groaning noise and dropped like a stone.

I turned and ran for the trees. I didn't head for the car simply because I had no idea if it was safe to do so. I had no idea whether it was safe to run through the open parking lot, either. After all, these men had weapons and had shown a penchant for using them.

The thought sent a fresh surge of energy flooding through my limbs, and I made it to the trees in record time. I didn't stop there, but ran deep into the middle. It might be only a small wood, but no one could get me in their rifle sights or creep up on me in here. The ground was too strewn with leaf matter and other rubbish.

I leaned back against a tree and tried to catch my breath. My limbs were trembling and my heart raced like a wild thing. I might have defended myself, but— just like in the past—it had scared the hell out of me.

Maybe I should leave this to the experts.

Maybe I should just pack up and go home.

Only it was too late for that now. They knew who I was, where I lived, and what I did. There was nowhere safe for me to run, not without endangering the lives of everyone around me.

Besides, I didn't have much left besides my integrity, and how could I live the rest of my life, knowing I'd walked away from my one chance to avenge Rainey and save her soul?

The strident blast of a car horn made me jump, and I looked out through the trees to see a green SUV come to a halt on the road almost directly opposite my position.

The fear leaped again, but even as I pushed away from the tree, ready to run, the window wound down and a familiar face appeared.

Damon. Relief spun through me. I raced toward him and jumped into the passenger side of the car. He took off immediately, the tires squealing and no doubt waking those still asleep in the park.

"There's more than one—" I said, grabbing the seat belt and buckling up.

"Yeah, I know," he cut in. "We're obviously dealing with a large organization, not just the half dozen or so I'd presumed."

"But how could such a large group exist without the council or the other cliques getting wind of it?"

"The fact that no one *does* know suggests Julio's fears could be right, and that there *is* a clique behind it somewhere."

"But a clique wouldn't back a draman uprising."

"No, but they *would* use draman as foot soldiers in a war. Dragons are great manipulators. The draman might not even realize what they're actually fighting for." His expression was grim as he glanced at me. "And remember, dragons are collectors. Wealth, land, and power are all prizes worth fighting—and backstabbing—for."

"So if all this is the beginning of a planned uprising against the kings, why kill a king's son and risk possible exposure?"

"It's possible they were given no choice. If there *is* a clique behind this, Lucian might have recognized one or more of the players."

"Lucian being Julio's son?"

"Yes." He glanced at me, expression cool yet again. "And considering a couple of the men involved are from your clique, that should probably be our first avenue of investigation."

I might not like my king's or my clique's ways, but I still felt honor-bound to defend them. After all, not everyone there had grown up to be an arrogant bastard—just a good percentage of them.

"That doesn't necessarily mean clique involvement. For all we know, it could be an underground movement of draman."

"But why would draman kill draman?"

I snorted softly. "Killing is an accepted part of dragon culture, and regardless of what dragons may think of us, we are a part of that culture. And for all we know, this whole mess could be nothing more than a territorial dispute between draman."

"A territorial dispute won't fly. Both towns were on separate, unclaimed dragon lands."

"And draman can't dispute property?"

"Of course they can, but a territorial dispute wouldn't lead to such complete destruction of life."

No, I guess it wouldn't. "If there *is* a clique behind it, will you have to go to the council and make this an official investigation?"

"I can't. Not until we know for sure what's going on here."

"That's not what I asked."

He glanced at me. "Yes. I can't move against a clique unless I have the approval of all the other kings."

"Then I'm praying like hell that there *isn't* a clique behind it all." Because if the council got involved, things could go *very* wrong. Not just for my own quest, but for draman in general. "So, what's next?"

"We find Deca Dent and its owner."

"You don't think they'll be expecting that?"

"Probably."

"And you don't care?" I said, squinting across at him.

"Something like that."

And he thought *I* was crazy? "Well, I'm not going to walk into anything blind," I said, and reached back to grab my bag, which I'd spotted earlier on the backseat. Once I'd located the phone, I punched in Leith's number.

"Who are you phoning?" Damon asked.

"A friend," I said, then added when Leith answered, "Hey, babe, I need some help again."

"You are going to end up owing me a fortune in food," he said, voice heavy yet hinting at amusement.

"Dinner for a year is worth the price, trust me."

"You say that now, but you'll be complaining when you actually have to foot the bill. What can I do for you?"

"I need you to find out what you can about a club called Deca Dent. Oh, and if you can also check out a guy called Hannish Valorn for me, I'll be eternally grateful." I paused, then added, "But tread carefully on that one—he's the Nevada king's son."

"Delightful," he said drily. "I'm gathering you need this ASAP?"

I grinned at the exasperation in his voice. "Of course."

"I'll see what I can do. Oh, and Janelle says to tell Death he's not only a fool, but he needs an attitude adjustment."

"Several people have already told him that, including me."

"I bet you have," Leith said, amusement in his voice. "Oh, and there's no death certificate for Seth Knightly. But there's been no activity in any of his bank accounts and he hasn't worked or paid taxes, as far as I can tell. For all intents and purposes, the man has disappeared and might well be dead."

Which didn't really help solve the matter one way or another. "So there's no rumor as to why he disappeared?"

"Nothing concrete." He hesitated. "But I did hear a whisper that he was involved in some land transaction that went sour, and had to leave the state fast."

Instinct prickled. Maybe it was coincidence that his disappearance might have been due to a land dispute, and maybe it wasn't. Either way, it was a rumor worth chasing.

"I gather you're hunting up information on that?"

"Of course."

He said it like I'd offended him, and I grinned. "Thanks."

"No probs. I'll get back to you as soon as I can, Mercy."

"Who was that?" Damon said as I hung up and shoved the phone back into my pocket.

His voice sounded a little tight, and surprise ran through me. "A friend, as I said. He runs Phoenix Investigations, a very successful PI agency."

"And this Janelle he mentioned?"

"You were listening? That's not very polite."

"If you wanted to keep the conversation private, you should not have had it in the car."

Again there was a touch of tightness in his voice, and I shifted to look at him. "You're annoyed."

"Of course I'm annoyed. I was just called a fool by someone I don't even know."

I grinned. "Janelle's a psychic who works for Phoenix. I think she's older than the moon itself, and she's very forthcoming with her opinions."

"Being old is no excuse for rudeness."

I laughed. I couldn't help it. "Oh yes it is. Just ask her, if you ever happen to meet her."

"It's probably lucky I won't, given her opinion of me."

I gave him a quizzical look. "Why is this bugging you so?"

"Because it does," he muttered, voice as dark as his expression. "You think this Leith fellow will come through with the information?"

Once again, he was changing the subject rather than discussing what was going on in his mind. It was frustrating, but if he thought I was going to give up, he was badly mistaken. I might not have much time with him, but I was going to use it to get past the barrier, to see and understand the core of the man. "Leith usually comes through with whatever I need."

"So you're close?"

"Yes."

He flexed his fingers against the steering wheel and it suddenly hit me. Death wasn't happy with the realization that there were other men in my life. And as realizations went, *that* was pretty damn good, if only because it was further evidence that he wasn't as immune to me as he was pretending.

"Is that a problem for you?" I added, a hint of my amusement bubbling through in my voice.

His expression seemed to darken, and I hadn't thought that was possible. "Of course it isn't. I just wanted to know if he could be trusted."

"He's been helping me find leads on this case, and I'd trust him with my life."

"Why?"

I raised my eyebrows. "Why does it matter?"

"Because you said earlier that you never trust anyone, and yet you'd trust this man with your life."

"I trust you, too. Which, according to you, makes me strange."

"That's true, too."

This time a smile teased his lips, breaking the tension and the darkness shadowing his features. But what he said was true enough. It *was* odd that I'd trusted him so readily, yet there was just something about the man that made me feel safe. And that was rare when it came to fire dragons and me—although given my history with them, the actual attraction I felt wasn't surprising. I did tend to have a thing for bad boys.

"So where are we headed now? Until we find out where Deca Dent is, we're sort of stuck."

"As it turns out, you're not the only one with friends." The last of his tension slipped away under the growing warmth of his smile. "And mine also have the capacity to use the Internet."

"So much for Death being a lone ranger who cares for no one."

"Friends are not loved ones. There is a difference."

"How would you know if you've never had any loved ones?"

"I had a mother."

"Had?" I glanced at him, and caught the hint of sadness that washed across his features. "She's dead?"

"Yes," he said, and then, frustratingly, shifted the topic again. "How do you feel about a cooked lunch?"

"That depends on where we're having it."

"It happens to be a pretty apartment overlooking a certain club of interest."

I couldn't help smiling. "And would you happen to know the person who owns this apartment?"

"No, but I'm sure they won't mind us making use of their facilities for a while."

"And where might they be while we're doing this?"

"The south of France, according to the neighbors."

"Convenient."

"Totally." He glanced at me. "I'll cook."

"This morning you said you couldn't cook."

"No, I said I couldn't do pancakes." He glanced at me. "There's coffee on the floor at the back."

I twisted around in the seat and saw two cups sitting in a take-out tray. "You took time to grab coffee? When there's who knows how many bad guys coming after us?"

"The bad-guy ranks are currently two down. If we keep picking them off, the odds will be on our side sooner or later."

His voice was philosophical, but it wasn't something I wanted to think about. I might be determined to find the people behind the cleansings and Rainey's death, but I really hadn't gone as far as thinking what I'd actually do once I'd found them.

Perhaps deep down I'd never really thought that I would. "Is there nothing that scares you?"

He considered the question for what seemed an inordinate amount of time, then simply said, "Yes."

I raised my eyebrows. "What?"

His gaze met mine, but those dark depths were totally unreadable. Once again I had no idea what this man was thinking or feeling, and in some ways, that was even more scary than the situation we'd found ourselves in.

"*You* scare me," he answered at last.

"Me?" I said, surprise making my voice little more than a squeak. "Why the hell would I scare you?"

He hesitated for a moment, then said, "Because you don't react as expected."

I had a strange feeling that wasn't what he'd actually meant, but I also knew he wouldn't admit to anything else. Not yet, anyway.

Chapter Eleven

I leaned back in the kitchen chair and stared out the dust-covered windows. Damon's idea of pretty was vastly different from mine—no surprise, I suppose, given he apparently found plain brown draman extremely attractive.

The apartment was part of an old confectionery factory, and it was still very industrial in feel. Old bricks, hard steel, bright chrome, and polished concrete were the flavor of the day.

But it was directly opposite Deca Dent, and provided the perfect refuge to spy on the club. Not that there was anything or anyone to spy on at the moment. The place was as deserted as an old cemetery.

Of course, we still did regular perimeter checks, just in case they used the rear entrance.

"Would you like any more steak?" Damon asked.

He was sitting opposite me, but his bare feet were caressing the bottom of my leg and there was a heated, hungry look in his eyes. The meal he'd cooked had catered to one hunger; now the other had come to the fore. Even after we'd spent a good percentage of the afternoon twined around each other, exploring and caressing and loving until exhaustion hit and the meal was ready.

But as much as I wanted nothing more than to touch and be touched, I also hungered to be something other than *just* another sexual partner. It might never amount to anything permanent, but I wanted to be remembered as more than just another woman in a long line of them.

So I ignored the simmering desire, and simply said, "If I eat anything else, I'll burst."

"What about some more red?"

I shook my head and watched him pour wine into his glass, then said, "Tell me, why do you see yourself as little more than a killer?"

"Because that's what I do and that's all I am."

"But it's not." There was a slight tic in the muscles along his jawline. This man really *didn't* like talking about himself. Was it was part of his training or did it go far deeper? "You like to keep people at arm's length, don't you?"

His expression closed over once again. "Why would you think that?"

"Because any normal person would be terrified by the statement."

"You weren't."

"We've already established that I'm far from normal." My voice was dry, and amusement briefly tugged the corners of his mouth. "Besides, the situation we were in was far from normal. I needed to get out of that place and if I had to use a killer to do that, then I damn well would."

"That still doesn't make your statement about me true."

"Of course it does. You're too at ease with calling yourself that, so you've done it more than once. Add to that the fact that you've already said you have no intention of ever getting emotionally involved, and your emotionally barren little world remains nice and secure."

"You really do like making snap judgments about people you barely know, don't you?"

"It's not a snap judgment. And besides, after last night and this afternoon, you can't exactly say we're strangers anymore."

"It makes us *intimate* strangers, Mercy, nothing more."

My smile felt tight. "You do realize your strategy is doomed to failure, don't you?"

He raised an eyebrow. "And why would you think that?"

"Because you are neither cold nor unfeeling, Damon, and sooner or later someone *will* break through that wall you've raised around your heart."

"I come from a long line of muerte who lost their heads, not their hearts. I expect to be no different."

"Then you're selling yourself short. You are not your forefathers."

"And you," he said gently, "are reading entirely too much into my actions. I will not fall, Mercy, no matter how great the attraction between us."

I snorted derisively. "Oh, never fear, I have no illusions when it comes to you and *me*. You've expressed your views well enough when it comes to draman and their usefulness."

"It's not because you're draman." He reached out and wrapped his hands around mine, squeezing lightly. "I don't see you as draman. I don't think I ever have, which is why I was so surprised when you told me you were."

"That's not the point—"

"But it is. I won't have you believing something that isn't true."

"Then what *is* your great truth?" I muttered, suddenly wishing I hadn't gotten into this whole subject. It didn't really matter which of us was right, because there was one truth that *wasn't* going to change. The magic we'd felt every time we came together—the intimacy and the possibilities—would *not* be explored once this case was solved. No matter what, he would walk away, and it would probably hurt a whole lot more then than the thought did now.

Because no matter what he said, there was something between us. Something that was worth exploring.

"You were afraid today when you saw that car, weren't you?"

I frowned. "Of course, but—"

"Well," he continued relentlessly, "imagine living with that sort of fear daily. Imagine living with me and not knowing at the end of each day whether I'd walk in the door at the end of it."

"If you love someone, you love the whole of them. And that includes what they are and what they do."

"It's easy to say that when you're not living the situation day in, day out."

"People do."

"Yes, and lots of marriages break up over it, too. That's a statistical fact."

"The difference between your statistics and what we're discussing here is two simple words—*soul mate*. When you meet her, Damon, your dragon will not let her go."

When it came to dragons, that was the truth—and yet not the whole truth. A dragon male might meet his soul mate, but that didn't necessarily mean he had to settle down and make a commitment to her. My clique's king was living proof of that. He kept his queen by his side but he refused to commit to her, and continued to breed with other women whenever the whim took him. I couldn't actually complain about that, because if not for our king's philandering ways, my brother would not exist. And Trae was the one thing in my life that I couldn't do without. He wasn't only my brother, but my savior. I wouldn't be here today if he hadn't saved me all those years ago when one of his idiot half-brothers had decided I'd needed to learn to fly. Which is how I'd gotten one of those damn scars—Trae had misjudged his claw position as he'd swooped from the sky to grab me, inches from the rocks.

"How do you know I haven't already met my soul mate?" Damon asked gently. "How do you know I haven't already walked away from her?"

Because you wouldn't be responding to me the way you are if you'd already met your soul mate. But I kept the words inside, and simply said, "If you have, then you are a fool. And I don't believe you are."

His smile was wry. "That's another of your snap judgments."

"But it's true, isn't it?"

"Only partially."

I raised an eyebrow. "So you're admitting to being a fool?"

"No."

"Then what are you admitting?"

He glanced at me, his face like granite. It'd be easier to read a rock than try to catch this man's thoughts and emotions. "Right now?" he said. "Nothing."

"Yeah, believing that," I muttered.

"Let's just enjoy what we have, Mercy, and be grateful for it."

Grateful could take a long, flying leap off the nearest cliff, I thought, but I was saved from actually having to say anything by the ringing of my phone.

"Well, I found the owner of Deca Dent for you," Leith said, the minute I hit the receive button. I didn't bother putting it on speaker—Damon had already proven that he could hear the other side of a phone conversation. "And it's owned by Hannish Valorn. I've e-mailed you some pics and the file with the information, but there's not a lot."

"Why not?"

"Because dragons are notoriously closed-mouthed when it comes to talking about their own. I *can* tell you he only got back into the country a few months ago, and took over ownership of the club almost immediately."

"So he owns it legally?"

"Yep. I had one of the boys track down the paperwork. The club itself is a known haunt for lowlifes, which makes it a rather odd acquisition for the only son of a dragon king. I tried to find out more about

Hannish," Leith said, "but the grapevine is amazingly quiet. We're doing an overseas search to see if we can find anything there, but it's probably going to take time."

Everything about this case seemed to. "But there's nothing you can uncover to suggest he's involved in anything nefarious?"

"No. But that also means there's nothing to say he's not, as well." He paused, and tapped some keys, meaning he was still at the office, because he generally refused to work at home. "The club isn't run by Hannish, though. It appears he has a manager—a fellow by the name of Franco Harkin, a draman from your clique. There's also a Jake Whilde working there. I can't find a picture or very much information about Harkin, but both men appear to have come into the country with Hannish."

"If they came into the country with Hannish, then they have to have passports."

"Obviously, but they're either overseas ones or they have them under other names."

"Is that even possible in this day and age?"

"Anything is possible if you know the right people, Mercy."

I guess so.

Leith continued, "About the only bit of gossip I could gather was the fact that Hannish and his dad had a serious falling-out about ten years ago, and they haven't seen each other since. Oh, and one guy commented that Hannish was out to get his dad."

"'Get' as in kill?"

"I'm not sure. When I asked him to clarify, he just

shrugged. I think he was too scared to admit anything more."

"Well, if Hannish *is* behind the cleansings, then he had a right to be wary." I shivered as the memories of the truck hitting us rose again, but shoved them aside and said, "Is that all?"

"Yes. But I'm digging into the council's records to see if I can find anything there."

Surprise rippled across Damon's features. "How are you accessing the council's records? The security around them is supposedly watertight."

"Nothing is watertight where a sea dragon is concerned." Leith's voice was amused. "Especially when the security involved is over a year old. Your council needs a serious update."

"I'll tell them." Damon's voice was grim.

"Please do," Leith commented cheerfully. "And if you want a recommendation, I can give you several names."

"No doubt friends of yours who can be pressured for passwords."

"I don't need passwords, my friend."

Damon snorted softly, but it was an amused sound. "You think you're good enough to find, and then get into, Hannish's bank accounts?"

"Yes. Although it might take a little while unless you can give me the bank and account number."

"If I start asking for that sort of information, I might just stir up interest in the wrong places. I'd rather not warn anyone we're suspicious at the moment."

"Why do you want to investigate his bank records?" I asked, a little confused by the sudden request.

"Because," Damon said, "Marcus cut his son off

financially when they argued ten years ago, and Hannish was left with little more than the clothes on his back and a few thousand dollars in the bank. It'll be interesting to see where he got the money to buy Deca Dent."

"Maybe he has investment partners," I said.

"He owns the club directly," Leith commented. "And if his dad did cut him off, then tracking down the source of his wealth just might expose a clue or two."

I frowned. "Dragons are notorious thieves, so sudden influxes of wealth come with the territory."

Damon was shaking his head even before I'd finished. "Most dragons are very judicious with their thieving these days. They have to be—not only because human security techniques are getting better, but because stealing too much in their own territory could bring the wrong sort of attention."

Meaning the council as well as the humans. "Yeah, but Hannish has been overseas, and I doubt he would give a crap about his clique anyway." And anyone involved in the slaughter of two whole towns wasn't ever likely to care about *that* sort of stuff. "And it still doesn't explain the destruction of the draman towns."

"Maybe the draman were in the way," Leith said.

"How?" I asked. "The towns weren't on dragon land and were in the middle of goddamn nowhere. How on earth could they be a threat to whomever is behind the destruction?"

"Maybe they *weren't* a threat," Damon said slowly. "Maybe they were simply, as Leith said, in the way."

"What?" I said, frowning at him. Why did it suddenly feel that these two men had gone to a whole other place from me? "What do you mean?"

"I mean, aside from the town that was destroyed when Angus was young, the two towns were in the same state, and both were close to the borders of the Nevada clique."

"And it would be interesting," Leith mused, "to see what happened to the *land* those towns were sitting on, wouldn't it?"

"Most definitely," Damon agreed. "And it might also be worth checking whether the land between the clique and the towns has recently been sold—and to whom. You think you can get that information without setting off any alarms?"

"If the council hasn't caught me yet, I doubt the real estate people will," Leith said, voice dry. "I'll get back to you as soon as I find anything. In the meantime, play it safe, you two."

He hung up. I pushed up from the chair and walked across to the bench, grabbing my bag and dragging out the netbook. "Maybe I'm a little thick, but why would the land the towns are sitting on be so important that they'd kill for it?"

"It's not just land, its territory. Unclaimed territory, technically."

I frowned as the computer fired up. "But it's not. As you said yourself, Nevada belongs to Hannish's dad."

"As a territory, yes. But the clique itself owns only a few thousand acres."

"So you think Hannish might be buying up the land around his dad's clique? To what end?"

Damon shrugged. "Who knows? Maybe he wants nothing more than to piss his father off."

I glanced at him as the computer began downloading e-mail. "But you don't believe that."

"No." He rose from the chair and walked over, stopping just behind me. His scent filled every breath, warm and delicious, making me tingle inside and out. "If they were only after land, they could have gone anywhere. There's more to this than we're seeing."

I raised my eyebrows. "Like what?"

He shrugged and raised a hand, lightly running his fingers through my hair—which we'd dyed red when we first arrived at the apartment. I rather liked it, but Damon seemed to prefer my natural color. He was a man of strange taste.

"Think about it," he said softly. "Julio hears rumors of a plot against the kings. Shortly after, his son—whom he named as his heir—is killed, and two large draman towns near clique grounds are wiped off the map. Now there's news of Hannish Valorn suddenly returning."

"We have no proof of a connection between Hannish's return and the possible landgrab."

"No, but it is logical, especially if Hannish *is* behind it all."

"I'm still not understanding why."

"Nevada is the smallest clique, landwise, and as such, has less say in the council."

He said it patiently, like he were talking to a child, and it rankled. But I guess he had no idea just how little I knew about the inner workings of the dragon world. "I thought all kings were created equal?"

He snorted. "They might present a united front but, trust me, the council is ruled by territory. Why do you think the head of the council is usually from Montana, Wyoming, or North or South Dakota?"

Because they were the biggest cliques, obviously.

"But Hannish has been cut off by his dad, so how would buying the land help the Nevada clique?"

"He might have been disowned, but officially he is still listed as the heir. So if something happened to Marcus, Hannish can step right into his shoes."

I twisted around to stare at him. "Surely he wouldn't kill his own dad?"

His smile touched his dark eyes and made them sparkle like diamonds. My heart did an odd little dance and desire stirred low down in my body. "Dragons have a long history of brothers killing brothers to claim the throne. In this case, Hannish's only competition is the dad who disowned him. I don't think he'll have many qualms."

"Wow. That's pretty cold." I clicked Leith's e-mail as it came in, then added, "But what about the council?"

"If it's done right, the council will have no choice but to accept the situation."

"I still can't see the twelve other cliques standing by and allowing someone like Hannish to make a land-grab and take over the council. Especially if they suspect Hannish took out his dad to get to the throne."

"There is precedent for it. How else do you think Montana became one of the largest cliques?"

I shook my head in disbelief. But then, why I was surprised when I knew from experience just how cold and bloody-minded some dragons could be, I have no idea.

The pictures attached to Leith's e-mail opened up. The first man appeared a few years older than me, and had dark red hair and a somewhat angular face. His blue eyes had a look that I'd seen a hundred times before—cold, inhuman, impassionate. A dragon who considered himself well above the rest of us.

I didn't know him, but I knew the look. I'd seen it a thousand times in Seth's eyes.

The other man had small brown eyes and a pinched, gaunt face. Recognition stirred, and so too did the ghost of fear. I might not recognize the name, but his face—although changed by time, weather, and what looked like repeated beatings—was certainly familiar.

"That one," Damon said softly, pointing to the red-haired man, "is Hannish. I'm not sure about the other man."

"His name when I knew him was Leon, not Jake." I glanced over my shoulder and met his gaze. "And his best friend and lover was Seth."

"From the fear I can taste, I take it Seth and Leon were the dragons who made your life so unpleasant?"

"Yes. And if Leon *is* involved, then Seth will be. The two are inseparable." He might even be this Franco no one had a photo of.

Damon linked his fingers together and stretched them forward, cracking his knuckles. "It will be my very great pleasure to meet them both."

I glanced at him. "And why would you want to punish someone for once beating up a current—and unimportant—bed partner?"

"Because dragons *that* size should know better than to pick on a woman of *any* size. Even if they do think they can protect themselves."

I smiled at this light barb, then downsized the pics and opened the folder. Leith had been right. There wasn't much more information in there than he'd already mentioned.

I sighed in frustration, then glanced out the window. There still wasn't any life in or around the building, although—according to the neighbors—it opened at five, which was only a few minutes away. I would have thought someone would have had to come in earlier to set things up.

"Turn around for a moment."

Damon's voice held a low, sexy note that had my insides twisting. My smile grew and I did as he asked. We weren't yet touching, but I could feel the heat radiating off him.

"We're here to watch for our suspects. If we make love, that's not going to happen. Even Death can't attend to two things at once." I paused, then added wryly, "And if you pay more attention to what's out that window than to me, I'll be most upset."

He chuckled softly and reached into his pocket, drawing out a small wrapped package. "I actually just wanted to give you this. I saw it when I was out buying food."

I stared at the package, a lump in my throat and more than a little dumbstruck, then met his gaze. "Why?"

He raised an eyebrow. "Do I need to have a reason?"

"Yes."

He smiled and took my hand, opening my fingers and dropping the little box into it. "You really have had a rough upbringing if you're suspicious of a simple gift."

"You have no idea," I muttered, turning the package around. It was roughly wrapped, and the Scotch tape was messy, but right then it was the most beautiful thing I'd ever seen.

"Are you going to open it, or are you simply going to stare at it?"

I grinned and carefully undid the wrapping. The box inside was hard white cardboard, and looked like something that would hold jewelry. I lifted the lid carefully and discovered a necklace. The delicate gold chain was paired with a brushed gold-and-silver pendant that had a subtle lotus flower embossed on it.

"The lotus apparently symbolizes renewal, transformation, and new beginnings," he said softly. "I thought it appropriate given everything that's happened to you over the last few days."

I lifted the necklace out of the box by the chain. The late afternoon light streaming in through the window glinted off the gossamer-fine metal. "It's gorgeous," I said, through the growing lump in my throat. This was the first time someone who wasn't related had bought me something pretty, and that thought hurt so much I wanted to cry. "Thank you."

"I thought it was a nice knickknack to start your new collection with."

He took the necklace from me and motioned for me to turn around. I lifted my hair as I turned, and he put it on me. I was thankful that my back was to him— he couldn't see the tears I was blinking furiously away.

"There," he said, his fingers lingering against my neck. "Turn around again."

I took a deep, somewhat shuddery breath, then faced him again, moving my fingers to the pendant and cupping it gently. "It's gorgeous," I repeated. "Thank you."

He smiled then leaned forward, holding my cheeks

between his hands and kissing me gently. "You're welcome. I hope it brings you everything you want in life."

"Me, too," I said, and wished it could bring me him. Not just for a moment or two, but a whole lot longer. A lifetime longer.

But that was a wish a simple good-luck charm was never going to be able to produce.

I looked beyond him for a moment, trying to get hold of my emotions, and suddenly saw movement on the street below us. A car had pulled up, and a blue-suited man with dark brown hair and hawkish features stepped out.

"One of our targets just showed up," I said, partly relieved, and partly irritated, by the interruption.

He spun around, the amusement and gentleness fading from his face as if it had never been there.

"That definitely looks like the man currently calling himself Jake."

It certainly did. And watching him walk into the club left me in little doubt that it was actually Leon. He had that same leashed-beast amble. "What's the plan, then?"

"We hit him straight away, before anyone else gets there."

"He's probably got security in there. If that place is regularly filled with lowlifes, they're not going to be without twenty-four-hour protection."

"Which is *why* we hit him hard and fast. You think you can cut the power?"

I gave him a wry grin. "Flicking a master switch isn't exactly hard."

"It is when there are security cameras on every corner."

"There's a minute-long gap between each sweep," I said, then grinned at his surprised look. "My brother is something of a security expert. He taught me well."

"A woman of many talents. I like it." He glanced at his watch. "Give me ten minutes to get inside, then cut the power. That'll drag Leon out of his hole and give me an easier chance of jumping him."

"Death taking the easy road? That doesn't seem right."

He smiled. "I may do this job, but it doesn't mean I have to make it harder than necessary." He glanced at his watch. "It's five sixteen. At five twenty-six, hit the switch."

I checked my watch, then stepped forward and gave him a quick kiss. "You be careful in there. Leon won't surrender easily."

"And I'm trained to deal with far worse than him." He caught my hand as I went to step away and dragged me back toward him, wrapping his arms around me and pressing me close. "And that was hardly a proper kiss."

I raised an eyebrow, a grin teasing on my lips. "And what is that going to do to your ten-minute plan?"

"It included kissing time," he murmured, then his lips met mine and there was no more talking, only enjoying.

Neither of us was breathing very steadily by the time the kiss finished. "We'll have to continue that later," he said, and lightly ran a knuckle down my cheek. "Better make that five twenty-nine. The kissing time ran over."

My smile bloomed. "Death has no self-control. How sad."

"Death has plenty of control. He's not, for instance, racing you off to the bedroom, as he'd love to do right now."

I clucked my tongue and let my gaze travel down his body and settle on his groin. "Is that going to cause problems?"

"Probably." He glanced at his watch again. "Make it five thirty. Come through the back door."

"Will do."

He gaze dropped to my lips, then he muttered something under his breath and walked around me. Two seconds later he was out of the apartment, leaving me with a foolish grin and a happy heart.

I closed down the netbook and tucked it safely back into my bag, then walked into the bedroom and opened the closet, sorting through the owner's clothes until I found a jacket with a hood. I pulled my hair into a ponytail, then pulled on the hood and headed out of the apartment.

Dusk was beginning to filter in, bringing with it glimmers of energy that raced across my skin. I breathed deep, drawing the evening's fire into my lungs, reveling in the sensation of power flowing into my body. It made me wish for the open skies and wings to fly, but that was yet another wish that was never going to come true.

The street itself was pretty much deserted, but cars were moving down the main streets blocks away, and the drone of the traffic carried toward me on the breeze.

I ran across the road and kept to the shadows of the building, listening to the slight buzz of the cameras as they made their sweeps. I kept my head down and my hands in my pockets until I reached the corner. I hesitated underneath one of the cameras, knowing that while I couldn't be seen by that one, I was still visible to the other two. I knew from our previous scouting missions that the breaker box was at the rear of the premises, while the back door was actually along this side of the building.

Several cars were parked along the street, but they'd been there most of the afternoon and I didn't think they belonged to anyone already in the club. The camera was moving toward me again, so I moved on, only glancing up as I passed the door. It still appeared locked, so Damon obviously hadn't gotten here yet.

I glanced at my watch. There were still a few minutes to go, so that wasn't really surprising. But tension rolled through me anyway, and breathing deep didn't do a lot to relieve it.

I kept walking, acutely aware of the tracking camera and trying to keep an eye out for anyone who might be paying anything more than cursory attention to what I was doing. No one was, but that didn't help my nerves. Dragons might be born thieves, but it wasn't something I'd practiced a lot—although my brother had insisted that I learn all the tricks of the trade, just in case journalism crashed and burned.

The camera began its track back up the street. I looked around the corner, saw that the camera on the far end was also going the other way, then quickly jumped the fence and raced for the electrical box. I glanced at my watch, then took off the cover and toggled the power off.

The cameras stopped moving. I put the cover back

and bolted for the fence, leaping over it then walking back up the street.

The side door was open. I slipped inside and closed the door behind me, then stood there for several seconds, staring into the darkness and listening for any sound of movement.

The place was deathly quiet. I couldn't even hear the ticking of a clock. I called to the fire within, and watched it flare bright across my fingertips, filling the shadows with its warmth. Leon would sense my presence whether or not I used the flames, so I could see no point in walking around in the dark. Still, I tempered the flames to a muted glow and walked forward, following a slightly musty-smelling passageway around to the right. It ended in a set of stairs with a door at the top.

The metal creaked under my weight and I paused, waiting to see if anyone responded. I couldn't hear or feel anyone close, but that didn't mean anything when you had senses as unreliable as mine could sometimes be. I wrapped my fingers around the handle, then doused the flames and slowly opened the door.

And heard the footsteps.

I froze, my breath stuttering to a halt. I flared my nostrils, trying to get a hint of who was approaching, but the only scent I could catch was the stench of stale cigarettes and alcohol.

I stepped into the room and let the door close, my fingers against the wood to prevent it from slamming. The footsteps were stealthy and moving away to the right. Though I was getting no scent, I sensed he was dragon. It wasn't Damon, so it was either Leon or someone else.

Someone we hadn't accounted for.

I bit my lip, torn between the sensible option of just getting out of there and the need to help Damon when I could. He might be muerte, he might be a killer, but he didn't know Leon like I did. The man was a bastard, and a devious one at that.

And even a trained killer could die if he was shot in the back. Leon wouldn't have any qualms about doing something like that.

I blew out a soft breath then carefully followed the steps, picking my way through stacks of furniture until I reached another doorway. I peered around carefully and saw the stranger. He was a dark-haired man with a thickset body and arms the size of tree trunks.

Not someone I wanted to tackle, no matter how well I thought I could protect myself.

And yet I couldn't let him sneak up on Damon, either.

After a moment's hesitation, I slipped out the doorway and pressed my back to the wall, creeping along after the stranger. The fires burned within me, ready to explode at the slightest provocation. Whether he sensed that, I don't know, but suddenly he turned around, and I was staring into eyes as flat and as dead as stone.

I flicked my fingers outwards, releasing my fire. It streamed forward, burning across the air, splitting into several ribbons before swirling around him, encasing him in flames.

But I didn't need to do any more than that, because Damon was coming. I could feel him—a presence whose heat burned somewhere deep inside me.

Then the guard laughed. It was a cruel, harsh sound.

He touched the flames with a finger, drawing then into his body, feeding on them.

"You'll have to do better than that, love," he said.

"She has no need to," said a familiar voice from the shadows. Damon appeared, chopping with one hand at the guard, who dropped to the floor, his hands grasping at his neck, making a strange gurgling sound in his throat. I realized that his larynx had been crushed, and that I was looking at a dead man.

My gaze rose and met Damon's. His eyes were as flat as the stranger's had been a moment ago, and yet they chilled me far more.

"Suffocation isn't a nice way to go, Damon."

Something flickered in the dark depths, then he stepped forward. With a quick flick of his hands, he broke the man's neck, killing him swiftly.

"Your soft heart is going to get you into trouble one day," he said, turning around and walking back up the hallway, not bothering to wait for me.

"I think it already has," I muttered.

I kept my gaze on his broad shoulders, determinedly *not* looking at the guard's broken body. He might have deserved it, and he probably would have done a whole lot worse to me, but it didn't alter the fact that he was dead and that I'd played a part.

Somewhere deep inside, I couldn't help wishing that neither Rainey nor I had started down this path.

And yet, if we hadn't, there was no telling where this would end, or how many more draman *and* dragons would have to die before the people behind it were satisfied.

I followed Damon through the next door, into what turned out to be the bar's main room. The front windows were blacked out, but four skylights allowed the fading sunlight to filter in. It wasn't enough, leaving a room that was gloomy and reeking of smoke and alcohol. Modern artwork lined the grimy walls, and tables and chairs were scattered haphazardly around. A small dance floor had been squeezed into a far corner, but it was obvious that dancing wasn't a priority here. The fourth wall was dominated by a long wooden bar, behind which were shelves lined with bottles and glasses.

Leon was stretched out on the bar, tape over his mouth and his hands tied by wiring that looped around his neck. A trick Damon was fond of, apparently.

He walked over toward the bar, his footsteps barely audible on the old wooden floor. Mine echoed, filling the silence.

Damon stopped in front of the man currently calling himself Jake and ripped the tape from his mouth. The swearing began instantly, and even though I'd heard it all before, my eyebrows rose. Leon had certainly become creative when it came to combining expletives.

I stopped several yards behind Damon, close enough to see what was going on but far enough to stay out of the way.

"Enough," Damon said, voice flat and quiet, and yet somehow easily heard over the other man's expostulations.

"Do you know who you're fucking with?" Leon snarled.

Goose bumps prickled down my spine, and it was all I could do not to step back in fear. But that fear belonged to the past and I would not give in to it now.

"I know your real name is Leon, and I know you're dead if you don't cooperate. Everything else I intend to find out," Damon said. "And I'd appreciate it if you cut the swearing. We do have a lady present."

Leon looked at me, and it left me in no doubt that he not only recognized me, but that he'd kill me given half the chance. "I can't see a lady, but I *can* see one fine fucking whore."

Damon hit him. Hard.

Leon spat out some blood and teeth, then said, "What do you want?"

"Answers," Damon said, and lightly touched the other man's shoulder. His fingers began to glow, but it wasn't caused by internal heat. He was stealing Leon's.

Leon swore and began to struggle, the wire around his neck starting to cut into his skin. He didn't seem to care. Damon pushed down on his hand, pressing the other man's shoulder into the bar's surface, forcing him to be still. "Stop, or I'll break it."

"Then keep your thieving hands to yourself, you bastard!"

"If you behave, and if you answer my questions, you'll keep your heat. If not—"

He didn't finish the threat. He didn't need to. Neither Leon nor I were in any doubt as to what he meant, although I certainly had doubts as to whether Leon would actually survive this encounter anyway.

"What do you want to know?" It was sullenly said, but the fire in Leon's brown eyes suggested he'd far from given up. Yet the Leon from my past knew when to fight and when to roll over, and his bravado here just didn't sit right.

The tension in Damon's body suggested he thought

the same. "Tell me about the draman towns you've been destroying."

Leon snorted. "Even if I *was* aware of such a thing happening, what would it matter to you? Draman are nothing more than parasites living off the riches of the cliques."

"Draman do all the dirty work," I cut in. "And we're responsible for the day-to-day running of the cliques. You need us, even if you won't admit it."

Damon gave me a warning look, then pressed his hand down harder, fingers glowing. This time a hiss of air escaped Leon's lips. "Do not play games with me, Leon. We know you're involved. We know Seth and Hannish are also involved. And you will answer our questions or I will ensure a fate far worse than death befalls you."

Sweat popped out along Leon's forehead and his skin began to get a drawn, ashen look. It wasn't dangerous, not yet, but it was evidence enough that Damon meant what he said.

"All right, I'll cooperate."

And despite the desperate edge in his words, I could taste the lie. Something was going on here— something we didn't understand.

"Then tell me why you're destroying the draman towns."

"We were paid to. The Nevada king wanted the parasites away from his boundaries, and when they refused to move, he acted."

It all sounded perfectly reasonable—or as reasonable as dragon culture sometimes got. And yet I didn't believe him. He might have had his reasons, but they weren't the ones he was currently quoting.

"Marcus Valorn would not have ordered such destruction, so quit the lies and give me the truth."

Leon's dark eyes narrowed. "Why would a muerte be worried about what's happening to a few small draman towns in Nevada?"

"If it was only draman being destroyed, perhaps I wouldn't be. But a king's son was killed in one of the incidents, and that's a whole different kettle of fish."

Leon absorbed that news with barely a flicker of his eyelids. "I don't know what you're talking about."

Like hell he didn't. Damon obviously thought the same, because the glow around his fingers flared again.

Leon screamed. "He saw Hannish! We had no choice."

"So he *is* behind the push to take over the Nevada clique and make it one of the largest?"

Again, there was little reaction, but the sudden flash of fear riding the air spoke volumes. "Why would Hannish want that? He and his dad aren't even on speaking terms."

"But if Marcus suddenly dies, Hannish steps in as king. And with his recent land purchases, he suddenly becomes large enough—and powerful enough—to take over as head of the council."

Damon's voice was matter-of-fact, like we had all the pieces of the puzzle in hand when in truth it was little more than guesswork.

"Why would Hannish be stupid enough to kill his king? The council wouldn't look kindly on such a deed."

"The council has been known to turn a blind eye, especially if other cliques back the move."

Leon snorted. "And in what world is that likely to

happen? The cliques *I* know wouldn't support a murdering upstart."

"They would if some of them were also controlled by other murdering upstarts." Damon raised an eyebrow. "Just when does Seth plan to kill *his* king?"

Leon didn't answer. Damon glanced at me. "You want to go up to his office and sort through his paperwork? It's through the door to the left of the bar, and up the stairs."

In other words, things were about to get a whole lot messier down here, and I probably wouldn't want to see it. He was right about that. Feeling little sympathy for Leon, and half wishing it were Seth lying there, I turned and walked through the open door at the end of the bar.

As I did so, Leon screamed. I closed my eyes for a second, part of me savoring the sound and part of me hating it. Because in many ways, it made us no better than those men, and that was a vile realization. Even if we were doing it in the name of justice.

And yet, if we didn't, more would suffer. And all those people who died in Stillwater and Desert Springs would not be alone in roaming the netherworld between this existence and the next.

Thankfully, the screams didn't follow me up the stairwell. I lit a flame across my fingertips, the light penetrating the darkness just enough to see. The old metal stairs were grimy and creaked under the weight of each step. The door at the top was also metal, although dented and holed in several places. Evidence, perhaps, of unhappy customers or deals gone bad.

I opened the door cautiously, keeping to one side until I was absolutely sure no one else was inside. The room was as dingy as the rest of the place, and again smelled heavily of cigarette smoke. A large desk dominated the middle of the room and the walls were adorned with bulletin boards. There were several windows directly opposite the doorway, but these had been boarded up. Leon obviously had some pretty nasty enemies if he felt the need to avoid sunlight, especially given that it was the fuel for a dragon's flames.

But then, maybe Leon relied more on his brawn and human weapons than his flames to protect himself.

I walked behind the desk and sat down on the old leather office chair. The desk was a mess. Loose papers sat in various unwieldy stacks among the Coke cans, take-out wrappings, and several overflowing ashtrays. I wrinkled my nose at the moldy, smoky smell, then grabbed the nearest stack and began sifting through it. It was nothing more than bills and other business stuff. The remaining stacks proved to be more of the same.

I tried the drawers next, and found his wallet in the top one. A quick investigation uncovered three driver's licenses and eight credit cards, all in different names, none of them Leon's. Seth was probably also using numerous aliases, which is why Leith had been unable to track him.

I tossed it back and continued searching the drawers. Other than a cache of weapons that included knives as well as guns, there didn't seem to be anything of interest.

But maybe Damon already knew that. Maybe his intent in sending me up here was nothing more than a need to get me out of the way.

I leaned back in the chair and studied the room again. My gaze fell on one of the bulletin boards, and there, right in front of my eyes, was the information I'd been looking for.

It was a map of Nevada.

Excitement surged and I leaped to my feet. Six towns had been ringed, five of them crossed out. Two of those five were the erased towns we knew about. The remaining one was a little place called Red Rock—not a place I'd heard of, but that wasn't surprising given these places were basically little more than bumps in the road that few people would drive past, let alone visit.

Along with the ringed and crossed-out towns were what looked to be boundary markings. The lands owned by the Nevada clique were shaded in black, but there were huge tracts of land between it and the towns that were either shaded in or marked by a red or yellow pin. I couldn't see a legend of any kind, but if Damon's theory was right, then those markings represented land already bought, being purchased, or wanted. If they succeeded in getting everything that was marked, then they'd own a sizeable chunk of land. It would certainly rival that of the three largest cliques, and would make Nevada the largest once the land was combined.

I searched the drawers again until I found two different colored pens, then set about replacing the pins with colored dots. With that done, I took down the map, folded it up and shoved it in my pocket. It was a start.

I continued searching, but I didn't see anything else that stood up and waved a clue. I couldn't find any sort of legal document—especially not anything relating to land purchases. Nor was there anything to suggest that Leon was working with anyone else.

But he had to be. Leon wasn't the voice I'd heard when I'd been half drugged, and Angus had referred to that man as the "boss."

Besides, Leon had always been the brawn, not the brain.

Which meant there *had* to be something else here. Frowning, I stood with my hands on my hips, studying the room and wondering what I was missing. It wasn't possible that someone so involved in this mess would have nothing more than a map in his main office.

Presuming this was his main area of work, of course.

I scanned the walls again, looking for anything that might be hiding a safe. But there was nothing.

Frowning, I turned around, looking at the placement of the furniture. I couldn't see him going to the effort of dragging out filing cabinets every time he wanted to get something out or put something in a safe. But a drinks cabinet had definite possibilities.

I walked over and opened a couple of doors. There were several racks of glasses and bottles of alcohol, but nothing that couldn't be easily shifted. And despite the fact that the cabinet was both heavy and old, it wouldn't be that hard to move. Not for a dragon.

I shoved my weight against one edge and forced the cabinet away from the wall. Sure enough, there was a safe behind it. I squatted, studying the lock. It wasn't particularly up to date, and even if it had been, it wouldn't have stopped a determined dragon. Or a half-dragon.

I cracked my knuckles, then set to work and had it open in a couple of minutes—almost triple the time my brother would have taken, but then he was a professional. I just played at it occasionally.

I opened the door. Inside sat several manila folders, some bulging with papers, others not.

I grabbed them all, shut the door and tumbled the locks closed, then moved the cabinet back. I grabbed the map, shoved it on top of the folders, then headed back down the stairs.

Leon wasn't moving. His skin was ashen, a sharp contrast to Damon, who seemed to positively glow.

"What are you going to do with him?" I stopped several yards away and studied Leon's chest. He was breathing, so he wasn't dead, and I wasn't sure whether to be happy about that or not. If anyone deserved to die, it was him. But if he *was* killed, then people would know, and that was the one thing we needed to avoid. "We can't afford to leave him here alive, and we can't risk taking him with us."

"Which is why I'll be flying him out to sea."

And Leon wouldn't be flying back, if the angle of his arm was anything to go by. He'd drown, because few dragons were good swimmers and Leon was worse than most. His death would be long and pain-filled, and I really couldn't get upset about that, if only because we needed as much time as possible before Seth realized his lover was dead.

But his death was one of the ones I needed to save Rainey.

"I found a safe filled with paperwork," I said, "and a map that might prove useful if we can find the key."

"Good. Go back to the apartment and sort though those papers. I'll be back by seven."

Meaning he was going to fly Leon a *long* way out to sea. "Be careful."

He gave me a smile that made my insides curl, but his eyes were still hard. Still doing the job, still concentrating on the kill, even if he hadn't yet killed.

"Keep an eye on the windows, Mercy, and see who else comes into the club."

I nodded, then turned and headed out. Once back in the apartment, I made myself coffee then settled down to read the paperwork. I started with the thinner folders, but it wasn't until I was on my third cup and had started in on the fattest of the folders that I found something.

And it was the one thing I didn't want to find.

The town of Red Rock was slated for destruction.

In less than six hours' time.

Chapter Twelve

*G*od, we had to stop it from happening. *Had* to.

And yet even if we flew there, what could one dra-man and one muerte do against the force that these people seemed to have behind them? Damon might be a trained assassin, but all it would take would be one bullet to bring him down, and I had no doubt these men would do just that. After all, it was what they'd done to Angus, and he'd been far less dangerous.

We needed help.

I ran to the phone and quickly dialed Leith's number.

He answered on the second ring. "Phoenix Investigations, Leith Nichols speaking."

"It's Mercy again."

He reacted to the note of panic in my voice, his own filled with urgency. "What's wrong?"

"Do you know of a place called Red Rock in Nevada? And if so, how long will it take me to drive there from San Francisco?"

"Hang on, I'll google it." The sound of tapping keys came down the line, and after a few seconds, he added, "Okay, you're looking at a good eight-hour drive from San Francisco. Why is this information so vitally important and why do you seem so stressed?"

"Because Red Rock is slated to be destroyed at midnight, meaning we need to contact someone in that town ASAP to see if we can arrange an evacuation."

"Shit." Leith blew out a breath. "Where's your muerte?"

"He's not my anything, and right now he's flying Leon—the man running under the alias of Jake—out to sea."

"Why the hell didn't he just kill him?"

"Because that would tell his kin something was wrong, and we need to avoid that right now."

"Fuck, Mercy, you're dealing with seasoned criminals here. The men behind all this probably already *know* you have him."

"Maybe. Maybe not. Can you help me with Red Rock?"

"I've got some friends in Las Vegas who might be able to fly out there, but it's going to be a close thing to get everyone out in time."

"All the inhabitants have to do is take flight." Except that not every draman could take flight, and our felons might already be watching the roads.

"Mercy, if this town is a target, the inhabitants won't be able to come back until these bastards have been dealt with. And most of them can't go back to their cliques, either. These towns are rogue establishments for a reason, remember?"

"I remember. But it's better to be homeless for a

while than dead for an eternity." Not to mention their spirits roaming the void between this life and the next. Because unless Damon and I could solve these crimes in the allotted time, that would also be their fate, just like it had been the fate of everyone in Stillwater and Desert Springs.

I closed my eyes, trying not to think about the fact that I had only two days left to solve Rainey's murder. I could do it. I *would* do it.

"Look," Leith said, frustration in his voice. "I'll make some phone calls and see what I can arrange. No promises."

"I know, and thanks." I hesitated, then added, "And because we *are* dealing with criminals and thugs, you'd better warn whoever goes out there to be very, very careful. It's likely these people have scouts."

"They might, but they'll keep any reaction discreet. Whatever this operation really is, secrecy appears to be the key."

"I hope you're right." And yet instinct suggested he wasn't. Not entirely. This operation was too big, too planned, to be left to chance. I wouldn't put it past them to just shoot as many draman as they could. After all, who would the draman report the crime to? The knowledge that we could never go to—or trust— human authorities was too ingrained, and there were few of us who put any faith in the dragon council to help out. "Damon and I will be heading out there as soon as we can."

"Just be careful, Mercy. If they see the town being evacuated, they might realize you were behind it. And have a trap waiting."

"I know. I'll phone you later to give an update."

"You'd damn well better."

He hung up. I put the phone back in its cradle, then spun and headed for the bedroom, searching until I found a backpack. In it I stashed some clothes and the stolen papers from Hannish's office. Once filled, I dumped it beside my other pack, then grabbed the netbook, firing it up to do a search for Red Rock while I waited for Damon to get back.

He was as good as his word, and arrived just before seven. He came in the door looking drawn and tired, but his smile was one of pure delight when his gaze met mine.

As if he was truly happy to see me. Like it meant something that he was back with me.

And it made my insides quiver, even if I knew the emotions so evident in his expression weren't likely to last. He'd warned me of that. Warned me he wouldn't get attached, no matter what.

I believed him. I had to. I'd been hurt too greatly in the past by reading too much into a gesture or a smile to be taken in by such things now.

His gaze swept me and the smile faded. "What's wrong?"

I handed him a cup of coffee. "There's another dra-man town slated for destruction in five hours."

"Fuck." He thrust his free hand through his damp hair. "How long is it going to take us to drive there?"

"Longer than we've got," I replied grimly. "I called Leith and asked him to get someone down there to warn the people. Hopefully, they'll evacuate before the hit men arrive."

"We can't chance that." He downed some coffee, then added, "We'll have to fly out."

I frowned at the weariness in his voice—the same weariness that was so evident in the set of his shoulders. "Are you going to have enough energy?"

His smile was warm. "Of course I will. It's just that a certain insatiable woman kept me up most of last night and then wore me out this afternoon."

I grinned. "I didn't hear any protests at the time."

"No sane man would have made such a protest." Amusement crinkled the corners of his dark eyes. "And despite rumors to the contrary, I *am* sane."

"Says the man who took off in dragon form in the middle of a suburban street," I said, voice wry. "I've packed us a bag—but if you think you'll need guns, we'll have to grab those handguns you've got stashed in the car."

"Good idea." He finished his coffee in several gulps that must have scalded his tongue, then walked past me and dumped the cup in the sink. "It's going to be cold up there. I'd wrap up some more."

"I can flame at night, remember, so I can keep myself warm."

"But not dry. It's raining."

"It is?" I glanced at the darkened windows and saw that he was right. I'd been so caught up in worry that I hadn't even noticed.

"And your flames aren't going to do much to keep the rain off," he said, amused, "so do me a favor and find yourself a coat."

I rolled my eyes but did as he asked and headed back into the bedroom. It took a couple of minutes, but I finally found a coat that was thick and waterproof.

"I looked up Red Rock on the net while I was

waiting," I said, shoving the coat on as I walked back out. "The nearest town is a place called Elko—"

My words faded and a sick feeling invaded my stomach as I walked into an empty kitchen. Damon wasn't there. I turned around and walked into the living room, but that was empty as well. In fact, I couldn't feel the heat of him anywhere in the apartment.

"Damon?" I called, knowing he'd gone and yet not wanting to believe he could just walk out like that.

No answer came. Not that I expected one.

My gaze fell on a piece of paper sitting on the coffee table, and I walked over to pick it up.

Sorry, Mercy, but this is going to be dangerous, it said, *and I just won't risk you. Wait here for me. Please*.

"Wait here indeed," I muttered, screwing up the note and throwing it back down on the table in disgust.

Waiting wasn't going to track down the man behind these killings.

Waiting wasn't going to save Rainey's soul.

And no damn *please* added to the end of the note was going to change either of those facts.

I grabbed the backpacks, slung them over my shoulder, and bolted for the door. When I hit the stairs, I ran down, not up. A dragon didn't take long to shift shape and fly, so there was no point in going to the roof. My best bet now was the car. I wouldn't get there in time to be of any help, but at least I'd get there. And I still had all the paperwork, so if Damon had totally abandoned me, at least I could continue my investigations.

I threw the backpacks into the car then jumped

into the driver's seat. The car started at the first turn of the key, and I reversed out with a squeal of tires.

Luckily, Damon had stolen a car with a navigation system. I typed in my destination and settled in for a long, fast drive.

Night still dominated the skyline by the time I neared my destination. Sunrise—and the power that came with it—was still a good few hours away. That was probably a good thing, because at least the dust being thrown up by the car on this godforsaken track wouldn't be as noticeable. Had it been daylight, I might as well have waved a flag and said, "Come and get me."

According to the navigation unit, Red Rock was less than two miles away. I slowed the car, glad that a long slope divided me from the little township. I didn't dare drive any closer, simply because I had no idea who—or what—might be waiting for me there. And even if they couldn't see the dust, the sound of the car's engine would surely carry in the stillness.

Which meant, of course, that I had to walk the rest of the way. It might be only two miles, but after the long night of driving, I felt like hell. Not even the faint, buzzing promise of dawn could wipe the exhaustion from my system.

I pulled off the road and drove the car as far as possible into a group of scrawny-looking trees. They wouldn't hide it from anyone driving by, but a dragon flying overhead might just miss it.

I opened the door and climbed out. The air swirled around me, warm and yet somehow stark. I reached back into the car and dragged out the backpacks, then squinted up through the scrubby branches of the trees and took a deep breath, trying to shake the cobwebs from my mind. I needed to be fully alert if I was to have any hope of getting through the next couple of hours.

At least it was still dark. Dawn might energize me, but it would also expose me. There weren't many places to hide out here. Besides, the warmth still hanging in the air suggested the coming day would probably be a scorcher, and while I might be draman—and therefore totally at home in heat—the human half of my soul insured I wasn't immune to the effects of sunburn. And a plain brown dragon with sunburn was never a good look. I knew *that* from experience.

Memories of the fun Rainey and I used to have at the beach as teenagers brought a smile to my lips, but it also sharpened the need to do right by her, to give her the future she so richly deserved. I closed the car door, pocketed the keys, and headed out through the trees. Once free of them, I pushed into a jog. Little clouds of dirt plumed around my shoes with every step, but I would have felt too exposed had I been running on the road.

I was puffing by the time I neared the top of the hill. I slowed to a walk and kept my head below the ridgeline until I found another strand of trees. Only then did I step out to see what waited in the valley below.

Red Rock was nothing but a small cluster of buildings, and looked more like a large ranch than an actual town. And maybe it was. None of the buildings were burned and I couldn't see any bodies, but that didn't mean we'd been successful in saving this place or the people in it. And I wasn't about to trust the fact that it all looked deserted. For all I knew, the men behind this mad scheme were still down there, patiently waiting for an unwary draman to waltz right into their trap.

Something I was desperate to avoid.

As I stood there staring at the town, a frisson of awareness shot through me, and my silly heart rejoiced.

Damon was here.

The thought had me smiling, but the smile—and the stupid internal reaction—faded quickly into concern. Just because I sensed him didn't mean that I could find him. And it certainly didn't mean he was free. These men had caught him once before, and even Death could be overwhelmed by the sheer weight of numbers.

I shifted my weight from one foot to the other and as I did so, another sensation swept over me.

I was no longer alone on this hillside.

And it *wasn't* Damon who approached so stealthily.

My stomach dropped and a sick sensation rose up my throat. I swallowed hard, concentrating on the approach of the stranger, my grip on the straps of the backpacks so hard my knuckles glowed white. The thick, musky heat of him got closer and closer, until his scent stained every breath and my muscles were trembling with the need to move, to react.

But I didn't, knowing I'd have only one chance at this.

The hairs on the back of my neck rose and my skin burned with the awareness of danger. Just as it felt like his thick fingers were going to descend on my shoulder, I swung around, ripping a backpack away from my shoulder and swinging it at the stranger as hard as I could.

He ducked, but not fast enough, and the pack caught him on the shoulder and sent him staggering. I had a brief glimpse of blond hair and a hawklike nose, then I dropped and swept with my leg, hitting the back of his knees hard and knocking him off his feet. He landed with a grunt that sounded more like a curse and tried to regroup and scramble to his feet, but I came at him fast, following with a punch to the face that flattened his nose and had him unconscious in an instant.

For several seconds, I stayed low, my body trembling as I listened to the faint breeze, trying to discover whether there were any other draman trying to sneak up on me.

But the night was free of any unusual noises, and the breeze was free from the taint of others.

Which didn't mean they weren't out there.

My gaze returned to the man at my feet. He was a big, rough-looking man, and more like the muscle than the brains. Besides, his face didn't look familiar, and if the man I'd heard talking to Angus—the man whose voice reminded me of Seth—*was* the leader, then surely I *would* recognize him.

The stranger had one of those small speaker microphones clipped around his ear, the talk switch clipped to the lapel of his jacket. Had he reported my presence? Surely not. The stillness of the night would carry sound too well, and I would have heard him speaking. Although I hadn't heard him creeping up on me until it was almost too late.

But then, some draman could move with the stealth of dragons.

I ripped off the mike to insure he couldn't use it,

then searched through his pockets until I found a wallet. His name was Ralph Jenkins and, according to his license, he lived in Las Vegas. Given the extent of this operation, that might or might not be true. Further inspection revealed several credit cards—all in different names—and a large amount of cash. Payment for destroying a town, perhaps?

I shoved everything back into his pocket then rose and took off his jacket, tearing it into long strips with which I tied his hands and feet. To make doubly sure he couldn't escape, I took off his shoes and socks, then grabbed his shoelaces and tied the ends to form a long string. I roped his thumbs together then ran the laces around his neck. It might not be as deadly as Damon's garrotes, but it wouldn't be comfortable, either.

With the stranger trussed as securely as possible, I touched his face and reached for his flame, sucking in the heat of him. It swirled through my body—a delicious burn of energy that replaced the reserves drained by the long night of driving. But unlike Damon, I left embers behind. I didn't have the skill—or the desire—to completely annihilate what nature had given him.

The stranger began to stir, his feet twitching against the ropes. I grabbed him under the armpits and, with a grunt of effort, dragged him into the shade. It wouldn't stop him from energizing himself once dawn arrived, but hopefully I'd have my answers and be out of reach by then.

But first, I had to find out who waited below.

I stood back and toed his thigh. He jerked in reaction, then his eyes snapped open and his face contorted in an odd mix of anger and pain. His gaze briefly roamed the trees then fixed on me.

"Scream and I'll fry you." My voice was flat and my fingers glowed in warning.

"Who the fuck are you?" he spat, his voice a growl of low fury.

"A question I was going to ask you," I replied, "because I don't for one minute trust the name on your license."

"Well, that's too bad, ain't it, because that happens to be my real name."

I doubted it, but it wasn't a point worth arguing. "Why are you here in Red Rock?"

"Visiting kin." He paused, and his features twisted again. This time, it was pure fury. "What the hell have you done to my flames?"

"Doused them. And unless you answer my questions, I'll make damn sure you never flame again."

His gaze met mine, his expression disbelieving and yet a touch fearful. "Draman haven't got the skills to do that. Only dragons have."

"And many dragons still believe that draman can't fly or flame." I shrugged and reached forward, as if to touch his skin. He jerked away from me and I let my hand drop. "Answer my questions and I'll leave you restrained but alive. Or would you rather risk your flames—and your life—in the belief I might be lying?"

He swore under his breath, then said, "They don't pay me enough for this sort of shit."

"Who doesn't?"

"Some fellow named Franco. That's all I know, I swear."

"You contacted him through the Deca Dent night-club?"

Ralph grunted, which I took for a yes. "I never went there," he added. "It was all done by phone."

"Is this the first town you've been sent to destroy?"

He frowned. "I ain't here to destroy no town."

"Then what are you here for?"

"I'm here with the darting team."

I raised my eyebrows. "Darting team?"

"Yeah. They wanted to capture some muerte that was causing them trouble." He paused and gave me the evil eye. "As well as his bitch draman. Someone obviously forgot to warn us the bitch could fight."

And suddenly Leon's bravado made sense. He might have paid a hefty price, but he'd been setting us up all along. Red Rock was a trap, not a town slated for destruction. Which made me wonder if Leith's people were okay. I had to hope so, because I couldn't phone to find out—I didn't have the time and there didn't seem to be any reception in this valley.

"And what happened to the muerte?"

"No frigging sign of him."

Relief rolled through me. At least he wasn't captured. Or dead. But it did beg the question—why was he hiding? "How many of you are there?"

"Six." He shrugged, the movement awkward. "I think it's overkill. It's only one dragon, after all."

Obviously, no one had ever explained to this man just what a muerte was capable of. But then, I shouldn't have been surprised—he was draman, after all. And I hadn't known about the muerte, either, until recently.

"How long have you been here?"

"We got here before eleven. Just as well I can flame, I tell you, because it gets damn cold here at night."

"So what did you do with all the people living here?"

"Oh, they were eliminated weeks ago. This was one of the first places we did."

"What did you do with the bodies?"

"Buried them, of course. We didn't want their kin knowing they were dead—not that most of them *had* kin who would even care." He stopped and gave a nasty grin. "Do you have kin who will care when you die, little draman?"

I didn't answer, but the sick feeling in my gut was growing. My gaze darted along the tree line. I couldn't see or feel anyone approaching, but that didn't mean they weren't out there, getting a line on me with a rifle at this very moment.

I licked my lips, torn between the urge to run and the need to stay and help out. Running wouldn't stop these murderers, and it certainly wouldn't save Rainey's soul.

And I had less than two days left.

I closed my eyes against the brief surge of panic, then said, "Why did Franco have it marked as un-cleansed on his wall map?"

"How else was he going to set the trap?" He shifted again. "Listen, lady, I'm being helpful here. You could at least make me more comfortable. Undo some ropes or something."

"Sorry, but I'm not that stupid."

He swore at me—long, loud, and inventively. I couldn't help smiling. "An interesting combination of words, but it isn't going to help. When did Franco contact you?"

"He didn't actually contact me. He contacted Tomi."

I rolled my eyes. No wonder no one knew who the head guy was—he was using too many intermediaries. "And Tomi is?"

"The guy who hires the rest of us."

"So what time did this Tomi contact you?"

"About six thirty. It took us a while to collect everything we needed."

Then it must have been Seth who'd contacted Tomi, not Leon, because by six thirty, Leon was well on his way to being dumped somewhere deep in the Pacific.

My gaze darted around, and again I saw nothing but darkness. But my unease was growing.

"So you've had no personal dealings with Franco—or anybody else?"

He shrugged. This time, the movement jerked the shoelaces against his neck, leaving a red mark. He glared at me balefully. "I heard some guy speaking on the phone a couple of times, when I was with Tomi."

"Was it Franco?"

"No. Franco's accent falls in and out. This guy's didn't."

I had no idea what Hannish sounded like, but if he and Seth had known each other for a long time, it was possible that Seth was imitating Hannish's accent. He'd always aspired to be more than he was.

"Ralph, what the hell are you doing out there?"

The voice was soft but clear. I jerked around, my heart racing and flames leaping across my fingertips before I realized the words were coming from the speaker at his ear. I glanced at my captive. "Who's that?"

"The boss. Tomi."

I picked up the speaker microphone. "I want you to answer him. Give me away—or even make me suspect you've given me away—and I will kill you."

His gaze met mine. Judging. Weighing. I have no idea what he saw in my expression, but after a moment, he nodded. I pressed the switch and held the mike near his mouth.

"I'm investigating the engine noise, as ordered," Ralph said.

"And?"

"Nothing. Must have been just the wind."

"Then get your ass back into position. The muerte is on his way, apparently."

"Will do."

I released the switch, ripped the speaker mike apart, then tossed the separate pieces as far away as I could.

"How long will it be before he starts missing you?"

I didn't actually expect an honest answer, and I didn't get one.

"Twenty minutes. Maybe more," he said, his lie practically staining the air.

Meaning I probably had a few minutes rather than twenty.

"You've been extremely helpful," I said, and with no warning, hit him as hard as I could. His chin snapped back and he was out before he even realized what was happening.

I checked his makeshift ropes a final time to insure they were still all tight, then sucked in the heat of his refueling flames, leaving him with embers and me with another few vital minutes.

Then I rose and made my way down the hill, keeping it between myself and Red Rock. I ran quickly, leaping over rocks and fallen trees, my senses twitching with awareness but finding nothing. Only bugs and silence.

I looped around to the back of the town then stopped, my breath rasping past my lips and sweat beginning to trickle down my spine.

I raised my face to the sky for a moment, letting the distant energy of the dawn yet to come caress my skin.

What the hell was I going to do now?

There were five men out there, and I had no idea where Damon was. I knew he was here, but not much more than that. It was possible that Ralph had been lying, and that Damon was inside and captive—or even dead—and they were all waiting for my arrival. Hell, for all I knew, Ralph had sent a coded message to his boss. His words had seemed innocent enough, but that didn't mean they actually were.

I blew out a breath, then shrugged the backpacks off my shoulder and tucked them securely into the broken remains of a tree trunk. It wouldn't hold up to a concerted search, but at least it was hidden from a casual glance. The netbook and the stuff I'd stolen from Leon, were as safe as I could make them.

I glanced toward the top of the hill, feeling like I was about to step into a dark void, then took a deep breath and moved forward. Once near the ridge, I dropped to my knees and crawled until I could once again see the valley below.

Red Rock remained quiet.

No smoke drifted from any of the chimneys, and there was no hint that anyone was down there at all. And for all I knew, there wasn't. The other five men might have been in the hills like me, watching and waiting.

But I had no choice. I had to go down there and see what was waiting for me, whether that was Damon or a trap.

I scanned the hillside and spotted a line of scrubby trees sweeping most of the way downhill. I wriggled back down the slope and then ran across to those trees, darting from trunk to trunk, keeping to the shadows as much as possible. My heart was racing and my stomach churning, but I made it to the last of the trees without being caught.

Whether I'd been seen was another matter entirely, and it wasn't something I was going to know until someone actually jumped out at me.

I peeked out from behind the tree trunk. A barren space of about twenty yards separated me from the back of one of the old wooden buildings and deep shadows. And yet it seemed as exposed as a field in bright sunshine.

Nerves—who needed them?

I licked my lips and drew in a breath that remained free of any taint of danger. After a silent count to three, I raced forward. Out of cover, into the open. And it suddenly felt as if the eyes of the world were on me.

With fear giving my feet wings, I flew across the small strip of land separating me from the deeper shadows of the building.

I was almost there, almost safe, when I felt the sting in my neck.

I slapped at it, saw something silver fly sideways, and realized with a sinking sensation that it was a dart.

I reached the building and grabbed at the window frame, my gaze swinging wildly to the left and right, looking for my attackers.

I couldn't see them. Couldn't smell them. But they were obviously there.

If I had wings, I could have flown somewhere safe. But I didn't have wings and I never would, leaving me yet again stuck on land and cursing the lack.

It was a curse that died on my lips as unconsciousness snatched away all awareness.

Chapter Thirteen

Waking was a slow and painful business. My head felt as if it were stuck in the middle of two bass drums, and the reverberations were making my eyes water. The rest of me fared no better—it felt like I'd been hit by a truck. Again.

Add to that the fact that my flesh was so cold my fingers and toes were aching from it, and you had one big bundle of misery.

It was that factor, more than anything else, that had awareness surging. Why was I so damn cold? It was a hot day and I was draman. There was no way I should have been this cold.

I forced my eyelids open. Darkness greeted me. Darkness and air so cold every breath hurt.

Memories surged, reminding me of another time when the darkness had been all-encompassing and the air so cold it could freeze the insides.

I was in another freezer.

Oh, *fuck*.

I closed my eyes against the surge of panic. I *wasn't* alone. Rainey might not be here to rescue me this time, but Damon was. He'd come. He wouldn't let me freeze.

I just had to wait. I just had to remain calm. I gulped down several freezing breaths, then forced myself upright. My fingers stuck to the shelf and, as I tore them away, left flesh behind.

I swore and reached for my flames.

To find nothing but ashes.

It was a realization that hit like a punch to the gut. For several seconds, I couldn't even breathe. Panic rolled through me, and it was all I could do not to start screaming. I'd only survived last time thanks to my flames; without them, I was dead.

No. I won't die. I won't let him win. He didn't last time and he wouldn't now. My flames had been stolen, *not* destroyed. The dragon still lay deep inside; she was slumbering, not gone forever.

She would recover, albeit slowly.

Damn it, I *had* to get out of this freezer.

I rubbed my arms to get some blood flowing back into my limbs, glad that my captors had at least left me fully clothed. I might not have woken otherwise.

My fingertips began tingling—stinging—which at least chased away the numbness. I thrust upright, but my feet felt like lead and I almost fell over again. I stamped them hard and wriggled my toes to get some blood flowing. After a few minutes, they came back to aching life. I raised my arms, sweeping ahead of me as I walked carefully forward. Three steps, and I hit a wall. I followed it along, feeling with my fingertips and wishing I could see something, anything. But the damn fridge was darker than night, and if there was a door then it was well and truly sealed.

I found a shelf, the metal as cold as the rest of this place, and felt along it. Plastic-wrapped packages and various-size boxes were stacked in what felt like an orderly arrangement. I continued along and found the junction of the walls. Following the second one soon had me touching rubber, then a door release. Relief slithered through me, and it wasn't cold that had my fingers trembling as I hit the emergency release mechanism.

Only nothing happened. The door remained firmly closed.

God, *no*.

I hit it again, with the same result. The fear and panic rose again and I hit the door as hard as I could, needing to get out of this icy hellhole. And then I hit it again, and again, and again, until the door was dented, my knuckles were bleeding, and the pain was so bad that common sense crawled over the panic and I regained control.

Hitting the door wasn't going to get me out of here, and the sooner I accepted that and concentrated on surviving, the better off I'd be.

Seth might want me dead, but Hannish *wouldn't*. Not yet. Not until they knew what I knew and who I'd talked to. I had to believe that. Angus had said as much, and I had no doubt it was as true now as it was then.

So, this chill was merely their way of insuring I was kept scared and helpless. My past aside, dragons, darkness, and chill was *not* a good combination. Under normal circumstances, it would render any one of us helpless.

But my flames had been my only major defense for

more years than I could even remember, and while my brother had taught me to fight, that skill had come later in life, *after* I'd learned control over my fire. And while even *I* couldn't totally refuel myself in this kind of hell, I could keep myself alive longer than most.

I just had to stave off panic and *think*.

I felt my way back to the little metal bench and sat down. The chill wrapped around me but I ignored it, closing my eyes and reaching deep within to the embers of the dragon. She was my heart, my soul, and she could warm me, even in this state. All I had to do was channel energy back into her, feeding the flames and directing the heat of them outward to my extremities, keeping the dangerous cold at bay.

It took a while, but gradually the embers began to burn brighter, and the heat—though nowhere near even quarter strength—slithered through my body, chasing the cold from my fingers, making my toes ache with renewed life.

Enough to keep me awake.

Enough to keep me alive.

I couldn't keep this up forever, though, and even as I concentrated on channeling the energy that fed the life-giving flames, part of me was praying that my captors came to check on me sooner rather than later.

It seemed like an age before my prayers were answered, but, eventually, the scuffle of movement came from outside my prison. In my disconnected state, it seemed like they approached and then moved away again. Something creaked harshly, then the heat of two men flooded the darkness, hitting me with all the force of an express train.

I breathed deep, sucking in the scent of them, letting

the heat radiating off them slither through me. It wasn't anywhere near enough to fan the fires to life, but it was a start.

"She'd better not be a popsicle. I will *not* be happy if you've killed her."

The voice was rich and arrogant and oh-so-familiar. Seth.

The urge to open my eyes was almost overwhelming, but I resisted.

After expending so much energy on keeping warm, I probably wouldn't be much of a threat to them, but if I could just get them a little closer, I might be able to steal a little of their heat. And I needed that heat. Needed it bad.

So I kept still, my eyes closed, and waited.

"She's alive." It was the voice I'd heard speaking to Ralph over the speaker. "You can see her breathing."

They came closer, their footsteps echoing harshly in the boxed stillness. I desperately wanted to jump up and grab one of them, but again I restrained the urge, even though the effort left me trembling. I could only hope it wasn't showing. They might not get too close if they realized just how alert I was.

The two men halted. Their scents hit me, filling each breath with musk, sunshine, and sage.

The sage was Seth. Even smelling it had an echo of pain slithering along the long-healed, S-shaped scar down my back.

But then, Seth had never really played on the same sane team as the rest of us. He was probably grinning like a madman right now at the mere thought of what all this cold was doing to me, and what memories it was bringing back.

"Wake her up," he said, his voice as cold as the air I was breathing.

The other man grunted and stepped forward. The heat of him was fierce against my skin and the inner trembling grew. I needed—wanted—that warmth.

He reached out—something I felt rather than saw—and grabbed my shoulder, shaking me roughly. My hand shot out and I latched on to his arm, gripping him so tightly I swear his bones cracked. But the moment my fingers touched his flesh, the dragon within sprang to life, sweeping into his body, sucking at his flames and drawing them back into mine. It was a fierce and ugly attack, because I didn't have much time.

He yelled—screamed—then his open hand smacked into the side of my face. My head snapped around and darkness loomed, but I held on grimly—both to consciousness and his arm.

He hit me again, this time harder, breaking my grip and leaving my cheek aching and my head ringing. I swear I heard a roar of anger within that ringing, but as I blinked back tears, it faded, leaving only a distant touch of thunder rolling through my mind.

Damon, I thought, for no particular reason.

And yet, if he knew what was going on, why hadn't he come to rescue me? What the hell was he waiting for?

Answers?

That *had* to be it. He was a muerte, first and fore most, and his allegiance lay with the council, not to any one person and certainly not to me. Given the basic choice between saving me and getting answers, there *was* no choice.

I blinked back tears, not entirely sure whether they were from my aching cheek or the stark knowledge that I would *never* come first in Damon's world, and opened my eyes.

"Well, well," Seth said. "It seems our little draman was foxing us."

He'd changed in the years since I'd last seen him. His nose was sharper, his cheeks more angular, and his body more muscular. He was obviously wearing contacts, because his eyes were blue instead of gray, and his hair had also changed—deep red rather than the dark gold he'd been born with. But the cold, unfeeling air that clung to him like a storm cloud was the same, as was the thin, straight set of his lips.

"I should have realized from the beginning that this insanity had your mark, Seth."

God, it hurt to remember that I'd once foolishly thought—however briefly—that this dragon had actually *liked* me. *Stupid* is the only word that adequately describes it—although even *I* was human enough to be flattered by the attentions of a dragon who, at the time, had been one of the "popular" kids.

"I have to admit to a little disappointment that you didn't catch on sooner." He crossed his arms, allowing a brief glimpse of his left hand—a hand that was twisted and scarred. My work, and one of the main reasons for his hatred of me. The other was my refusal of his advances. Seth didn't like to be told no. Of course, it was his inability to accept that word that had led to the scarring.

"Especially," he continued, a slight smile touching one corner of his lips—only it held no warmth, no compassion, just the chilling sense of superiority that was so much a part of this man—"after being locked in that metal-lined cellar. It was a particularly delicious salute to the past, didn't you think?"

I didn't say anything. There wasn't much *to* say.

"And Leon certainly hasn't changed that much, so it was surprising that you didn't recognize him in the truck." He paused, and something cold and cruel twitched his lips. "He did so enjoy ramming into the two of you."

Something close to excitement leaped through me. "So you ordered the hit? Not Hannish?"

His smile was arrogant. Overconfident. It had been his downfall once before—and would be again, hopefully. "Hannish was foolish enough to believe it was better to let the two of you wander around aimlessly, but he doesn't know your tenacity like I do."

I briefly closed my eyes. One death stood between me and saving Rainey's soul. I didn't have to kill Hannish—didn't have to kill a king's son.

Only Seth, who might also be a king's son, but as far as I knew, he wasn't heir—even if he intended to be.

Seth added, "Of course, I *did* have to reprimand him for not checking that both of you were dead."

"Which you no doubt enjoyed doing." My smile was just as cruel and harsh as his. "But I bet you didn't enjoy it half as much as we enjoyed killing his fire, breaking his body, and then flying him out to sea to drown."

The barb hit home. His eyes narrowed fractionally and his anger stirred the air. Most people might have missed the signs, but I knew this man very well.

And he had cared for Leon, although he would never admit it. They weren't mates in the soul-mate sense of the word, but as bisexual males who didn't really care *where* they took their pleasure from, they'd been enjoying each other's company for most of their lives.

"That," he said heavily, "was a mistake on your part. I might have let you live otherwise."

I snorted softly. Given our past history, I was never likely to believe that. "I'm sure Leon's ghost will be pleased to see how badly you're taking his death."

He shrugged, a seemingly casual movement that was oddly edged with anger. "Sometimes sacrifices must be made if we wish our plans to come to fruition."

Meaning that, even though he cared for Leon, not even the man who'd been his lover for over twenty years was going to get in his way.

"Of course," he continued, "now that I *have* decided to kill you, I shall insure your death is a long and painful one. He'd appreciate that."

I'm sure he would. "Was Leon aware that he was bait?"

"Of course. But he was extremely confident in his ability to handle the muerte." His gaze pinned me. "Tell me, where exactly did you dump him?"

"That, I can't say. I can't fly, remember?"

"Ah, yes. It was such fun prodding Waylin to drop you mid-flight. A shame your brother intervened." His voice was almost philosophical, yet the anger remained, burning deep in his eyes. "I shall try to retrieve Leon. He was a good lieutenant. Hell, I might even try and save his soul, once we kill the muerte."

There was nothing I could say that wouldn't actually get me into more trouble, so I kept my mouth shut and my arms crossed. They couldn't see my hands and didn't know that the heat I'd stolen now burned in readiness. I could protect myself if I needed to.

But I was no longer alone in this battle.

Damon was out there and on the move. The awareness of his presence was a distant but ever-strengthening song that made my inner dragon want to dance.

Seth glanced briefly at his watch. "As much as I'm enjoying reliving old times, I really need to get moving. Tomi, if she moves, shoot her."

Shoot her, not kill her, I noted. But Seth was like that. Maiming always seemed to taste better to him than actual death. "Why am I here, Seth?"

"Two reasons," he said, almost cheerfully. "First, you're bait for the muerte."

I laughed. "If you think Damon will go out of his way to save my butt, you're chasing down the wrong street."

"Maybe, but I do think he'd go out of his way to find the leaders of this little operation, and here I am, in a nice little package."

"And if you think he's dumb enough to simply walk into a trap, you're deluded."

"We caught him once, dear Mercy, and I believe we can catch him again."

I didn't. And we'd see soon enough which of us was right.

"So, just how do you plan to take over the Jamieson clique? Because that's you're intention, isn't it?

He raised an eyebrow. "You know more than we presumed. Or did Leon talk too much?"

"Leon couldn't do much of anything once we'd

finished with him." They weren't wise words, but I couldn't help the urge to bait him.

He merely smiled. It was a cold, cruel thing, and a chill ran down my spine. "Those actions will haunt you when your time comes, Mercy."

The chill increased. I ignored it, keeping my voice even as I said, "Our king is never going to name you heir."

"Oh, but he already has. Even if he doesn't know it yet."

I frowned, and he laughed. "It's always amusing how little you draman know about the culture you live in. Kings name heirs in legal documents kept in the council vaults. They are easy enough to access if you know the right people to bribe, and even easier to alter if you know a good forger."

So one step in the plan was already completed. I wondered how much time our king had left; how much time Marcus Valorn had left. If we didn't catch Hannish, he might yet go ahead with the plot, with or without the backing of the Jamieson clique. After all, we had no real evidence connecting him to any of this as yet.

But maybe Damon didn't need it. Maybe Hannish would simply disappear again.

"So why kill the draman in Stillwater and Desert Springs? Couldn't you have just relocated them?"

"They refused to sell their land." He shrugged. "They paid the price for that refusal."

"But why take that risk?"

He snorted. "What risk? Jamieson wiped out the Whale Point settlement years ago, and not one council member bothered investigating it."

"You're wrong. The council has been watching Jamieson—and our king—ever since."

"Yeah? And done what, precisely?" His voice was mocking. "It was a draman settlement, like Stillwater and Desert Springs. We both know draman don't matter."

Well, he was at least right about *that*. "But how does killing them make anything any better? The land would be bequeathed to their heirs, not you."

Seth raised an eyebrow. "Would you hang on to land on which your whole family had been slaughtered?"

The answer was no, and we both knew it. There would be too many ghosts living on this land for anyone with even a hint of dragon blood to remain.

I would feel them at night's onset, because the time between day and night gave every dragon power, even those caught between worlds, but I wondered if Seth would. Could someone who appeared to have no connection to life really be aware of those who lingered in death?

My gaze flickered past him, studying the view beyond the fridge's doorway. Flags of red and gold were beginning to tint the horizon, meaning the night and the shadows would soon be gone. If Damon was going to make a move, then he'd better do it soon.

I met Seth's gaze again. "So you simply stepped in and bought the land from the surviving heirs? Where the hell did you get that sort of money? And how can you even sleep at night?"

"We have our backers, Mercy, and I sleep very well, trust me."

Of that I had no doubt. A man so out of touch with anything resembling humanity wasn't ever likely to be attacked by guilt. "Even so, you can't possibly think the other cliques are going to let two murderers usurp the council."

"Oh, but they already have. I'm sure the muerte has already mentioned Montana. It set a precedent—one the current kings will sorely regret." His smile was cold and arrogant. "Our king's succession document is not the only one that has been changed."

So Damon's guess had been right. This was about taking over the council. "The council knows about the plot. You won't succeed."

He gave me a condescending smile. "If the council knew, the muertes would have been unleashed and we would be dead. No, this will be done properly, the deaths will all take time and look accidental, and no one will be the wiser. Not until it is far too late, anyway."

I glanced past him again, studying the growing shadows and wondering what the hell Damon was doing. His song continued to reverberate through my soul, growing in strength, but it gave me no real idea of his location. He could have been just outside the door for all I knew.

"The mere fact that it's you who's becoming one of the kings is reason enough to stop this mad scheme." His attitude toward draman was worse than most. "You said there were two reasons I'm here."

"The other is, of course, information. We made the mistake of trying to kill you far too early once before. We shall not make the same mistake again."

"What do you need to know?" I asked, my gaze shifting briefly as one of the shadows behind him moved ever so slightly.

Damon, here in this room. My inner dragon felt him, but there was no sense of awareness otherwise, no scent to give him away. He was a shadow who didn't seem to exist in any physical way. Part of me wanted to dance, the rest of me just tensed up. I knew a muerte should have been more than capable of taking out a couple of dragons, but Seth had never been just an ordinary dragon.

It was a point he proved by suddenly producing a gun from under his jacket and spinning around. The sound of the shot reverberated loudly in the metal confines of the refrigerator and light flared briefly, causing little pinpoints of brightness to momentarily burn into my retinas. Fear twisted my heart. But I thrust it aside and launched myself at Tomi, who was slower on the uptake than Seth and yet probably no less deadly.

Even with the heat I'd stolen, my reflexes were still far too slow. Seth saw me coming and twisted around, firing the gun a second time. I twisted around, felt the bullet burn past me, leaving behind a stinging, bloody streak on my side. I fell into Tomi and he wrapped an arm opportunistically around my neck, but I grabbed the hand holding the weapon, forcing the gun up as he fired. The bullet bit through the ceiling above us and bits of metal and freezer lining showered down.

"Let go, bitch," he muttered, shaking me roughly from side to side like a rag doll.

"Not on your goddamn life."

The words were forced through clenched teeth as I fought to retain control of his hand while keeping my shoulders hunched in an effort to stop him from strangling me.

I was vaguely aware of Seth fighting with Damon, who was still little more than a shadow, but that awareness bloomed as the two of them hit us. The sheer force of their weight sent us all sprawling to the floor, with me on the bottom. For several seconds, stars danced across my vision and my breath came as little more than labored grunts. Even so, my dragon snapped to life, the contact with Tomi allowing her to suck in more of his heat. He swore softly and thrust an elbow backward; the blow barely missed my cheek. Body weight shifted, then Seth was up and running, with the shadow that was Damon in pursuit.

Leaving me with Tomi.

I wrapped an arm around his neck and hung on grimly as he struggled and swore. His body flamed, and the heat of him burned against my skin—a delicious fire that helped melt more of the iciness from my bones.

He snuffed it out the minute he realized he was helping rather than hindering me, then somehow wrenched his arm around and fired at my legs. The bullet bit into the side of my calf, and pain bloomed, forcing a yelp from my lips. My grip weakened. He scrambled up in an instant but I rose with him, striking low and hard at his kidneys. He fell backward again, forcing me to sidestep in a hurry. As he hit the floor, I stuck again—this time with two stiffened fingers at the point just below his Adam's apple. It left him gasping for air, and I used those few precious seconds to rip the gun from his hand then leap over his body and bolt for the door. I had barely closed and locked it before his weight hit the other side.

"Bitch!" he yelled, "Let me out."

"Not on your goddamn life," I muttered, glancing down at the gun in my hand, then dropping it into the barrel of water at the end of the building.

For a moment I did nothing more than stand there, sucking in the ever-growing power of the dawn. It chased away the last of the cold and stoked the embers deep in my soul.

Then I turned around and looked for Damon and Seth. A scream of inhuman rage jerked my gaze skyward, and my heart just about slammed into my throat. High above me, two dragons battled, one gold, one black, both equally huge.

Seth screamed again, wheeling about in the brightening skies, slashing at Damon's dark hide with razorsharp claws. He caught flesh, tearing deep, and blood sprayed. A scream tore out of my throat, but I clapped a hand over my mouth, stopping it before it could pass my lips. Damon didn't need any distractions right now, and Seth certainly didn't need to know I was out of the fridge and free.

Damon dived, the growing sunlight playing across his dark scales, setting them ablaze with fires of purple and red. He twisted around, then somehow bellyrolled, coming up under Seth. His bared teeth sank deep into the other dragon's tender underside, then he shook his head, whipping Seth to and fro. Seth's fury boiled across the air, his scream so high it hurt to hear it. His claws raked the air, missing Damon's bleeding side by mere inches, then he lashed out with his tail, the whiplike strike forcing Damon to release him. Damon dropped away, spitting out a chunk of flesh. Then, with a mighty sweep of his wings, he drove upward, obviously trying to get above Seth.

Seth saw him and banked around, coming in fast, teeth bared and a blazing look of hatred twisting his serpentine features. Damon slashed with his claws and spun away, still driving upward, still trying to get the advantage of height.

But the gold dragon was just as fast as the black.

Maybe I could do something about that. Maybe I could distract him enough to give Damon the upper hand.

I spread my arms wide and called the power of the dawn, letting it burn unchecked through my body—a maelstrom of energy that my dragon struggled to contain.

When I opened my eyes, the black dragon was chasing the gold, the powerful sweep of their wings causing wind to batter the trees and rooftops below them as they swept down from the sky.

I clenched my fists, heat blazing across my fingertips—a whirlpool of power that made my hands glow. Closer and closer the two dragons came, until the air around me filled with dirt and debris and all I could see was the fury in the gold dragon's eyes.

I raised my hands and flung a wide band of flames directly at his face. Even as they arced upward, I reached deeper into myself, gathering all the energy I had, channeling it into my fingertips and then outward—this time as two needle-sharp spears that moved with blinding speed.

The broad band of flames slapped across Seth's face. He snorted, shaking his head, his scales absorbing the impact, using it to fuel his own energy.

But he didn't see the second, smaller spears. He couldn't have, because he looked right back at me.

And in that moment, the spears hit, burning deep into his retinas and destroying his sight.

He screamed—a harsh and painful sound. His wings jerked upward and he struggled to maintain position. And that was when Damon hit him, his claws sinking deep into Seth's back, the weight forcing him earthward as Damon's head snaked around and latched on to Seth's throat.

They hit the dirt so hard the earth under my feet shuddered, and went rolling in a tangle of bodies and legs that made me fear for Damon's wings. Blood spurted and there was another horrible scream that ended abruptly as Damon bit again.

The gold dragon stilled.

The black dragon struggled to untangle himself from the other then rose, one wing dragging as the blue shape-shifting fire began to crawl across his body, encasing him in its unearthly light as he transformed from dragon to human.

I was limping toward him before that transformation was completed, and launched myself at him the minute he reappeared. He grunted, a sound that contained pain, and yet his good arm held me with a fierceness that said he didn't care.

"Thank God it's over," I murmured, trembling as I wrapped my arms around his neck and held on tight. He smelled of sweat and blood and fading anger, and never in my life had I inhaled anything sweeter.

For several seconds he didn't say anything, just held on tight. In that moment, it would have been very easy to believe I was the most precious thing in his world.

After several minutes more, he shifted back slightly, then lifted my chin with a gentle finger and kissed me.

It was a kiss that was rich and warm, sweet and yet so filled with emotion that it made my heart ache. A kiss that said so much, yet one that left so much more unsaid.

When we finally parted, he brushed my cheek with the back of his hand, then stepped away and said, "I have to go."

No. Not so soon. It can't be over so soon. "But your arm is broken. You can't fly."

"I can steal a car, and there's a medical kit in one of the bunk rooms. I can reset broken bones. It won't be the first time I've done it."

"But—"

He touched my lips gently, silencing me. "It's not over yet. Hannish still needs to be caught—and now, before he has any chance to run."

"But the only real evidence we have that Hannish is involved is the land purchase documents. Both Seth and Leon are dead, so they can't really testify against him." I hesitated, then added, "And the council isn't likely to give too much credit to what either Tomi or I say. We don't matter in their eyes."

"You matter," he said, voice gentle and dark eyes suddenly blazing with emotion. "Don't ever believe otherwise."

Say the words, part of me wanted to beg. *Admit what you feel.* But his admitting what he felt was a moot point, so I held my tongue. He was still going to walk away regardless. He'd decided that long before we'd met, and I had no reason to believe anything we'd shared would change that.

Not even the fact that his song rang clear and true in my mind.

"No matter what you might think, the council is not likely to take the word of two draman against that of a king's heir," I said softly, "which means it comes down to your word against his."

"Not so," Damon said. "Didn't you wonder why I left you in that fridge, and in Seth's hands, for so long?"

I studied him, hating the distance he was keeping between us and wishing I had the courage to lessen it myself. But I didn't want him retreating any farther, and I suspected that's just what would happen if I did attempt to move closer. "Well, now that you mentioned it, I think I did throw a few curses your way for not riding to the rescue sooner than you did."

He smiled. "The ability to shadow is not the only reason certain dragons are chosen for this job."

I raised an eyebrow. "Well, what a surprise. There's something else you've failed to tell me."

He laughed—a warm, rich sound that sent delighted shivers racing across my skin. "You have no idea just how much I actually *have* told you. More than anyone else, even my family."

Maybe he had, but it wasn't nearly enough, because he wasn't telling me the most important thing of all.

He wasn't telling me what he felt.

It didn't matter that his emotions were evident in his kiss and his touch, or in the way we were so in tune with each other. I still needed to hear those words. Maybe there wasn't any hope for the two of us, but surely he could just admit what he felt. I wanted to hear it, just once, so the words would keep me warm through the long nights ahead.

That wasn't asking too much, was it?

But he didn't say the words and probably never

would. For several seconds I had to resist the urge to just turn and run from this man and the heartache that was waiting.

In the end, I simply asked, "So tell me what else muertes can do, and how it will solve the problem."

His gaze flicked down my body, as if he had been expecting me to say something else. And maybe he had been. It wouldn't have been the first time he'd sensed what I'd really wanted to say.

But, like me, he held his thoughts back, and simply said, "Muertes can link to broadcasters."

I raised my eyebrows. "What the hell is a broad-caster?"

"Broadcasting is a psychic skill, and those who have it can telepathically link to several people at once."

The delay suddenly made all sorts of sense. "Meaning you linked to this broadcaster while hidden in the shadows, and whoever *he* was linked to heard the whole of it?"

"Yes—both this morning, and when I was question-ing Leon. The twelve members of the council heard every word said. Hannish's fate has already been de-cided."

"And now you have to execute that decision?"

"Yes."

"And afterward?"

He knew what I meant, and brushed his knuckles lightly against my cheek, letting them slide down to my chin. "There is no afterward, Mercy. You know that."

I stepped back, away from his reach, away from the smell and heat of him. "There's one other thing you for-got to tell me about muertes, Damon."

His fingers twitched, as if he were tempted to reach

for me again, then he dropped his hand and simply said, "What?"

"You never told me they were cowards."

"Mercy—"

"Don't bother," I cut in, taking another step back and steeling myself against the rising ache in my heart. An ache that pierced like a knife. "You may not be afraid of death, Damon, but you're sure as hell afraid of life."

This time he did reach for me, but I slapped his hand away. "Nothing you say or do can alter the truth. You're walking away to protect yourself, not me. You're afraid to love because you're afraid to lose. That's cowardice, Damon, nothing more."

"Mercy, that's not true. What I do—"

"Is an excuse. One you can keep on believing, but don't expect anyone else to." I took another step, my eyes stinging with tears I refused to let fall. "Goodbye, Damon."

With that, I turned and walked away. The air was filled with turmoil—his and mine—but he didn't move, he didn't stop me, and I kept on walking.

My dreams might be ashes and my world might be falling apart, but I still had the soul of a friend to save and less than twenty-four hours left to find the point where our car had gone off the road.

That, at least, gave me something to focus on.

I could worry about the rest of it later.

Chapter Fourteen

The air began to hum with power long before the first vestiges of night began to creep through the day. Energy flitted across my skin—little sparks of power that were very visible in the fading brightness that surrounded me. There were ghosts here, too—other souls who'd died along this stretch of road. They were little more than fragile wisps of humanity whose pain, bewilderment, and sorrow infused me, making me want to cry. But there was nothing I could do to help or save them.

They were neither kin nor friends, and the task of saving their souls was not on my shoulders.

I was here to help Rainey move on.

I took a deep breath, drawing in the power of dusk, wishing it had the strength to ease the ache in my heart. But I doubted anything could do that right now.

I studied the horizon, waiting, as the hum of power grew and intensified, and the slivers of red and gold streaked the sky—bright flags of color that heralded peace for Rainey.

As dusk's energy flooded my body, the power in the air framed the ghosts around me, briefly illuminating their forms, giving them shape if not substance. Tears stung my eyes. Rainey was there somewhere.

"Rainey Carmichael, I call on your soul and your spirit and ask that you stand before me this night."

My voice was little more than a whisper, but the power surged and danced around me, filling the sunset with its beauty. Wispy fingers of energy stirred amid the gathered ghosts, searching, feeling, until they swirled around one wispy form and urged her forward. Her face was little more than a radiant blur, but I knew it was Rainey. I could feel her—in my heart, and in my soul.

I took a deep, shuddering breath, and continued with the ritual.

"May the gods of sun and sky and air bear witness to the fact that those who killed you have paid the price." As I spoke, her form seemed to grow brighter and brighter, as if the sun itself was finally burning her, taking the flesh that no longer existed and freeing her soul from its constraints. "With the power of this dusk, I free you. May the gods guide and protect you as you continue your journey, Rainey."

The radiance and power in the air seemed to reach a crescendo and, just for a moment, I heard the sound of laughter. Rich, carefree, and joyous.

Rainey, free at last.

Tears stung my eyes, and my throat was so constricted I could barely speak the final words. "May you find the peace and happiness in the forever lands that you could not find in this, my friend."

The streaming fingers of sunlight seemed to twirl and dance, as if in answer, and then they were gone, lost to the shadows of the oncoming night.

The radiance caressing my skin died, taking with it the underlying hum of energy. All that remained were the fading remnants of ghosts who would never find the release that Rainey had.

She was free, but she was also gone from my life forever.

I closed my eyes, took a deep shuddering breath, then slowly turned around and headed back to the hotel, where I finally let go of the pent-up hurt and anger, and grieved for the friend I'd lost.

A month later, just about everything had returned to normal. I'd gone back to work and found myself a new place to live—albeit one empty of everything I'd spent a lifetime collecting. Instead, my new place had little more than secondhand furniture and some basics borrowed from friends until the damn insurance people decided to pay me.

But the barren apartment was a constant reminder of everything I'd lost, and it just added weight to the loneliness that was crushing me.

My upbringing might have been rough at times, but the one good thing about it was the fact that I'd never really been alone. I'd had my brother, and I'd had Rainey, and I'd grown up used to having them there when I needed them. Now Rainey was gone forever, and Trae nowhere to be found. It felt like there was a chunk of me missing, and even now, long after I prayed for her soul and sent her on her final journey,

I still found myself picking up the phone to talk to her. I kept expecting her to walk through the door with her wild red hair and big toothy grin.

But all that was nothing compared to the ache in my heart. Maybe it was even worse, because Damon was alive, and some small part of me refused to give up hope, even though I told myself a thousand times a day to get over it—to get over him—and move on.

And yet there were times when I thought I felt him close by. Times when the faintest whisper of a warm and familiar presence ran through my mind, teasing my senses and making my heart leap in hope. But no matter how often I looked, there was never any sign of him, and I knew it was probably nothing more than an overactive imagination combined with that never-say-die sliver of hope.

Life, I thought, sipping my coffee as I stared out the window, watching sunset flare across the building opposite and turning its windows a brilliant shade of bronze, was a bitch. Just this once, it could have given me the fairy tale instead of the nightmare.

The doorbell rang sharply in the silence. I jumped, and the coffee rocked over the sides of the cup, splashing across my hand. I cursed softly, then placed the cup on the sill and shook my hand dry as I ran over to the intercom.

"Yes?"

"So, would you like to explain how, exactly, you managed to burn down my apartment?"

The voice was warm and rich and familiar, and a grin split my lips. "That's a rather long story, brother dearest. And where the hell have you been? I've been trying to get hold of you for over a month."

"I got sidetracked by a pretty lady in distress. I've brought her along so that you can meet her."

That raised my eyebrows. Pretty ladies and my brother went together like bread and butter, but never before had he gone to the trouble of actually introducing me to one. This *had* to be serious.

I pressed the buzzer to let them in. "You'd better come on up, then. Apartment 408."

I walked into the kitchen to turn on the coffeemaker—one of the few luxuries I refused to live without—then walked across to the door and opened it.

My brother, all rugged good looks, blond hair, and sunshiney disposition, walked into the room and gave me the biggest hug of my life.

"I've been worried about you," he said, once he'd finally put me down. His blue eyes studied me critically. "Are you okay? You look tired."

"I'm fine," I said, and avoided the intent behind the question by looking past him. The woman standing at the door was tall and somewhat lanky, with eyes that were the green of a deep ocean and framed by long, thick lashes the rest of us would die for. Her hair was black, but highlights of dark green and blue played through it, as if the sea itself had kissed it.

She was a sea dragon. My gaze skimmed her body.

She was also pregnant. *Very* pregnant.

Meaning this really *was* serious.

"I'm Destiny." She stepped forward and offered her hand. "And I'm the previously mentioned lady in distress."

I moved past my brother and shook her hand. Her skin was on the cool side, but her eyes were warm and friendly, and dimples were lurking about the corners of her lips.

"You don't actually look too distressed," I said, waving them both into the living room.

"Oh, I'm not." She smiled up at Trae as his fingers twined through hers. The love so evident in that brief glance had my heart aching. "Although your brother has been the cause of a fair bit of stress over the last few months or so."

"He's like that," I said wryly. "No thought or concern for those who care about him."

"Ha," he said, seating Destiny on the one sofa I had before folding himself to the floor at her feet. "This from the woman who apparently got herself into so much trouble that she gave her mother nightmares?"

I raised my eyebrows as I sat on the chair opposite them. "Why on earth would Mom be worried about me?"

"Because she was getting visions of you in trouble, and no one knew where you were or how to get hold of you. And you weren't answering your phone."

"I broke it." I hadn't even thought to ring Mom, but even if I had, I wouldn't have. Especially not after Rainey's death. "So that's why you're here? So you can tell Mom that you've seen me and I'm okay?"

"That, and to tell you I'm going to be a dad."

"Like *that* wasn't obvious." I glanced at Destiny with a smile. "You're a brave woman to take him on. He's a little bit crazy. You know that, don't you?"

She nodded, green eyes twinkling. "I discovered that awhile back."

Both of them were grinning broadly, and Trae was

looking happier than I'd ever seen him, but even as my heart rejoiced for them, it broke a little more.

And Trae saw it. The brightness in his eyes dimmed a little and he frowned. "*Are* you okay?"

"Yeah, brother, I am." I said it softly, forcefully, and even if I didn't entirely convince myself, it seemed to convince him, because he relaxed a little. I pushed to my feet. "Now, while I grab us all some coffee, why don't you tell me how you two met?"

So they did. And I wasn't the only one who'd had a harrowing time recently, it seemed.

"So," Trae said, several cups later. "You want to explain how you burned down both my apartment and yours?"

"That's sort of a long story." And it wasn't one I really wanted to get into right then. Not when it was all still so raw.

He raised an eyebrow and gave me the sort of look that suggested he was prepared to wait a very long time indeed. "We have nothing to do for the next couple of hours."

So much for him believing that I was okay. Thankfully, the doorbell chose that moment to ring. "Gotta answer that," I said, rather unsuccessfully hiding the relief in my voice as I jumped up.

"We'll just help ourselves to the contents of your fridge," he said, voice dry. "And don't think we're going to be put off by whoever it is at the door."

I flashed him a grin over my shoulder in acknowledgment and pressed the intercom button.

"Yes?"

"Mercy? It's Damon."

My body went hot, then cold, and my hands were suddenly shaking.

"Who?" My fingers reflexively touched the lotus pendant around my neck. I must have heard wrong. He *couldn't* be here. Not after walking away. Not after all his fine speeches about being a muerte and wanting no one to care about.

"It's me, Mercy."

He sounded so heartbreakingly real, like he really *was* standing down there. But part of me didn't want to believe it. He'd walked away. Surely he wouldn't just walk back, like nothing had happened.

When I didn't say anything, he added softly, "I need to talk to you."

"Why?" I asked automatically. Then I remembered Trae and Destiny standing in my kitchen, undoubtedly listening to every word, and I added hastily, "I'm coming down."

I grabbed my jacket from the coatrack, flung an "I'll be back" over my shoulder, then dived out the door. I didn't wait for the elevator but took the stairs two at a time, slowing only when I neared the ground floor.

It *was* him.

He was leaning a shoulder against the wall of the building, staring off down the street. His sharp features were drawn, as if he'd been getting as little sleep as I had, and there were shadows under his eyes.

I slowed as my foot hit the foyer floor, wanting to drink in the sight of him just a bit longer, enjoy the feeling of him flowing through my mind. But he sensed my presence and looked my way.

Those dark eyes caught mine so easily, and yet they were completely neutral—showing nothing, revealing nothing. I stopped, suddenly unsure whether I really should open that door.

What if he wasn't here to tell me he missed me?

What if he was simply here to sort out something relating to Hannish and the Jamieson king?

My stomach suddenly twisted. God, what if he was here to drag me in front of the council?

I took a step back, then stopped.

This was stupid. I was braver than this. I'd proved that time and again.

"What do you want, Damon?"

"I didn't come here to talk to you through a glass security door, Mercy. Either let me in, or come out."

"Why should I come out? You left." My voice broke a little, but I sucked it up and added, "What more is there to discuss?"

"Plenty." He paused, and a sweet, almost tentative smile teased the corners of his mouth. "I've arranged for chocolate cake . . ."

Despite my fears, I couldn't help feeling a glimmer of amusement. He'd remembered. That had to be good, right? "I don't see any chocolate cake."

"It's waiting in the restaurant down the street."

"And why would it be waiting there?"

"Because I thought you were more likely to talk to me on neutral ground." He paused again, and I swear fear flashed through the dark depths of his eyes. It made that small sliver of hope that had been with me since he'd left burst into a bonfire. "Please, Mercy. Come out and talk to me."

"You have precisely twenty minutes," I said, knowing even as I said it that he could have the rest of my life if only he said the right words. "I have guests waiting upstairs."

I opened the door then grabbed the loose edges of my jacket and wrapped them around me—more to keep from reaching for him than any real need to keep out the cold.

But I couldn't help drawing in the scent of him, letting the richness of it flow through my lungs, filling and warming me.

"This way," he said, raising his hand to guide me, then dropping it before he actually touched my back.

We walked down the street like two strangers, and yet every time he moved, every time he breathed, I was aware of it.

He opened the restaurant door and ushered me through, once again careful not to touch me, then guided me over to a table in the corner. The place was small, homey, and packed. Our table was the only empty one.

A waiter came up immediately, depositing two coffees and a large serving of chocolate cake before removing the "reserved" sign and walking away.

I wrapped my fingers around the cup and drew it close, but I didn't dare pick it up. My hands were still shaking too much.

"So," I said finally, meeting his dark gaze. "What do you want to talk about?"

"How about my stupidity?"

"A good place to start," I acknowledged, desperately battling the urge to smile. He didn't deserve that yet. After a month of heartache, he owed me the full explanation. And perhaps a bit of groveling. "What particular area of your stupidity do you wish to discuss?"

"The part where I said muertes can't get involved."

I picked up the fork and cut into the cake. I had to do something, anything, to stop myself from giving in to the growing desire to reach across the table and silence him with a kiss. The part of me that had hoped for so long suddenly didn't care about explanations; it just wanted him. But the stubborn part still wanted to hear the words; still wanted to hear him say them before I truly believed. "And why would you want to discuss that? You were very emphatic about it."

"It was a lie when I said it, and it's a lie now."

He caught my hand, gently pulling the fork from it and enclosing it in his warm, firm grip. My breath caught and my heart began pounding so hard I swear it was trying to jump out of my chest. I was suddenly glad he didn't seem to expect me to say anything, because right then I was totally incapable of speech.

"I tried to forget you," he continued softly. "I tried to get on with my life and my job, but you've invaded every part of me—even my dreams—and there *is* no me without you. I love you, Mercy."

I closed my eyes for a moment and savored the words, letting them wash away the loneliness and the fear of the past month. Letting them warm my soul and heal my heart.

Even so, it couldn't end there. There was one more question I needed to ask.

"What about that whole speech you gave about the power of the muerte being the fact that he has no family—and no loved ones—to fear for? Are you saying that was a lie, too?"

"No. It's as true then as it is now. But this last month has given me a taste of what it would be like to live the rest of my life without you. And I'd rather live with the fear of losing you than live without you entirely."

"Are you sure, Damon? Because *I'd* rather live alone than live the rest of my life with the fear that you'll walk away again."

"I'm more sure of that than anything else in my life. Please, say you'll forgive me. Say you'll take the risk and become a part of my life."

I studied him for a moment, aching to say yes but all too aware of the shadow that still stood between us— a shadow he hadn't yet mentioned.

"You say you love me, that you can't live without me," I said slowly, "but I'm draman and that will never change. Where will your allegiance lie if the council issues an order that all draman are to have their powers ripped from them?"

"I doubt the council will order something like that."

"But if it did?" I persisted.

"I would not let that happen to you," he said softly, but with such determination it warmed the chill of uncertainty from my bones.

"And the other draman? Do you really think they deserve to lose their powers simply because the full-bloods are so insecure about our position in their lives?"

"I can't promise that the council won't vote to cull draman powers, but I can tell you that they've set up a scientific study of the coastal cliques in the hope of discovering just what is going on. They've also agreed, in principle, to a summit meeting between representatives of the draman and the cliques."

It wasn't acceptance, but it was certainly a whole lot more than I'd ever thought I'd see in my lifetime. "You did this?"

"I recommended it. Julio and several other kings backed me." He shrugged, like it was nothing. Except it was everything, because I had no doubt he'd done it for me, to prove just how much he *did* care. He reached out and brushed my cheek lightly. "I've answered your questions. How about answering mine?"

Love and fear were in his voice, in his expression, and I couldn't help the urge to tease him. "I can't say yes. You haven't promised me a regular supply of chocolate cake."

A smile twitched his lips. "Oh, I think I can arrange that easily enough."

"What about children? I want lots of them. Boys *and* girls—and no favoring the boys, thank you very much."

"I promise." He drew me across the table, his breath washing heat across my lips. "Anything else?"

"Yes," I murmured, my lips brushing his and my gaze on his, losing myself in those dark depths and the love so evident there. "Promise me we'll fly every single day."

"Forever and ever," he murmured, his lips so close I could taste his words.

"Then you'd better come back to my apartment and meet my brother. He needs to approve."

"He'll approve. I'm a very lovable sort of fellow when I want to be."

I laughed at that, and he grinned. Then the amusement twinkling in his bright eyes faded. "Do you promise to be mine, Mercy?"

"Forever and ever," I murmured, then took his lips with mine and sealed our deal with a kiss.

Be sure not to miss
Darkness Unbound,

the first book of Keri Arthur's thrilling new
Dark Angels series!

Read on for a special preview. . . .

Darkness Unbound

On sale Summer 2011

I've always seen the reapers.

Even as a toddler—with little understanding of spirits, death, or the horrors that lie in the shadows—I'd been aware of them. As I'd gotten older and my knowledge of the mystical had strengthened, I'd begun to call them Death, because the people I'd seen them following had always died within a day or so.

In my teenage years, I learned who and what they really were. They called themselves reapers, and they were collectors of souls. They took the essence—the spirit—of the dying and escorted them to the next part of their journey, be that heaven or hell.

The reapers weren't flesh-and-blood beings, although they could attain that form if they wished. They were creatures of light and shadows—and an energy so fierce that their mere presence burned across my skin like flame.

Which is how I'd sensed the one now following me. He was keeping his distance, but the heat of him sang through the night, warming my skin and stirring the embers of fear. I swallowed heavily and tried to stay calm. After all, being the daughter of one of Melbourne's most powerful psychics had its benefits— and one of those was a knowledge of my own death. It would come many years from now, in a stupid car accident.

Of course, it was totally possible that I'd gotten the timing of my death wrong. My visions weren't always as accurate as my mother's, so maybe the death I'd seen in my future was a whole lot closer than I'd presumed.

And it was also a fact that not all deaths actually happened when they were *supposed* to. That's why there were ghosts—they were the souls uncollected by reapers, either because their deaths had come *before* their allotted time, or because they'd refused the reaper's guidance. Either way, the end result was the same. The soul was left stranded between this world and the next.

I shoved my hands into the pockets of my leather jacket and walked a little faster. There was no outrunning the reapers—I knew that—but I still couldn't help the instinctive urge to try.

Around me, the day was only just dawning. Lygon Street gleamed wetly after the night's rain, and the air was fresh and smelled ever so faintly of spring. The heavy bass beat coming from the nearby wolf clubs overran what little traffic noise there was, and laughter rode the breeze—a happy sound that did little to chase the chill from my flesh.

It wasn't a chill caused by an icy morning, but rather the ever-growing tide of fear.

Why was the reaper following *me*?

As I crossed over to Pelham Street, my gaze flicked to the nearby shop windows, searching again for the shadow of death.

Reapers came in all shapes and sizes, often taking the form most likely to be accepted by those they'd come to collect. I'm not sure what it said about me that *my* reaper was shirtless, tattooed, and appeared to be wearing some sort of sword strapped across his back.

A reaper with a weapon? Now *that* was something I'd never come across before. But maybe he knew I wasn't about to go quietly.

I turned into Ormond Place and hurried toward the private parking lot my restaurant shared with several other nearby businesses. There was no sound of steps behind me, no scent of another, yet the reaper's presence burned all around me—a heat I could feel on my skin and within my mind.

Sometimes being psychic like my mom *really* sucked.

I wrapped my fingers around my keys and hit the automatic opener. As the old metal gate began to grind and screech its way to one side, I couldn't help looking over my shoulder.

My gaze met the reaper's. His face was chiseled, almost classical in its beauty, and yet possessing a hard edge that spoke of a man who'd won more than his fair share of battles. His eyes were blue—one a blue as vivid and as bright as a sapphire, the other almost a navy, and as dark and stormy as the sea.

Awareness flashed through those vivid, turbulent depths—an awareness that seemed to echo right through me. It was also an awareness that seemed to be accompanied, at least on his part, by surprise.

For several heartbeats neither of us moved, and then he simply disappeared. One second he was there, and the next he wasn't.

I blinked, wondering if it were some sort of trick. Reapers, like the Aedh, could become energy and smoke at will, but—for me, at least—it usually took longer than the blink of an eye to achieve. Of course, I was only half Aedh, so maybe that was the problem.

The reaper didn't reappear, and the heat of his presence no longer burned through the air or shivered through my mind. He'd gone. Which was totally out of character for a reaper, as far as I knew.

I mean, they were collectors of *souls*. It was their duty to hang about until said soul was collected. I've never known of one to up and disappear the moment he'd been spotted—although given the ability to actually spot them was a rare one, that probably wasn't an everyday occurrence.

Mom, despite her amazing abilities—abilities that had been sharpened during her creation in a madman's cloning lab—certainly couldn't see them. But then, she couldn't actually see *anything*. The sight she did have came via a psychic link she shared with a creature known as a Fravardin—a guardian spirit that had been gifted to her by a long dead clone brother.

She was also a full Helki werewolf, not a half-Aedh

like me. The Aedh were kin to the reapers, and it was their blood that gave me the ability to see the reapers.

But why did *this* reaper disappear like that? Had he realized he'd been following the wrong soul, or was something weirder going on?

Frowning, I walked across to my bike and climbed on. The leather seat wrapped around my butt like a glove and I couldn't help smiling. The Ducati wasn't new, but she was sharp and clean and comfortable to ride, and even though the hydrogen engine was getting a little old by today's standards, she still put out a whole lot of power. Maybe not as much as the newer engines, but enough to give a mother gray hair. Or so *my* mom reckoned, anyway.

As the thought of her ran through my mind again, so did the sudden urge to call her. My frown deepening, I dug my phone out of my pocket and said, "Mom."

The voice-recognition software clicked into action and the call went through almost instantly.

"Risa," she said, her luminous blue eyes shining with warmth and amusement. "I was just thinking about you."

"I figured as much. What's up?"

She sighed, and I instantly knew what that meant. My stomach twisted and I closed my eyes, wishing away the words I knew were coming.

But it didn't work. It never worked.

"I have another client who wants your help." She said it softly, without inflection. She knew how much I hated hospitals.

"Mom—"

"It's a little girl, Ris. Otherwise I wouldn't ask you. Not so soon after the last time."

I took a deep breath and blew it out slowly. The last time had been a teenager whose bones had pretty much been pulverized in a car accident. He'd been on life support for weeks, with no sign of brain activity, and the doctors had finally advised his parents to turn off the machine and let him pass over. Naturally enough, his parents had been reluctant, clinging to the belief that he was still there, that there was still hope.

Mom couldn't tell them that. But I could.

Yet it had meant going into the hospital, immersing myself in the dying and the dead and the heat of the reapers. I hated it. It always seemed like I was losing a piece of myself.

But more than that, I hated facing the grief of the parents when—*if*—I had to tell them that their loved ones were long gone.

"What happened to her?"

If it was an accident, if it was a repeat of the teenager and the parents were looking for a miracle, then I could beg off. It wouldn't be easy, but neither was walking into that hospital.

"She went in with a fever, fell into a coma, and hasn't woken up. They have her on life support at the moment."

"Do they know why?" I asked the question almost desperately, torn between wanting to help a little girl caught in the twilight realms between life and death and the serious need *not* to go into that place.

"No. She had the flu and was dehydrated, which is why she was originally admitted. The doctors have run every test imaginable and have come up with nothing." Mom hesitated. "Please, Ris. Her mother is a longtime client."

My mom knew *precisely* which buttons to push. I loved her to death, but god, there were some days I wished I could simply ignore her.

"Which hospital is she in?"

"The Children's."

I blew out a breath. "I'll head there now."

"You can't. Not until eight," Mom said heavily. "They're not allowing anyone but family outside of visiting hours."

Great. Two hours to wait. Two hours to dread what I was being asked to do.

"Okay. But no more for a while after this. Please?"

"Deal." There was no pleasure in her voice. No victory. She might push my buttons to get what she wanted, but she also knew how much these trips took out of me. "Come back home afterward and I'll make you breakfast."

"I can't." I scrubbed my eyes and resisted the sudden impulse to yawn. "I've been working at the restaurant all night and I really need some sleep. Send me the details about her parents and the ward number, and I'll give you a buzz once I've been to see her."

"Good. Are you still up for our lunch on Thursday?"

I smiled. Thursday lunch had been something of a ritual for my entire life. My mom and Aunt Riley—who wasn't really an aunt, but a good friend of Mom's who'd taken me under her wing and basically spoiled me rotten since birth—had been meeting at the same restaurant for more than twenty-five years. They had, in fact, recently purchased it to prevent it from being torn down to make way for apartments. Almost nothing got in the way of their ritual—and certainly *not* a multimillion dollar investment company.

"I wouldn't miss it for the world."

"Good. See you then. Love you."

I smiled and said, "But not as much as I love you."

The words had become something of a ritual at the end of our phone calls, but I never took them for granted. I'd seen far too many people over the years trying to get in contact with the departed just so they could say the words they'd never said in life.

I hit the end button then shoved the phone back into my pocket. As I did so, it began to chime the song "Witchy Woman"—an indicator that Mom had already sent the requested information via text. Obviously, she'd had it ready to go. I shook my head and didn't bother looking at it. I needed to wash the grime of work away and get some sustenance in my belly before I faced dealing with that little girl in the hospital.

Two hours later, I arrived at the hospital. I parked in the nearby underground lot, then checked Mom's text, grabbing the ward number and the parents' names before heading inside.

It hit me in the foyer.

The dead, the dying, and the diseased created a veil of misery and pain that permeated not only the air but the very foundations of the building. It felt like a ton of bricks as it settled across my shoulders, and it was a weight that made my back hunch, my knees buckle, and my breath stutter to a momentary halt.

Not that I really *wanted* to breathe. I didn't want to take that scent—that wash of despair and loss—into myself. And most especially, I didn't want to see the reapers and the tiny souls they were carrying away.

I was gripped by the sudden urge to run, and it was so fierce and strong that my whole body shook. I had to clench my fists against it and force my feet onward. I'd promised Mom I'd do this, and I couldn't go back on my promise. No matter how much I might want to.

I walked into the elevator and punched the floor for intensive care, then watched as the doors closed and the floor numbers slowly rolled by. As the doors opened on my floor, a reaper walked by. She had brown eyes and a face you couldn't help but trust, and her wings shone white, tipped with gold.

An angel—the sort depicted throughout religion, not those that inhabited the real world. Walking beside her, her tiny hand held within the angel's, was a child. I briefly closed my eyes against the sting of tears. When I opened them again, the reaper and her soul were gone.

I took the right-hand corridor. A nurse looked up as I approached the desk. "May I help you?"

"I'm here to scc Hanna Kingston."

She hesitated, looking me up and down. "Are you family?"

"No, but her parents asked me to come. I'm Risa Jones."

"Oh," she said, then her eyes widened slightly as the name registered. "The daughter of Dia Jones?"

I nodded. People might not know me, but thanks to the fact that many of her clients were celebrities, they sure knew Mom. "Mrs. Kingston is a client. She asked for me specifically."

"I'm sorry, but I'll have to check."

I nodded again, watching as she rose and walked through the door that separated the reception area from the intensive care wards. Down that bright hall, a shrouded gray figure waited. Another reaper. Another soul about to pass.

I closed my eyes again and took a long, slow breath. I could do this.

I could.

The nurse came back with another woman. She was small and dark haired, her sharp features and brown eyes drawn and tired-looking.

"Risa," she said, offering me her hand. "Fay Kingston. I'm so glad you were able to come."

I shook her hand briefly. Her grief seemed to crawl from her flesh, and it made my heart ache. I pulled my hand gently from hers and flexed my fingers. The grief still clung to them, stinging lightly. "There's no guarantee I can help you. She might have already made her decision."

The woman licked her lips and nodded, but the brightness in her eyes suggested she wasn't ready to believe it. But then, what mother would?

"We just need to know—" She stopped, tears gathering in her eyes. She took a deep breath, then gave me a bright, false smile. "This way."

I washed my hands, then followed her through the secure door and down the bright hall, the echo of our footsteps like a strong, steady heartbeat. The shrouded reaper didn't look our way—his concentration was on his soul. I glanced into the room as we passed him. It was a boy of about eight years old. There were machines and doctors clustered all around him, working frantically. *There's no hope,* I wanted to say. *Let him go in peace.*

But I'd been wrong before. Maybe I'd be wrong again.

Three doorways down from the reaper, Mrs. Kingston swung left into a room and walked across to a dark-haired man sitting near the bed. I stopped in the doorway, barely even registering his presence as my gaze was drawn to the small form on the bed.

She was a dark-haired bundle of bones that seemed lost amid the stark whiteness of the hospital room. Machines surrounded her, doing the work of her body, keeping her alive. Her face was drawn, gaunt, and there were dark circles under her closed eyes.

I couldn't feel her. But I couldn't feel the presence of a reaper, either, and that surely had to be a good sign.

"Do you think you can help her?" a deep voice asked.

I jumped, and my gaze flew to the father. Before I could answer, Fay said, "This is my husband, Steven."

I nodded. I didn't need to know his name to understand he was Hanna's father. The utter despair in his eyes was enough. I swallowed heavily and somehow said, "I honestly don't know if I can help her, Mr. Kingston. But I can try."

He nodded, his gaze drifting back to his baby girl. "Then try. Either way, we need to know what to do next."

I took a deep, somewhat shuddering breath, and blinked away the tears stinging my eyes once more.

I could do this. For her sake—for *their* sake—I could do this. If she was in there, if she was trapped between this world and the next, then she needed someone to talk to. Someone who could help her make a decision. That someone had to be me. There *was* no one else.

I forced my feet forward. The closer I got, the more I could feel . . . well, the oddness.

Pain and fear and hunger swirled around her tiny body like a storm, but there was no spark, no glimmer of consciousness—nothing to indicate that life had ever existed within her flesh.

It shouldn't have felt like that. And if death was her destiny, then there would have been a reaper here waiting. But there wasn't, so either the time for her decision had not arrived or she was slated to live.

So why couldn't I *feel* her?

Frowning, I sat down on the edge of the bed and picked up her hand. Her flesh was warm, though why that surprised me I wasn't entirely sure.

I took a deep breath and slowly released it. As I did, I released the awareness of everything and everyone else, concentrating on little Hanna, reaching for her not physically, but psychically. The world around me faded until the only thing existing on this plane was me and her. Warmth throbbed at my neck—Ilianna's magic at work, protecting me as my psyche, my soul, or whatever else people liked to call it, pulled away from the constraints of my flesh and stepped gently into the gray fields that were neither life nor death.

Only it felt like I'd stepped into the middle of a battleground.

And it was a battle that had gone very, *very* badly.

Fear and pain became physical things that battered at me with terrible force, tearing at my heart and ripping through my soul. My chest burned, breathing became painful, and all I could feel was fear. My fear, her fear, all twisted into one stinking mess that made my stomach roil and my flesh crawl.

And then there was the screaming. Unvoiced, unheard by anyone but me, it reverberated through the emptiness of her flesh—echoes of agony in the bloody, battered shell that had once held a little girl.

Her soul wasn't here, but it hadn't moved on.

Someone—*something*—had come into the hospital and ripped it from her flesh.